ALL MY BONES SHOOK

K-9 SEARCH AND RESCUE BOOK 8

LINDA J WHITE

WINDY BAY BOOKS

Cover Design, Hannah Linder.

First printing, April 2026

White, Linda J. 1949-

All My Bones Shook/Linda J. White

ISBN: 978-1-7372356-9-9 paperback

ISBN 979-8-9911696-2-2 ebook

For Becky and Amanda,
my right hand and my left,
and often, my brain.

May God bless you for
your diligence and grace.

Amid thoughts from visions of the night,
When deep sleep falls on men,
Dread came upon me, and trembling,
Which made all my bone shake.
Job 4:13-14

1

JESS

I felt a drip of sweat run down my neck and between my shoulder blades, tracing my spine. I gripped my Glock. My hand shook. This was my last chance, my very last chance. Everything depended on this shot. And I knew it.

I calmed my breath. Relaxed my jaw. I focused, willing my eyes to work together. And then, at just the right time, target in sight, I squeezed the trigger.

BANG! Bang, bang, bang! Bang!

Adrenaline surged through me. A sweet, smoky smell filled my nose. I lowered my weapon and peered downrange.

Success. Yes!

I turned to my husband and grinned. "I beat you, Scott! Look at that."

"What? No way!" Scott pretended to squint as he looked. "I don't believe you."

But the paper targets told the tale. Five of my six shots had hit the bulls-eye dead center. Only four of his were on the mark. Just four.

Scott turned, his blue eyes bright with affection. He hugged me. "My girl is back."

A terrorist's vicious blow to the side of my head six months prior had broken multiple bones around my left eye. For a while, doctors thought I'd lose vision in that eye but, thank God, I didn't. My depth perception, however, was MIA for a long time. My eyes refused to work together, making it difficult to judge distance. I tripped a lot, walked into more than one doorjamb, and got a lot of headaches.

So my victory at the shooting range meant much more than just beating Scott. My vision was finally healing.

Maybe now I could get back to real life.

My injuries after being attacked had landed me in the hospital for a week, and I was incapacitated for some time even after I'd gotten home. The same incident had injured Scott. Thankfully, our friend Kathryn was willing to take an emergency leave of absence to come stay at our house and help us out. She'd returned to her teaching job in Highland County in late January, but I had a feeling she wasn't going to renew her contract up there. During the time she was with us, she'd begun dating a local deputy, an older man whose wife had died of cancer.

And our Little Mike? How did all this affect him? Beside the fact that he and my dog Luke became inseparable.

My son was just over a year old when I got hurt. Thankfully, he was used to Kathryn, Nathan Tanner, and my earth-mother friend, Ellie, and between the three of them, he was well cared for. But they weren't his mother.

"Would me being jerked from his life count as an Adverse Childhood Experience for Mike?" I asked Scott one day.

He took a deep breath. "I'm sure it would. You two were very bonded."

Tears came to my eyes.

"*Are* very bonded. Jess, you're still his mom. And you can't protect your kid from everything."

"If I hadn't ..."

"If you hadn't I'd be dead and then he'd have a different trauma to deal with. You're back. I'm back. And Little Mike learned he can trust other people to change his pants and feed him. He'll be fine."

"Whatever doesn't kill you makes you stronger?"

"Something like that."

THAT EVENING, after I'd put our nineteen-month-old son to bed, I came back downstairs. Scott sat in his recliner, reading. He looked up and smiled, then went back to his book.

A question played on my heart, but I remained quiet. We'd spent the last six months doing everything together. We both had felt the horror of nearly losing each other. So we worked at home together, played together, attended church together, and even went to counseling together, determined to mend and build our relationship. Now, we were in a pretty good place. Mostly.

I curled up on the leather couch and picked up my book. Luke, my German shepherd search-and-rescue dog, huffed down on the floor next to me. I tried to read, but my question formed and reformed itself across the pages. I wondered if this was the right time.

Out of the corner of my eye, I saw Scott glance at me. I looked at him. My mouth opened. We both spoke at the same time.

And we both laughed. "You first," he said.

"No, you."

I expected him to say, *No, you,* but to my surprise, he dropped the footrest of the recliner and leaned forward. "Jess," he said, "it sounds crazy to say, but I'm actually thankful, in a way, that we both got hurt. I have loved the last six months. I'm so grateful you've recovered. I've loved hanging out with you and Mike, teaching him things and playing with him, being with you, but ..."

"...there's something missing!" I said, tossing my book aside and moving forward to the edge of the couch.

Scott looked confused. "What?"

"You miss ... you miss what? Going to work? Using your brain? Law enforcement? Criminals?"

"Well, it's not exactly ..."

"What is it exactly? Tell me! Because I've missed it too!"

He blinked. "What? You? The FBI?"

"No!" I laughed. "You first. Go ahead."

"Right! I've missed working." Relief showed as the muscles in his face relaxed. "I thought you'd be angry."

"Angry? No, I understand. Scott, you're too smart to just hang around here all the time. You need to do something. It's not your job that bothered me, it was your hyper-focus on your job, the time away, the lack of togetherness, not just for me, but for Mike too."

He nodded.

"So how could you work again but put boundaries on it?"

His answer was to pull out his phone, scroll through it, and then hand it to me. He'd pulled up an email from one of the higher-ups at the bureau, asking him to come back, either as an agent, or a consultant once his medical retirement came through. Or maybe as a special investigator.

When I looked up, Scott's eyes were shining. "Basically," he said, "they want me as a major case specialist. School shootings, mass attacks, that sort of thing—the psychology behind it, studying it, preventing it, guiding investigations, training new agents. I can work from home when possible."

"They really want you."

He nodded toward the phone. "Barnes is an older guy. We've talked a lot. He gets it."

"And does he have the authority to let you work this way?"

"Yes. From the director." Scott waved his hand like he was shooing a fly. "We can talk about this again after you've had time to think about it. How about you? What were you about to say earlier?"

I cocked my head and frowned. I took a deep breath. "Scott, it sounds crazy to say, but I'm actually thankful too, in a way, that we both got hurt. I have loved these last six months. I'm so grateful you've recovered. I've loved hanging out with you and Mike, but—"

Scott laughed. He stood and held out his hand for a high five. I smacked it. "Oh, gosh," he said, sitting back down. "You too?"

I grinned and nodded. "I'm restless. I want to work again."

"I get it. And all we need to do is figure out how to patch it all together."

"Easy-peasy," I said, knowing full well it wouldn't be.

THE NEXT DAY, Scott drove in to talk to Justin Barnes at the FBI. After exploring the options, Scott decided to stay active as an agent, although in a limited capacity. He'd been a fine street agent and a brilliant part of the Behavioral Analysis Unit. He wasn't quite ready to give up his badge yet. I understood that. But he did promise me that if the bureau went back on their part of the deal, he'd take medical retirement.

We sketched out a plan with the understanding we might have to modify it. I'd be Mike's primary caregiver Monday, Tuesday, Thursday, and Friday. Scott would work those days, at Quantico at first, until he got caught up, and then at home whenever he could. I'd cluster my PI cases on Wednesday when Scott would be on duty with Mike. On weekends, we'd both be flexible, but mostly he'd take care of Mike so I could resume SAR.

I STARTED ATTENDING the Battlefield Search and Rescue Group's Saturday training days, which were scheduled for every other week. Luke and I were both rusty, and I felt out of shape. We'd need to be recertified after our leave of absence. But my old friends were happy to see us, especially Nate.

I also sent an email to various lawyers and police departments in my part of Virginia updating them on my health and offering my PI services on a limited basis. I started getting the usual cases—background checks and a couple of prelude-to-divorce jobs. Then I got one that twisted my heart—a custody battle case.

The Albemarle County Family Court had awarded joint custody of two children when Brett and Brittany Hudgins got divorced two years ago. Brett, convinced that Brittany was mentally ill, was worried that Nora, now age nine, and Ava, seven, were not being well-cared for.

"She doesn't show up sometimes on her days, and she's usually late on others. I hear stories from the girls and, well, I don't like what I hear," Brett told his lawyer, Frank Sinclair. I was hired to find out what I could about Brittany Hudgins. Sinclair emailed me the custody schedule, addresses, and phone numbers.

"What do they do work wise?" I asked Frank. I'd taken cases from him before and liked the guy.

"Brett," he said, "is actually a lawyer."

"Really? What kind of law?"

"Corporate. And yes, he could hire a PI himself, but he's trying to keep his personal life separate from his professional life."

"I see. And his ex-wife?"

"Living on alimony, mostly. I think she also subs at a school or something. Otherwise, unemployed."

My heart in these cases automatically shifted toward the mom. Why? Because I am one. I imagined her staying home with these kids when they were little while dad climbed the corporate ladder. Now they're divorced, she sees the kids only half the time, and he's calling her bipolar. She didn't do everything the way he wanted to in marriage and now it's worse, and he's trying to take what little contact she has with her babies away from her.

I shifted in my chair and tried to step back from the brink. *Calm down, Jess. Find the facts first.*

I told Frank I'd get right on it, and I did.

I studied the pictures Frank had sent. Brett looked like a corporate lawyer. At thirty-eight, he had short, dark hair, stylishly cut. In the picture he wore a well-tailored, dark-blue suit and a crisp white shirt with an impressive, flowered tie. Brittany, age thirty-five, dressed in an oversized T-shirt and jeans, looked slightly overweight, slightly frumpy, and slightly worried.

Then I looked up their addresses, and I got my first shock.

2

JESS

"I must have these reversed!" I muttered out loud as I looked at the Hudgins's houses. According to Google maps, Mr. Corporate Lawyer, Brett, lived in an old, two-story farmhouse on ten acres west of Charlottesville. Ms. Mom's home was an upscale, five-bedroom townhouse in Charlottesville. What?

I checked the email Frank had sent me. Nope. I had them right. Why would the lawyer live so far out of town and in a place that clearly needed a lot of outdoor (and probably indoor) maintenance? And how could she afford a five-bedroom townhouse?

I stopped myself as an image of Scott, Mr. FBI, intruded into my thoughts. I mean, we live out in the sticks in a 150-year-old house, but put my husband in a business suit and he definitely looks like a city slicker. I thought he was one for the longest time. Now I know he's at his most natural when he's wearing Wrangler jeans, a plaid western shirt, and boots. And who knows? Maybe Brittany's family had money and was helping her out.

Drop the stereotypes, I told myself.

. . .

I'D ASKED Frank Sinclair if it was okay to contact his client directly. I wanted to hear more about his concerns. Frank said yes, so I called Brett Hudgins, and he agreed to meet me on Friday at a coffee shop called Serein Café in Charlottesville at 8:00 a.m. At seven, I kissed Little Mike and Scott goodbye, gave Luke a hug, and took off in my old Jeep. On the drive down Route 29, I braced myself. My guess was this lawyer was going to complain about the wife he'd outgrown. He would exaggerate her "emotionalism," and express hope I'd find enough dirt on his ex for him to get full custody and a lower alimony payment. I was determined not to be taken in. I'd made up a plan. I was ready for him.

I'd totally forgotten that "drop the stereotypes" bit.

The coffee shop was in downtown Charlottesville, not far from Hudgins's law office. I found street parking, walked to the shop, pulled open the door, and stepped in. I was immediately struck by the shop's modern, earthy design—the light ash furniture, the plants hanging from beams and sitting on windowsills, the murals. Nature brought inside. I felt like I was in the woods. Or maybe Heaven. Only the smell of coffee reminded me why I was here.

"Miss Cooper?"

I turned to see a strikingly handsome man, eyebrows arched, smiling at me. He wasn't much taller than me, maybe five feet eight, trim and fit, dressed in a black suit and a white dress shirt. His dark hair set off his blue eyes. I could smell his woodsy shower soap. My heart did a double-beat. "Mr. Hudgins?"

"Would you like to sit down?" He motioned toward a table off by itself. I walked toward the table. "What can I get you?" he asked.

I gave him my order, and he left. I realized I'd been thrown off my pace by the beauty of this place and by, well, his good looks and gracious manner. He was not the corporate lawyer I'd been expecting. I took a moment while he was gone to gather my wits. *Get real, Jess. Don't be taken in by aesthetics.* I set my jaw.

Hudgins returned a few minutes later with two handmade pottery mugs filled with black coffee. The smell of the bold brew filled my nose. It was the scent of early summer mornings on my own front porch, birds singing, deer emerging silently from the woods. "I haven't been here before," I said, fingering the rough surface of the mug.

"It just opened up two weeks ago." He started to sip his coffee and quickly put it down. Too hot. "Tell me about yourself."

I blinked.

"I like to know a little about the people I'm working with."

So I gave him a verbal resume, telling him about my past as a detective in Fairfax County, my PI work, and about volunteering with a search and rescue organization. "My husband," I told him, "is an FBI agent, and we have a toddler son."

"You are a busy lady."

"Yes. Speaking of which," I pulled a notebook and pen from my bag, "Frank Sinclair tells me you're concerned about your children."

"And my ex-wife. But yes, primarily about the children." He began speaking. I madly took notes. He and his wife had married right out of college. Had some early adjustment problems but then seemed to settle in. He went to law school at Harvard, while she worked as a teacher. "Then I got this job offer," he said, "and we moved to Charlottesville. A few years in, Brittany seemed to get restless, unhappy. I wasn't sure why, but we mutually decided maybe it was time for kids."

"You have two, right?"

"Yes, girls, Nora, who's nine, and Ava, seven." A smile crossed his face. "They are the light of my life."

I nodded. "So did having kids fix Brittany's unhappiness?" I thought I knew the answer to that already.

Brett shook his head. "Temporarily. She got a lot of attention from her mother, her sister, friends. But that soon wore off, and she was left with the diapers and the laundry and all the stuff. Sad, really. I thought she'd love having kids. She didn't."

He paused and took a sip of his coffee. "The really weird behavior started a year after Ava was born. Brittany got pregnant again, accidentally this time. She was furious and blamed me. She actually talked about an abortion."

I raised my eyebrows.

"I didn't support it. But then she miscarried in the first trimester. I honestly don't know if she did something to make that happen or if it was totally natural. But that's when she started going off the rails."

"Like how?"

"Spending money we didn't have. Flirting with other men, including my boss, in a very seductive manner. I'd come home from work and nothing had been done at the house. Nothing was picked up, there was laundry all over the couch, and when I asked my nine-year-old what she'd had for dinner, most of the time she said a peanut butter and jelly sandwich. She'd made one for Ava too."

The first hint of anger tightened his face. He took a long drink of coffee. I followed suit, the dark brew a comfort in my throat. "It sounds like your wife needed help," I suggested.

"I begged her to get it. I told her I'd come with her. I said I thought she was depressed and should see a counselor. She refused. She said the problem was me. I worked too much, didn't do enough around the house, neglected her. And the girls! I spoiled them." He sighed deeply.

"Well, did you help with the housework? I'm sure you're busy—"

"True. My job can be intense. It keeps me late sometimes.

But when I'd get home and find the house a mess, I didn't yell, I didn't shame her, I just cleaned it up."

"*You* cleaned it up?"

"Somebody had to. She wouldn't or couldn't. So I did. And I'd put the kids to bed, and I'd make their lunches for school the next day. Brittany was just ... checked out."

"Did you ever talk to your doctor about it?"

"I talked to her doctor, a primary care doc. She just kept prescribing my wife meds." He shook his head.

"Antidepressants?"

"Antidepressants. Sleeping pills. All kinds of meds. I didn't know what Brittany was taking. I was worried about her. She sure wasn't getting any better. So I waited until she was out and looked at the bottles in her vanity drawer and wrote down the names of the drugs. I found out some had black box warnings, saying they could cause 'suicidal or homicidal ideation.' That worried me even more."

"She didn't have a psychiatrist?"

"She wouldn't go. She didn't have a problem. It was all me. Or the girls." He ran his hand through his hair. "I was worried that while I was at work she'd hurt them in one of her rages."

"Rages?"

"It was mostly emotional abuse—screaming at them, throwing their things in the trash, breaking their toys in front of them."

"She didn't hit them?"

"Not in front of me. One day, though, I walked in from work. She didn't realize I was home. And I saw her smack Ava across the face."

I had a sick feeling in my stomach. I'm not opposed to corporal punishment, but there is a big difference between a measured swat on a diapered bottom and a blow to a child's face. "How'd you react?"

His face reddened. He looked down. "I was furious. I yelled

at her, dropped my briefcase, and rushed into the room. Nora stood between her mother and her little sister. That's not something a kid her age should have to do. I picked up Ava, who was sobbing, and told Brittany to get away from the girls."

"You didn't hit her?"

"No. I never struck my wife, although she'd hit me a couple of times. But seeing her slap Ava, well that ... that woke me up. This wasn't going away. In fact, it was getting worse. Brittany wouldn't get help, not real help. My kids were in danger. So I filed for divorce." He turned and stared out of the window for a moment. "The court, well, you know courts these days. The court decided on joint custody. I objected. I'd documented everything I'd observed, everything I'd tried to do to help her, over the prior eighteen months. I even got two expert witnesses, a psychiatrist and a social worker, to testify about the danger she posed to the children. But of course, she had her witnesses too. And the court awarded joint custody."

"How long ago was that?"

"A year and a half ago. I want to try again to get full custody. I'm worried about my girls."

"What's Brittany been like recently?"

"She doesn't show up when it's time for her to have the girls. Or she shows up late. Twice she hasn't brought them back when she was supposed to. Once she took them out of state, to the Outer Banks in North Carolina, which violates the custody agreement.

"Whenever she has them, the girls come back withdrawn, quiet. A few times I've seen bruises, and when I ask, I'm told they fell or were roughhousing together. Always an excuse. I'm stressed every time they're with her." He tapped his finger on the table. "Here's another thing. I don't know where she's getting her money."

"What do you mean?"

"I pay her alimony and child support, but that house she's

in? Worth at least six hundred thousand. What I pay her won't cover that."

"And she's not working?"

"Not at anything I can see."

"Her parents?"

"They don't have money."

"Is she involved with another man?"

"The girls tell me when there's a man at their mom's, but it always seems to be a different man. I don't like that one bit." His mouth formed a straight line.

"So the house where she lives," I looked down at my notes and recited the address, "isn't where you lived when you were married?"

He shook his head. "No, we had a simple three-bedroom townhouse near Pen Park. When I left, she got the house. A year or so later, she sold it, and the next thing I know she's buying that five-bedroom behemoth."

"What does she need with five bedrooms?"

"I don't know! The girls each have their own room, and Brittany has one. The girls tell me the other two are locked."

"Locked?"

"Right. Padlocked."

"That's weird."

His face looked red. "Her buying that house made me angry because the girls had to change schools, and it meant I had to move too. I wanted us both to live in the same school district."

"To make transportation to and from school easier."

"Right. So I rented a townhouse in the same community. And you know what? I don't like living there. I'm doing it for my kids. But I don't like it."

I frowned. "The address Frank Sinclair gave me for you isn't in town. It's out near Crozet."

"Yes. I bought that country house out of sheer frustration." His face reddened. "My dad had to help me buy it. I didn't have any money. It's a two-hundred-year-old farmhouse. Didn't even have indoor plumbing when I got it. I'm fixing it up with him. Maybe someday I'll get to live there full time. In the meantime..." He paused, running his finger over the rim of his mug. His eyes focused on the center of our round, wooden table. "I stay out there whenever I can. It's beautiful, listening to the birds, watching the sun come up. I have a fox on the property, and deer, possums, raccoons, owls. I love it." He looked at me. "It's peaceful."

"I get that," I said, softly.

"I'm mostly living in town for the sake of my children. I guess I didn't make that clear to Frank. He's mixed the addresses up. I'll clarify that."

"I'd like the address too."

He wrote it down and glanced at his watch. "I've got to run. Thank you for helping me. Us." He stood and extended his hand.

I stood and shook it. "I'll do my best. If I have other questions?"

"Oh, here," he said, pulling a business card out of his pocket. He quickly turned it over and jotted a number on the back. "That's a burner phone. I'm positive she doesn't have access to it."

I handed him my card. "Call me if anything comes up that concerns you."

"Thank you." He picked up his attaché case and left.

And as I watched him walk out of the door, I thought, it's true. Life is like a box of chocolates. You never know what you're going to get.

After leaving the coffee shop, I took the time to drive by Brittany Hudgins's house. White with dark-red shutters, it stood on the end of a row of nearly identical townhomes, next to a paved walking/biking trail. Twenty yards beyond the trail was a wooded area. Those trees connected to the woods that stood directly across the street from Brittany's house, forming an "L."

This wouldn't be an easy place to conduct surveillance. No dead-end street was. Directly in front of her house was a small turnaround. Any cars coming past her house had to swing through the turnaround to leave.

What I could do, I thought, was bring Little Mike and/or Luke and walk the neighborhood. I could chat with anyone I saw on the street. I'd be just a mom or dog owner out for a walk.

I continued through the neighborhood, driving past Brett's much-smaller house and then on to the local elementary school, a couple of miles away. After scouting out local stores, I found my way back to Route 29 and headed home.

As I drove, I thought about this case. It sounded to me like Brittany was struggling with some form of mental problem—bipolar disorder or chronic depression. Maybe narcissism. In the last six months Scott's grown daughter, Amanda, had shared with me how she'd learned that some of her erratic (and damaging) behavior had stemmed from childhood trauma. I wondered now if the same was true for Brittany and if she could be helped like Amanda had been.

That, I decided, was not in my job description.

3

AMANDA

On April 1, Amanda Cooper stood in front of a classroom of brand new US Fish & Wildlife Service interns. If there was a flutter in her stomach, there was also excitement in her spine. She was about to introduce them to the Chincoteague National Wildlife Refuge, a sprawling, federally protected area on Assateague Island off the Virginia coast.

"Welcome," she began, "to the refuge. I sat where you are last year, and I can tell you, working at the refuge changed my life. I hope it changes yours too for the better."

A twitter of nervous laughter spread through the room.

"Working at the refuge taught me to slow down, to detach from my phone, to appreciate the birds, the sea life, and the rhythms of the natural world. Before I worked here, I thought marshes were wasted land, stinky, smelly swamps just waiting to be developed. I thought if you'd seen one gull you'd seen them all. I cared nothing about protecting endangered or threatened species, except for maybe buying an animal tracking bracelet at the zoo.

"After working here for a year, I can tell you I was wrong.

Marshes are some of our most important ecosystems and need to remain undeveloped. Gulls are incredibly diverse and interesting. And I've found that supporting declining species, like the piping plover, is well worth my time.

"Working at the refuge has taught me to tolerate discomfort like heat and mosquitos and annoying humans, to ask questions rather than make assumptions, to ... to have curiosity, and to hope, even when disaster strikes." Her heart thumped when she said that. Some disasters are self-induced.

"You will soon learn, as I did," she continued, "to identify herring gulls in each of their four color phases, to differentiate between terns, and to spot piping plover scrapes and American oyster catcher nests from thirty feet away. You'll recognize when a storm is brewing that could affect you. You will experience the wonder of seeing newly hatched piping plovers and the heartbreak of a predator's strike. You will feel overwhelmed by the beauty of the sunrises and sunsets. Nature is all out there to discover, to experience, and to study.

"I hope you enjoy your summer as much as I did."

Amanda sat down to the applause as her boss, Amy Creasey, took the microphone. "Thank you, Amanda. Now ..." Amy went on outlining the history of the refuge, the mandate from Congress, and the purposes and goals established by the Fish & Wildlife Service and their partnership with the National Park Service. Amanda listened to the familiar presentation while a question raced through her head. *How in the world did I get here?*

A year ago, she felt like a crazy woman—insecure, unstable, unsure. Like someone trying to balance while standing on a mat floating on the ocean. Keeping a lid on the emotions boiling inside her took all of her energy. People thought she was beautiful and smart. They couldn't see the storm inside.

Now, over time, this place—the beach, the ocean, the birds,

the people—had brought her peace. She hardly knew what to do with it.

After the initial orientation meeting, the interns had a seemingly endless parade of forms to fill out for human resources. At the request of her boss, she hung out with them, answering questions. They broke for lunch, and then Amanda took them on a tour outside, showing them the marshes, the water impoundments, the dunes, Tom's Cove, and the Hook, the end of the island. She showed them Pony Marsh and the southern herd of the Chincoteague ponies that lived there.

Then she drove them up the service road to see the northern part of Assateague, and along the way, spotted some of the northern herd as well. They had lots of questions about them, most of which she knew the answers to. She warned them not to feed or try to pet the ponies. "They're feral," she said, "and we want to preserve as much of their wildness as we can. Plus, they're acclimated through generations of living on the island to eat salt grass. Anything else, even an apple or sugar, could give them colic."

By the end of the day, she drove home tired but satisfied.

That evening, Amanda sat on the front porch of the house she'd been renting, waiting for Henry Bunting III, handsome veterinarian and her guy. Who'd have thought she'd find such a man in this tiny place?

But then who'd have thought she'd find joy tromping through marshes on the Chincoteague National Wildlife Refuge and working with horses on a farm? A top-notch student, now her classroom had moved outdoors, and she was loving it.

By the time Henry's black Toyota Tundra pulled up in the

driveway, the sun had set, the night had turned cold, and Amanda had put on her squall jacket. Still, he'd want to sit outside, she knew. She rose to greet him, holding open the screen door. "Hey, look at that cute guy!"

Joking, he turned to see who she was talking about, then mounted the stairs. "Amanda!" he said and he kissed her, and the thought flashed through her mind, *this is home.*

She got his coffee—hot and black—and they sat side-by-side in the porch rockers. He told her about his day, about the cattle he'd inoculated, the horse he'd stitched up, and the new foal down at the family farm. She listened and then told him about her day at the refuge. "Talking to those interns made me realize how much I've changed," she said.

Henry looked at her in the semi-darkness, his eyes catching the glow from the streetlight. "How? How have you changed?"

She blinked. "First of all, I had no idea a year ago that I'd love working at the refuge. I took that job because I needed the money. I couldn't tell a piping plover from a crow. Now, I love all that stuff. To me, a crab is beautiful. Plovers are a wonder. I love working in the marsh."

"And oysters are delicious. Especially raw," he teased.

"No. They're disgusting."

"Ah, we still got work to do on you."

A truck went by on Main Street. Across the water, Amanda could see the lights of cars on the causeway connecting Chincoteague to the mainland. She'd made that drive for the first time in February fourteen months ago. What a long way she'd come. "I was such a mess a year ago. You know. I don't need to tell you that."

"Then you met a handsome prince, who kissed you and turned you from a frog into a beautiful princess."

She playfully punched his arm. "I was not a frog! Plus you have the fairy tale wrong. It's the guy. The guy is the frog."

Henry scratched his chin. "Well, I don't see how that fits."

She laughed. Henry could be such a nut. When she first met him, she thought he was too serious. He seemed older, quiet. She'd even given him a "grandfather" nickname—Pops. Now, his playful side emerged often and she found him funny.

They sat quietly for a few minutes, each lost in their own thoughts, watching cars on the causeway. Then Henry said, "I thought you were beautiful the first time I saw you. I've seen a lot of stunning young women, especially in college, so at first I shrugged it off. I wasn't looking for a relationship. But I kept bumping into you. I became intrigued. I saw beauty, drive, and vulnerability all mixed together. At first I just wanted to protect you, but then, before I knew it, I was in love."

"When? When did you know you were in love?"

Henry stroked her hand with his thumb. "One night, sitting here on the porch. I thought I was just being a good human, you know, checking on you after—"

"After I walked into the ocean and almost killed myself?"

"Yeah, that. All of a sudden, I realized, *I love this girl.* And that was it, man. I was doomed. Caught like a fly in a spiderweb. A rabbit in a trap. A lamb bound for slaughter. A—"

Amanda stood up and faced him, laughing. "That's enough! I did not trap you. I didn't even pursue you. You are not helpless, Henry Bunting."

He pulled her down onto his lap and held her close. "You are beautiful, intelligent, and driven," he said, his voice soft, "and I would rather spend time with you than anyone else in the world. I am hopelessly in love with you. I can't believe how lucky I am."

She relaxed in his arms. "And I love you, Henry Bunting. I really do."

4

JESS

A week after Luke and I had been recertified for SAR, I got a callout on a Saturday morning. Scott and Mike were out riding Scott's black gelding, Ace. I quickly got the details. Twin boys, age three, went missing from a daycare center near Lake Simon. That was just over the mountains from our farm. My mind quickly catalogued what gear I'd need to respond. My dog for one. My pack, some food, water ...

I gave them a tentative yes. "Let me confirm with Scott," I said.

Then I called my husband. "We've had a callout. They could use me and Luke, because it might end up being a water search. Okay with you if I go?"

Scott gave his okay. He and Mike were doing well. Luke was with them, but Scott would start back toward the house.

I saw them when I looked out of the kitchen window. They had just emerged from the woods about a quarter mile away in the pasture. At a walk, it would take them some time to get here. So I gathered food and water for myself and Luke and loaded my SAR pack. I ran upstairs and changed into search clothes. I put on my boots and grabbed a second complete outfit, including a jacket, in case I got wet. Glancing out of our bedroom window, I saw Scott's horse moving toward home in a gentle lope. I hurried downstairs.

"Hey!" I said, emerging from the house as they got to the front yard. I set my pack down as Luke came running to greet me. I ran my hands over his glossy black-and-gold coat. "Have you been a good boy?" I asked him. I looked up as Mike started to cry. "Did you miss me?" I asked my son.

Apparently not, because when I approached them, Mike pulled away, clearly saying, *Don't take me off this horse!* He thought his ride was over. "Well! I guess I know where I stand." I touched Mike's leg.

"I'd lean down and kiss you but I can't," Scott said, smiling. He had Mike strapped to him. "Hope your search goes well."

"I'll text you updates. Thanks, Scott!" I turned to my dog. "Ready to go search?" I said. That usually sent Luke into an explosion of joy. This time, though, he hesitated. He looked up at Mike. "It's okay," I said. "Scott will take good care of him. Let's go!"

Released from his responsibilities as a guardian, my dog ran toward my Jeep, barking. I grabbed my pack. "Love you!" I called over my shoulder.

"Love you too!"

So much had changed since my accident. I wasn't sure I liked it. But at least here I was, about to go on my first search since Scott and I had resumed working.

April in central Virginia can be all over the place weather-wise. Warm, cold, and anywhere in between. The last couple of days had been warm—around sixty degrees—and sunny. This afternoon, a front was forecast to come through, bringing rain and falling temperatures. By the time I arrived at the address I'd been given, the clouds were already moving in.

The daycare center was actually a private home. I saw a bunch of cars gathered in front, a fenced yard in the back, and plastic riding toys in the open garage.

My heart lifted when I saw my friend Nathan Tanner's black Tahoe. Just beyond it, he stood talking to the coordinator. I smiled, put my Jeep in PARK, and got out.

Nate walked toward me. "Look who's back!" he said. "First one, right? Since—"

"Since I was assaulted and nearly killed? Why, yes, yes it is." I smiled.

He wrapped his arms around me. "God is good!"

Together we walked over to join the Battlefield group for the briefing. I still was not used to seeing Nate without his springer spaniel, Sprite. The winter had been hard on the old dog. She got to the point where she was hurting too much to keep up with him at work, but she would cry when he left her at home alone.

After seeing what was going on, Nate's stepdaughter, Kathryn, offered to take her. She was a teacher, so Sprite could go with her to school, lie on a bed in the classroom, not move around a lot, and yet be with people. It was a hard decision, because Nate loved Sprite and had worked with her for fourteen years. But he decided to do what was best for the little dog.

"She's livin' the life!" he told me a couple of weeks later. "Kathryn says the kids love her. Sometimes they come sit by her and read. Tell her secrets. And Kathryn, she likes having her. 'It's another heartbeat in the house,' she told me."

The search coordinator this day was Joe Stewart. He was relatively new to Battlefield but not to SAR. In his fifties, he had been an integral part of SAR in New Hampshire for over thirty years.

I counted four handlers from Battlefield, but I quickly

found out Nate had responded just to be my walker. Was he worried about me? I looked at him, smiling. He shrugged, "Just like old times."

"Here's what we have," Stewart said. "Two little boys, twins, age three, disappeared at approximately 0730." He handed out copier pictures of two little blonde boys. "Jacob and Joshua. The daycare owner was receiving newcomers at the front. When she returned downstairs, she found the boys missing. Sheriff's deputies did an initial search with a dog and did not find them. Here's the topo map of the area." He handed out three printouts. "I've marked off three search areas. Jess, you're the only one who's water certified, so you take Section 3."

I nodded and stared at the map, showing a large area east of the house. "Is there a boat on the lake?"

"The sheriff's bringing a johnboat."

I handed the map to Nate as Stewart went on talking. Water first is a principle in SAR. Kids are always attracted to it.

I hoped those boys hadn't gone near the lake today. At age three, they wouldn't know how to swim. The water would be cold. And the area around a lake is often mucky. I could imagine a three-year-old getting stuck in it.

Stewart finished the briefing. I looked at Nate. "I'll get Luke. Want to check out that backyard?" He nodded. "Here, take the map. I'll meet you back there."

I got my dog and joined Nate behind the house. "That fence must be fifty years old," I said. "Do they even make thirty-six-inch, chain-link fences anymore?"

"I ain't seen one in years. The question is, can a couple of three-year-olds get over one?"

"Depends if they're just three or almost four," I responded, imagining my active son at that age.

"Look here." Nate pointed to mud on the chain-link. "And at that." He indicated a riding toy lying on its side, a smudge of mud on its edge. "Reckon those kids stood on that and climbed out?"

I raised my eyebrows. "Maybe." I looked at the ground outside the fence. If there were any smaller prints they'd already been obscured by adult-sized treads. I nodded toward the map in Nate's hand. "Did you figure out a plan?"

"We go around the lake first. If we don't see any evidence of the boys, we try this area." He pointed to a wooded area in our sector. "And we work our way back."

"Perfect," I said. "Let's do it."

We moved toward the lake a little way. I turned on my Garmin inReach and had Luke sit beside me. I checked the wind. Out of the corner of my eye, I saw Nate mark our position on his handheld GPS and take a reading on his compass. Then I leaned down, shot my hand forward, and said, "Seek, Luke! Seek!"

Luke was trained in both air scenting and HRD, human remains detection. *Seek* was the command to use air scenting to find any human in the general direction I'd pointed him in.

My dog was off in a flash, quartering as he headed toward the lake. Luke didn't track a specific scent trail, so he didn't need an article to sniff.

When the lake came into full view I could see it was small, maybe five acres. I immediately scanned it, searching for little heads, but I couldn't see any. That was neither good nor bad, because if the boys had drowned, their bodies would likely be underwater.

I glanced at Nate. "Counterclockwise," he said, reading my thoughts. I began moving that direction around the pond, watching Luke, but also looking down at the mud for footprints. Twice Luke stopped and sniffed the air, as if he'd scented something, but then he continued around the water. About a third of the way around, Luke stopped, turned toward the woods, and moved away from the water, sniffed the air, and started into the woods.

We got a message on the radio saying the johnboat had arrived and officers would be carrying it down to meet me. "Stand by," I said, reading my dog's actions. "Just hold on."

Luke disappeared into the woods. Nate marked the spot on his GPS. We followed the dog, my ears alert for the sound of his movement, picking our way through the brambles and low undergrowth. He was tracking back and forth, left to right, and moving away from us rapidly.

Then, silence. Nate and I both stopped. Where was he?

Suddenly, we heard an exuberant crashing, a joyful, hopeful smashing through dry leaves, punctuated by excited, low whimpers. "There he is!" I said, and Luke ran to me, grabbed the tug on my belt, and ran away again.

"He's got 'em." Nate clapped me on the back. "Go, go!" I could go faster since he was hobbled with his artificial leg. "Go!" he encouraged me.

So I went. What would I find? The boys alive and well? Or injured? Or worse? What was back there? My heart pounded. I pushed aside small branches. I climbed over a fallen tree. Luke returned, impatiently pulled the tug, and took off again. "I'm coming, I'm coming!"

And then there he was, tail wagging, standing over ... over what?

I saw a massive oak lying on the ground, its root ball ripped from the earth. It looked like it had been there for a while. Luke pawed at the ground. When I caught up to him I looked where he was looking. Two little boys lay snuggled together in the hole left by the root ball. It was at least five feet deep, too deep for them to get out on their own. Were they unconscious? Hypothermic? Worse?

Luke barked, his whole body quivering with excitement. I saw one of the boys move. "Nate! Nate, we've got them!" I heard the radio chatter as he called it in. Then I turned to my dog. "Good boy, Luke! You are a good, good boy!"

I whipped out my phone and took a picture of the pit and the boys, then I dropped my pack and used protruding roots to ease myself down into the hole. "Jacob? Joshua?" I said. The boys stirred. "Boys are you okay?" The edge of the hole was at my eye level. I wasn't sure even I could get out of it by myself, much less two little blond-haired boys.

Barking and whining, Luke began digging at the edges of the hole, flinging dirt down on me. "Stop! Luke, stop." He was worried about me. He didn't like me down there.

Thankfully, Nate showed up and praised Luke, then made him back off. "Are they okay?"

"Yes, I think so."

The boys started to cry. One of them reached for me. "You're okay, buddy. You're okay, " I said, pulling him into my arms. Then the other one held up his hands. "You, too, little man. We're going to get you out of here." They were muddy, and their bodies were cold. I gave them a hug, and then put one down. "You wait. I'm going to hand your brother up to Nate."

I lifted first one, then the other, up to my partner. Thankfully, they were wiry little dudes, and lifting my own son had strengthened my arm muscles. "Don't let them get away!" I said, as if Nate didn't know better. "There are water bottles in the outside pockets of my pack and emergency blankets in the middle compartment."

Nate sat them down on a nearby log, found the water bottles, and gave each boy one. He wrapped each in an emergency blanket. Then, for good measure, he put Luke on a down-stay in front of them. "Make them stay put," he told my dog, who, of course, didn't really understand him.

I tried getting myself out of the pit by grabbing an exposed root and pulling myself up. Major fail. It pulled out, and I fell backwards. "Wait!" Nate said. "Let me get a rope."

"Just tie it to a tree!" I said, determined to free myself. But in the end, two burly cops showed up and pulled me out. I brushed the mud off my butt. And it began to rain.

FINDING twin boys alive and well—that is a worthwhile day. I held my own son particularly close that night, rocking him to sleep while thanking God for the successful search. A steady rain clattered on our metal roof. I shivered thinking of those little guys. If they'd stayed in that pit ...

In my mind, I could still see their mom, a small, blonde woman, sobbing as she embraced her muddy boys. Such relief! I rested my head back on the rocker, satisfied, my son's weight on my body a blessing I would never take for granted.

I must have fallen asleep while rocking Mike to sleep, because the next thing I knew, Scott was gently lifting our son off my lap. "Scott?" I said, opening my eyes.

"Shhh ... it's okay. Come to bed with me."

He'd let Luke out for his last time, locked up the house, and turned out all the lights. He put Mike in his crib and led me to our bedroom. Five minutes later I was sound asleep again.

5

AMANDA

On Tuesday after work, Amanda went to her volunteer job at Hope Ranch, an equine therapy organization on Virginia's Eastern Shore. Across from her Chessie, a quarter horse gelding, and Sam, a former racehorse, and two other horses stood dozing in a corral.

The founder of Hope Ranch, Katherine McClellan, PhD, had a vision to connect hurting people, mostly children, with horses to help heal their emotions. For more than ten years, she'd been watching that vision come true.

Amanda had herself benefitted from Hope Ranch, both from contact with the horses and from individual counseling with Kate. So when Kate asked her if she'd like to start passing on what she'd learned, working with clients as a volunteer, Amanda readily agreed. She and three other potential volunteers had now finished the classroom work and were in the practical part of the training.

Nearby, a mare named Scarlet stood in a roomy paddock with her friend Milo, a fat gray pony. She was a beautiful mare, her red coat glossy in the sun, her head finely chiseled. When

Amanda had first met Scarlet, the mare's wide eyes and flared nostrils were terrifying. She'd come out of an abuse situation. Kate had taken her on, she said, because now and then she liked a challenge.

Something about Scarlet had attracted Amanda, and she'd gotten Kate's permission to work with her. She'd started by hanging out near her stall, reading to her, talking with her, getting her used to her presence. Gradually, Amanda progressed to giving her a carrot without getting bitten. Then came scratches. Light grooming. And after months and months of patient effort, Amanda was able to take her on a victorious walk on a lead rope near the paddocks.

That's when they discovered little Milo loved the red mare. Scarlet's bluster didn't faze him; her craziness didn't upset him. He was the opposite of reactive. He was just what she needed. Now they were buddies, grazing together and hanging out in the paddock, and another milestone in Scarlet's healing had been reached.

A word from Kate brought Amanda's attention back. "As you learned in our classroom work, here we are all about relationship. This is contrary to the rest of our human lives, where our major concern is getting something done. Working. Cleaning. Driving. Making progress. Achieving. And usually, when people approach a horse, they want him to *do* something. Take me for a ride. Jump over that fence. Follow me.

"Our goals here are different. Our purpose is connection with the horse. Partnership. We want to build trust. Mutual understanding. Two-way communication. Cooperation. Affection. Then, when we introduce a client, the horse is set up to offer a calm, relaxed relationship.

"Today we are going to learn how to halter a horse using these principles. How many of you have ever haltered a horse?" Three people, including Amanda, raised their hands. "Unlike what you may have learned, it's not about catching a horse and forcing a halter on it. It's about inviting the horse to join you in what you have planned.

"This may seem contrary to everything you've learned before. It may feel slow to you. Bear with me. I promise you it pays off over time. The chestnut gelding on the left is Chessie. The bay on the right is Sam. He's a former racehorse and is a little more 'hot' or reactive than Chessie. So we'll start with the chestnut. First off, before you even go in the paddock, calm yourself. Let go of your to-do list, your human busyness. Take a deep breath. You want to bring calm energy into the ring. Actually, Amanda, you've done this before. Why don't you demonstrate, and I'll narrate?"

"Okay," Amanda said, taking the halter, lead rope, and training stick from Kate. Feeling a little nervous, she practiced her anti-anxiety breathing while Kate explained further.

"Notice Amanda has a rope halter in her hand. We use those for several reasons. It's light. The knots apply gentle pressure right where we need it, on the horse's head, cheek, and jaw. Next, there's a twelve-foot lead rope already attached to the halter. And finally, she has the training stick in her hand. Anybody remember what the training stick is for?"

An older woman with dark hair raised her hand. "To communicate to the horse and give us some horizontal reach down the length of the horse's body since we humans are mostly vertical."

"Right. Okay, Amanda, how's your energy?"

"I'm pretty calm," she replied.

"Okay, go halter Chessie like you learned to do with Scarlet."

Amanda walked to the gate and slipped inside the paddock. Focused on her task, Kate's voice faded into the background. All of the horses were standing, one back foot cocked, heads down, dozing at the far end. She slowly walked their direction, being careful to give them a soft focus, rather than a hard stare.

Chessie looked up. Amanda stopped and bladed her body so she wasn't directly facing him. She waited, watching in her peripheral vision, to see what he would do. Curious, he slowly walked toward her. She backed up to give him space. He came to her, sniffed her hand, and moved in, asking for a scratch on his withers.

She gave it to him. He turned his head toward her. She stroked his throat. After a while, she put her arm around his neck, caught the off side of the halter, and held it while he inserted his muzzle. She brought the strap around and tied the knot to secure it.

"Now, Amanda and Chessie are connected," Kate said. "But does that mean she should just start walking and expect him to follow at her command? No. She'll invite him along on whatever she has planned. Go ahead, Amanda."

Amanda extended her arm in the direction she wanted to go, and she and the horse stepped out. Together they walked around the paddock to where Kate had opened the gate for them. "Come on out," she said.

Amanda did, stopping in front of the other students.

"Now let me ask you," Kate said, "if you had an anxious child with a history of abuse standing with you, what kind of horse would she find here?"

"Calm."

"Gentle."

"A horse who would invite her to pet him."

"All correct," Kate said. "We treat the horses gently, they treat our clients gently, and everybody wins. All it takes is time, understanding, and patience."

"And love," Amanda said. She felt her face grow hot. *Where had that come from?*

Kate beamed at her. "Most certainly, love."

. . .

THEY SPENT the rest of the two-hour session practicing those techniques with the other horses. After the session, feeling satisfied, Amanda picked up a grooming kit and walked over to spend some time with Scarlet. The red mare came right over when Amanda approached.

"Oh, are you going to be on your best behavior?" Amanda said, scratching the mare's nose. "Were you jealous when I was working with Chessie?" She pulled a lump of sugar out of her pocket and gave it to her. "You're my favorite, Scarlet. You know that."

"She's doing amazing," Kate said, walking up to the paddock. "You've done wonders with her."

Amanda smiled. "I don't know what it is, but working with her relaxes me. I guess it's because I have to be calm for her to be calm."

"They do pick up on your energy."

Amanda looked over at Kate. "Do you think she'll ever be able to work with kids?"

Kate smiled. "Based on what you've done so far, maybe. It'll take a while. You're just about the only one besides me that she's really comfortable with."

"And Henry. She's good with Henry now."

"She probably smells Henry on you and vice versa." Kate checked her watch. "I'd better go. I've got a client coming. Are you going to groom her?"

"Yes. And Milo. He always insists I give him equal time."

"He wants to look his best for his girlfriend," Kate said, laughing.

A CHILLY RAIN began to fall that evening, dripping off the roof as Amanda waited for Henry. She felt a little flutter in her gut. The decision she'd made that day was life-changing. How would she tell her dad?

Finally, Henry's familiar black Tundra swung into the driveway. Her heart lifting, she stood up and opened the screened door, smiling, welcoming him with a kiss. He took her in his arms and she closed her eyes, soaking in his presence along with some of the rain on his jacket. Then she pulled back and looked at him. "Hot or cold?"

"Coffee if you've got it," he said.

Of course she did. Because nine out of ten times, that's what he wanted. Familiar, she'd decided, felt pretty good.

Amanda went inside, picked his favorite mug out of the cabinet, and filled it with hot, dark coffee, grabbed a second mug for herself, and took both out to the front porch. "Good day?" she asked, handing him his mug.

"Yeah. That mare that was colicky? She's much better. And I checked Kate's other horses. One gelding has a hot leg. I told them to ice it. The rest are fine."

Amanda reached over and stroked his arm. "I'm sure she felt better after you examined them."

He gave his head a shake. "Horses can be tricky. Lots of things can go wrong. Gives you respect for the wild ones. I need to go to that family farm down near Machipongo tomorrow."

"The one with all the goats?"

"Goats, chickens, beef cattle, sheep. I can handle everything but the honeybees. They're on their own with them." Henry took a sip, then turned to Amanda. "How about you? How was work? Did you decide?"

She'd told him that morning that her deadline was coming up. She took a deep breath. "Yes. I'm not going to law school. I'm taking applied bio classes instead."

"At Salisbury?"

She nodded.

"Good for you." His mouth formed a soft smile. Then he reached over and squeezed her hand. "I'm so happy."

Applying for the program, based an hour away in Maryland, meant staying in Chincoteague. "Henry, I feel like I'm going backward. I have so many prerequisites to take if I want a master's degree."

He nodded. "You are, a little. But if it's really something you want to do ..."

"When I look at the list of courses I can take in biology, and then look at law school, well, there's no comparison."

"You want the bio classes."

"I could get through the law school ones, but they look so boring."

"Then don't do it."

"I've really loved working at the refuge, learning about the plants, the birds, the animals. Plus, if I don't go to law school, I can stay here."

"Don't stay here for me."

She smiled. "I don't need to stay here for you. I know, Henry Bunting, how to find you anytime I want. Right on this island. You're not going anywhere, that's for sure."

He laughed. "You got that right." He lifted her hand to his lips and kissed it. Then he turned and stared out over the water. "So," he said, his voice steady, "let's get married."

"What? Henry!"

"Why not?" He shrugged. "I love you. You seem to think I'm okay. So let's get married. I'm kinda getting tired of the commute."

"What? The one mile between your house and mine?"

"A mile can be a long way."

"I can't marry you!"

"Why not?"

"I'll ruin you."

He shifted his jaw and frowned, thinking. Then he nodded. "I'm willing to take that chance."

A silence grew between them. The creak of his porch rocker and the swish of tires on the wet street were the only sounds.

"I'm afraid," she said, finally.

"I know."

The rain came down harder, pounding on the pavement in little explosions. Exactly like what was going on in her heart.

Henry squeezed her hand. "Ask your folks if we can come visit. Like next weekend. You can tell your dad about law school, and I'll ask him if I can marry his daughter."

She jumped to her feet and faced him. "I haven't said yes!"

Henry stood up, leaned over, and kissed her, then he drew her to himself. "I love you, Amanda," he said, whispering in her ear. "I want to be with you. To make a life with you. To protect you and take care of you. Even sleep with you. Will you please marry me?"

She didn't respond.

"It's yes or no, Amanda. Just yes or no. And if it's no, I promise I'll leave you alone."

Her voice stuck in her throat. If yes was scary, no was terrifying. Losing Henry? This incredible man? She saw her future slipping away like a riptide. Her head spun. She looked into Henry's beautiful brown eyes. Touched his cheek and felt the stubble of his beard. She could not lose this man. "Oh, Henry, yes! I'll marry you."

He gave a whoop, picked her up, and swung her around. "Girl, that's the best news ever! I love you!" He kissed her hard.

6

JESS

On Wednesday morning, Scott slept in. Mike and I had breakfast and fed Luke. Then we went out to the barn and gave the horses some hay. Luke made his morning perimeter search of our property. Then, as Mike and I walked back from the barn, we saw two does stick their noses out from between the trees on the other side of our driveway. "Mike, look!" I said, quietly.

He immediately pulled away from me and took off, chasing them. They ran away, bounding through my butterfly garden and into the field beyond. Mike would have followed if I hadn't caught him. "Those are deer," I said, grabbing his hand. "They run fast, like horses. Here, let's watch." I picked him up, and we watched the deer run through the field and back into the woods.

"All gone?" Mike said, holding his hands up.

"Yes. All gone." I set him down. "Let's go see if Daddy's up."

We walked back to the house and met Luke coming up from the pasture. "Come on, buddy," I said, and as we mounted the stairs, Scott emerged from inside.

"What a beautiful day!" he said.

Indeed it was. Chilly, maybe forty-five degrees, but the sun was shining and the air felt fresh. The ground was wet from last night's rain, but that would soon dry out.

Mike grabbed his daddy's legs, and Scott reached down and picked him up. "Have you had breakfast, little buddy?"

"We've eaten and so have Luke and the horses," I said. I gave Scott a kiss.

We went inside. I made Scott some eggs while he made coffee. Mike acted like he wanted eggs too, so I put him in his high chair and gave him some. Really, I think he just wanted to be like his daddy. He soon wanted to get down, so I lifted him down and pulled out a special box of toys I keep in a cabinet so he could play and Scott and I could talk.

That's when he told me the news. "While you were putting Mike to bed last night," he said, "Amanda called. She and Henry want to come visit."

"Really!" So much had changed. "When?" I asked.

"They wanted to come the weekend after next, but I looked on the calendar and you've got that SAR training going on."

"Here."

"Right. So, they're coming this weekend!"

"Seriously?"

"If that's alright with you."

My mind started calculating all that I needed to do. *Get food. Prep two bedrooms. Check our supply of paper goods. Wash some clothes.*

"Is that okay?" Scott asked.

"Yes! Fine. Great, in fact!" I'd actually hoped to go back to Charlottesville with Mike in a stroller to walk past Brittany Hudgins's house, but hey, I could do that any day. "Can we invite Nate over? I'm sure he'd love to see them."

"Yes!" Scott paused. "Do you think they'll want to ride? Should I brush out the horses?"

I smiled. "I think it would be a very good idea."

SINCE LAST FALL, Amanda and Henry had come up to visit three or four times. Henry didn't have much in the way of family, just a father who was MIA most of the time and a brother who worked on an oil rig in the Gulf. They even came up for Christmas, and we went all out. Tree, decorations, Christmas Eve candlelight service, turkey dinner, presents. Nate had brought his banjo and his guitar and played songs we knew, more or less. And we played board games too. That was new.

While they were here, Amanda and Henry walked up behind the barn to the gravesite where Amanda's baby, Mia, was buried. Amanda, raped by a stranger, became pregnant and miscarried at five months. Trauma followed by tragedy. I watched them stand there, holding hands, for quite a while.

I took that for a good sign. Amanda had initially refused to grieve the loss of Mia. Now, she finally seemed strong enough to face that reality. Between her job, counseling, and Henry she seemed more anchored.

I loved Henry. So did Scott. I would have preferred Amanda's anchor to be Jesus, but Henry was a good first step. At least she was anchored to someone who seemed like a good guy. Plus she was happy.

We were ready when they arrived on Saturday at eleven, stepping out on the front porch to greet them. Amanda's blonde hair had grown back and fell below her shoulders. She was model-thin, with long, lanky legs, and tall, like her dad, with the same blue eyes. Henry was almost the same height, with broad shoulders and strong hands. His golden-brown eyes reminded me of Luke's, and I don't think he'd mind me thinking that.

We hugged them hello before they bent down and said hi to

Mike. Henry pulled something from his pocket. It was a six-inch plastic horse, black. "Here you go, Mike. It's for you!"

Mike said his word for "horse" and lifted it high, so I could see it. "That's so cool!" I said. "A horse."

They brought their things inside. "Same bedrooms as last time," I said, and they took their bags upstairs. As soon as they came down, Scott asked me, "Do we have time for a ride before lunch?"

"Of course. Go for it," I said. "We'll eat about one."

"Good." He looked at our visitors. "Let's go to the barn."

He shouldn't have said "barn." Mike immediately ran to the door and tried to open it, reaching high for the doorknob.

"We'll go down with you," I said, "but before you saddle up, I'll bring Mike back here. If he sees those saddles go on, he'll want to go too."

The day had warmed up. Perfect weather for a ride.

The horses were in their stalls, all brushed out and ready to go. Henry immediately began examining them, running his hand over their bodies and legs, picking up their feet, feeling their necks, and stroking their withers while narrating their condition. "They're good," he said to Scott. "They're in fine shape. Both of them."

Scott's grin conveyed his pride. His black gelding, Ace, was pretty much in the prime of his life, but the red mare, Abby, was almost twenty.

Henry looked at Amanda. "How 'bout you go first with your dad?" Then he winked at her.

I saw that wink! What was that all about? "Let me take Mike back to the house," I said.

"I'll go with you," Henry said. "C'mon, Mike! Jump on my back." He squatted down.

Mike knew exactly what that meant. He climbed on and threw his arms around Henry's neck. Henry galloped like a horse all the way back up to the house. I had to jog to keep up.

Forty minutes later, just as Henry was perfecting his Duplo tower technique, the front door burst open and Amanda came in, smiling. "Your turn," she said to Henry.

"I'll be back, Mike," he said. He gave Amanda a quick kiss and walked out.

"Let me wash my hands and I'll join you," Amanda said to Mike and me. We were sitting on the floor, Mike's toys all around us. She smelled faintly of horse, but that was normal for our house.

"Have a nice ride?" I asked when she returned. I kept my tone neutral, but I was dying of curiosity about that wink. I mean, maybe it was nothing.

"Really good."

"Which horse did you ride?"

"Abby." Amanda focused on the toys. "Want to build a barn, Mike, for your new horse?" He readily agreed and the two of them started working on that. "I told Dad I'm not going to law school."

"Oh?"

"I know it's prestigious and everything, but the more I thought about it, the more boring it seemed, both the classes and the career afterward."

"How did he react?"

"Surprised at first, but then he regrouped." She looked up at me. "I like what I'm doing at the refuge. Most of the time I'm outside. When I'm inside, I'm either in the lab or charting statistics. And it's interesting to me. It seems important."

"That's good. It's important to like what you do for a living."

"That's what Dad said."

She attached a second floor to half the building. "Look, Mike. That's the loft. Should we use green blocks for the hay?" He grunted his approval and Amanda continued. "I'm going to take some biology courses at Salisbury University, and if I like it and do okay, I'll go for an advanced degree."

"Very smart. Your job may pay for some of that."

"I hope so."

Mike suddenly smashed the hayloft, looked at her, and giggled.

"That's his love language," I said.

"You little devil!" She tickled his belly. "Come on, let's build it again." She started picking up blocks.

I waited a bit, then said, "Your dad was very excited you two wanted to come up this weekend." I paused. "You were smart to tell him about law school in person."

"Yes, well ..." Amanda stopped what she was doing and turned to me. "There's something else."

My heart thumped.

"Henry asked me to marry him."

"What! Oh, Amanda, I'm so happy for you." I rose to my knees, leaned over, and gave her a hug. "You said yes?"

She nodded. "I told him he didn't have to ask Dad. But Henry is old-fashioned. He said no, he wanted to do it the right way. He says I'm worth it."

"Scott will be so pleased. We love Henry. And you, of course. Oh Amanda! Tell me all about it, how he asked and all. I want all the details!"

So Amanda told me about the porch and the rain and what he said.

"When I said yes, he went crazy! Grabbed me and started dancing all around, singing some crazy song about falling into a fire. I got to laughing so hard I couldn't breathe!"

"What? That Johnny Cash song?"

"I don't know! He went crazy is all."

"He loves you."

She smiled and nodded.

"He's a good guy, Amanda. Hang onto him."

Smash! Mike destroyed the barn again, knocking it apart and kicking the blocks. Then he looked at Amanda with impish eyes and grinned. That boy's smile could bring joy to a turnip.

THE REST of the weekend went so well, I could hardly believe it. After years of skirmishes with Amanda it appeared the worst of the battle was over. She actually seemed happy. While I fixed lunch, Scott and Henry took another ride, this time with Mike up in the saddle with his dad. After lunch I put Mike down for a nap. The three of them went to work on something in the barn.

Nate arrived around four with his black German shepherd, Ember. By that time I was up and so was Mike. Henry asked us about search and rescue, and rather than just talk, Nate decided to demonstrate. He asked Amanda to go hide in the woods while I kept the dogs inside. "Find a hard place," I heard him say to her.

After about ten minutes, Nate texted me to come outside. I'd put Luke's SAR vest on to let him know we were working. Leaving Ember inside, I joined the others out behind the house. Mike immediately ran to Luke, but Scott intercepted him.

Nate acted as the search director. He assigned Henry to be my walker. And he pointed out the portion of the property Luke and I had been given to search. "Now normally, that would be on a map, and she'd be carryin' a forty-pound pack " Nate told Henry. "I'm lettin' her off easy today."

Nate showed me where he wanted me to begin, and I put Luke in a sit-down beside me. I puffed a little baby powder in the air to identify the wind direction. Nate, standing behind me, narrated what I was doing. Then I drew Luke's attention to an area that included the barn, paddock, and the woods beyond. Scott and Mike were behind us, and I kept seeing

Luke's ears flick back when Mike made a noise. I kept speaking to him quietly, and when I thought he was focused, I said, "Seek, Luke. Seek!" and I shot my hand forward.

My dog took off like a gold-and-black fireball, and I followed. Almost immediately he began quartering, and why not? He was looking for "any human" and we'd all been around the barn area that morning.

When he got to the barn itself, he stopped and looked at me. I caught up and told him, "Go ahead." He went into the barn and sniffed through all the stalls. He even looked up the ladder to the loft, but then decided no one was up there and left the barn.

"Wow, that's cool," Henry said, following me.

"So if this were a real search, you'd make a note that he'd hesitated at the loft ladder in our log or on a handheld GPS and that we didn't check it."

We exited the barn and Luke was nowhere in sight. "Where'd he go?" Henry asked.

"Into the woods, I'd guess, since we can't see him. So in this case, I listen for him, or just walk in the general direction of a point I'd picked out ahead of time. He'll range pretty far left and right while he's searching." I stopped to listen, then said, "This way."

We kept on walking through the woods and across our driveway. Then, finally, I heard Luke racing back. He grabbed the braided rope tug on my belt loop and took off again. "He'll keep doing that until he leads me back to the search subject," I said. "Then comes the most important part."

"What's that?"

"His play reward."

Amanda, it turned out, had hidden behind a tree and halfway down in the ditch that runs parallel to the road. "I'll tell you," she said, laughing as Henry offered her a hand up, "that dog is intimidating when you're on the ground and he's coming at you with all that energy!"

"Did you come straight to this spot from the backyard?" Henry asked.

"No, I went through the barn, then beyond it into the woods and then here."

I was already throwing Luke's favorite Kong toy for him. We walked back toward the house where everyone else was waiting in the front yard. Scott was holding Mike, but as soon as he saw us, our son kicked to get down and came running toward us, toward Luke actually. My dog put his brakes on to keep from running over his favorite little boy. Mike threw his arms around the dog's neck, and Luke licked his face. Then Mike grabbed a fistful of hair, and the two of them walked back to the house, side-by-side, at Mike's pace. *Someday, that little boy will be old enough to work with his own dog.*

We had dinner at six. I made a pasta and Italian sausage dish with salad and bread, and apple cobbler for dessert. We talked for a while in the living room. Henry sat on the floor. Most of the time he had a dog lying next to him.

I took our son upstairs to bed at eight-thirty. With all the activity, Mike had a hard time settling down to sleep. By the time he was down, I was ready for bed. I didn't even go back downstairs. Scott didn't come up until midnight, and I found out later that Henry and Nate stayed up talking until three in the morning.

I wondered what that was all about.

We all woke up early Sunday morning. Amanda and Henry had to head back to Chincoteague because Henry was on call that afternoon. I made breakfast for everybody and extra coffee so they could fill their travel mugs. We hugged them goodbye, and afterward Scott held me in his arms for a long time. I could feel the relief in his body. "What a miracle," he whispered.

What can I say? God is good.

We basked in the light of that good visit all day Sunday. That night, Scott and I had gone to bed when at 11:10 p.m., my phone beeped.

A text. From Brett Hudgins. I slipped out of bed.

7

JESS

When I read the text from Brett I knew I had to act on it. *Brittany has the girls,* he wrote. *Supposed to be back at seven. No response to my calls/texts. I'm furious. I don't know what to do.*

I responded, *Call the non-emergency number for the police and report it to establish an official record.*

He was a lawyer. He should have thought of that. He was probably frazzled. I needed to talk to him. *Can I call you?*

Three minutes later I was downstairs. "Do you have any idea what she was going to do with them this past week?" I asked Brett. Luke, who had followed me, took one look at the phone pressed against my ear and laid down on the kitchen floor.

"No!" Brett said. "And that's the problem. I don't know what she's doing or who with. Ever." A mix of anger and fear tightened his voice.

"She's done this before, right?"

"It's not unusual for her to be late. Six, seven o'clock. But it's after eleven! The kids have school tomorrow. I have work. It's ridiculous."

"Do your girls have iPads or iPhones?"

"Yes, iPads, but she won't let them bring them."

So much for the tracking feature. "Did you go by her house?"

He hesitated, then admitted he had. "It's dark."

"Okay, do what I said. Call the non-emergency number of the police department. Report it. And call me back." I thought of something else. "You know her license plate number, right?"

"I should. It's my car."

"What?" My eyes widened.

"My name is still on the title. I let her keep it so she'd have something to drive."

"Brett, if your name is on the title and registration, I can put a tracker on it." No response. "Look, call the police. And then we'll go from there."

A FEW MINUTES LATER, I got a text. He'd called the police and they'd come and taken a report. Finally, at 1:08 a.m., Brett called me. "They found them. At her house. She told them she'd taken the girls to 'see friends' in Northern Virginia and they'd gotten into traffic on I-95. So they were late. By the time they got to her house, the girls were tired, and she put them to bed. She told the cops she'd planned to call me in the morning.

"What did the cops do?" I was almost afraid to ask.

"One of them thought they shouldn't wake them up but the other said the custody arrangement was a court order and they needed to enforce that."

"God bless him!"

"Her. But yes, I'm thankful." He sighed. "They're in bed—here—asleep now. Sometime I'll ask them what exactly happened. But for now, they're safe."

"Good. Be sure to tell Frank Sinclair about this."

"I've already emailed his office. And Ms. Cooper, I'm sorry if I woke you up. My emotions ran away with me."

"No worries. Let's talk again in a day or two."

Of course, there was no way I was going to sleep after that mess! Instead, I went upstairs and opened my laptop, opting to move the case forward if I could. First, though, I ran a criminal background check on Brett Hudgins. It would be irresponsible, and in fact illegal, for me to put a tracker on Brittany's car if Brett had a criminal record. That was unlikely, since he was a practicing lawyer, but I needed to cover that base.

Thankfully, his record was clean as a whistle. And so, in fact, was Brittany's, except for a speeding ticket last year. Not a big deal.

I was still wide awake, so I thought I'd go a little deeper on her. I checked the normal social media platforms—all of them. There seemed to be more every year. Brittany's pages on which she used her maiden name or some iteration of it, were carefully curated. Gone was the somewhat-dumpy housewife look. Instead, she was beautiful. Successful. Loving.

I'd give her the "beautiful" part. She was that, now anyway. Her pictures showed a slim brunette, her hair thick and wavy, her eyes perfectly set in her face, her brows arched. Honestly, it looked like she'd had a glamour makeover.

I checked her posts carefully for recurring faces and locations, copying some of them for a file I'd begun on the case. I checked her friends and followers, making list after list of names. I made notes on who she followed on X, most of whom were "influencers."

I pulled out a small notebook and started writing down questions. Who were her close friends? Did she go to church? What did the other neighborhood moms think of her? Her girls' teachers?

Then I had an idea. Was she on any of the dating apps? Could that explain the multiple men visiting the house? I hadn't checked those for a case in a long time. I used her email address, which Brett had given me, and the names she used on her social media accounts, but didn't come up with anything. I even got creative and developed other forms of her name, seeing if I could get a hit. Then I discovered I could use her picture and reverse-search the apps, using facial recognition.

I had some success via that method. I think I found her on two sites initially, and then one more that I wasn't familiar with. But then, I thought, wasn't it possible for someone else to use her picture? I copied the information I'd found and then made myself stop looking. I needed to know more about these dating sites before using this information. Plus there was nothing illegal or immoral about being on them, right? I mean, I'd been hired to develop information which might support Brett's petition for full custody. Anything else was just snooping.

At 3:12 a.m., I closed my laptop and went to bed. I still couldn't sleep. I kept wondering what Brittany was up to and about that new dating app and whether I could trust the information I'd gotten and most of all, did it matter?

Around four, I fell asleep. Luke nudged me awake at 6:30 a.m. Little Mike was calling me. Nate says short nights make for long days. And I was in for one.

Scott was gone. It was Monday, his day to work, and when he drives into Quantico he leaves before six. I vaguely remembered him kissing me goodbye.

I dragged myself out of bed and went in to greet my son who was in the process of throwing everything out of his crib—his lovey, his blanket, his stuffies, and his water bottle. Despite my sleepiness, I smiled. "Well, good morning, sweet boy!" I said. "Are you ready to get up?"

Clearly he was. If he could have climbed out he would have. Scott and I had talked about moving him into a big boy's bed.

Mornings like this, though, he'd be all over the house before I was even awake.

While I fed Mike breakfast I checked the weather. I needed to figure out how to survive until my son's afternoon naptime. With just a couple hours of sleep, I knew I wasn't going to have a lot of energy or patience. My weather app predicted a high of sixty-two today, sunny and breezy. I toyed with the idea of taking the stroller and walking through Brittany's neighborhood. It would keep Mike occupied, help me work on the case, and if I waited until ten or so, it wouldn't be too chilly for him.

I lifted Mike out of his high chair, and we put on jackets to go check the horses. Luke came with us. When I got to the barn, I realized Scott must have fed them before he left. The horses were in the field and there was hay in the hayracks.

We played for a time in Mike's play area in the fourth stall. Then I let him add a handful of hay to the racks. He wanted to go out in the field and pet the horses, but I wasn't up for that, so I diverted him to our front yard, where we threw the ball for Luke.

We all went back inside and our morning continued. I had work to do from the weekend—sheets and towels to wash and extra dishes to put away. Mike "helped" me. Around nine thirty, I got a call from Brett.

I swooped up Mike, moved to the living room, and set him down near his toys. I put the gate up to block the doorway and sat down near him. Thank goodness I'd put a pen and my black notebook in my back pocket when I got dressed!

Clearly, trying to sound professional while building a Duplo barn was a skill I needed to learn. I switched the phone to my left ear, holding it in place with my shoulder, and took notes as Brett updated me.

"I let the girls sleep late. I just dropped them off at school. Over breakfast they told me what happened."

"What did they say?"

"Brittany drove them somewhere a long way away. They were on a highway with a lot of trucks. My older daughter saw a sign that said Springfield."

"So, Northern Virginia."

"Right. Then ..." He paused and took a deep breath. "She took them to a small apartment. A woman with an accent was there. And she left them! Left them there overnight! Unbelievable!" He added a strong word which I won't repeat.

"Was anyone else there? A man? Anybody? Did anything happen to them?" The alarm in my voice caught Mike's attention.

"Look, my girls know about inappropriate touches and all. Apparently, nothing happened. Apparently, it was just the woman. But I am furious!"

"What did they do all day?"

"They were allowed to watch TV, read books, play with their toys. The woman had no kids, so really, she was just babysitting as far as I can tell. She fed them. They slept in a bed big enough for both of them. And their mom came back and picked them up the next day."

"What time?"

"Noon."

"So she should have had plenty of time to get back to Charlottesville to hand the girls over at five."

"Yes. It's about a two-and-a-half-hour drive. But she didn't drive straight here. In fact, she drove them to Massanutten."

"Massanutten?" It was too warm for skiing and too cold for swimming. "What in the world were they doing there?"

"We used to go there sometimes as a family. There are things to do even at this time of the year."

"Ah," I said. "She wanted to give the girls something to tell you about, hoping they wouldn't mention the overnight."

"Exactly."

My gut was tight with tension. I felt his anger. "Look. Since you're on the registration, I can put a tracker on her car. But if I were you, I'd get Nora an Apple Watch. With cellular. She's old enough for that. Tell her not to wear it, to keep it in her backpack. That way you can see where she is, and she can even call you if she's scared."

"I will do that today."

"Is Brittany dating?"

"I don't know. If she's not, what are all the men coming around for?"

"I found her on two dating apps. There may be more."

"I figured." Brett blew out a breath. "Look, I just got to my office. I've got to go."

"Tell your lawyer what you told me. If you want a tracker, have Frank send me an email requesting it. Then I'll get on it ASAP."

I CLICKED off my phone wondering if I could wait until Wednesday to add the tracker. Then I realized Mike had escaped. He wasn't in front of me, playing with his toys. I glanced around—he was upside down on Scott's recliner, playing with the chair's remote, his head on the footrest. When he saw me looking at him, he giggled.

"You little rascal!" I said, jumping up.

He laughed and pressed a button, which made him slide forward, over the footrest. I caught him just before he hit the floor face-first. "Come on, you little bug," I said, picking him up. "Mommy has to work upstairs for a while."

Once we were upstairs in my office, I pulled out the very special box of toys I kept there for Mike. Then I opened my laptop, created a document cataloguing all I'd found, and what Brett reported. I saved it to my Hudgins file and emailed a copy to his lawyer, Frank Sinclair. Then I played with Mike a little.

My plan for the next step in my case ran continually in the

back of my mind. Something about this whole situation was making me feel hinky. If I went to put the tracker on Brittany's car, I wanted to carry my weapon. Why did I feel like I needed to be armed? I can't explain it, but I wasn't going to ignore my instinct.

That meant I'd either have to leave Mike with a sitter or wait until Wednesday when Scott would be home. While Mike pushed buttons on an electronic piano, I texted my friend Ellie to see if she'd be available tomorrow. She was, bless her.

That night, after I put Mike to bed, I told Scott what I was planning to do. He questioned me about the legality, but I told him Brett's name was still on the registration and, if Brittany had the girls, he could track them. Then Scott asked for both Brittany's and Brett's contact information. That was one adjustment we'd made since last year: We'd agreed that whenever either of us was going out on a case, we'd give the other all the details and ask enough questions to hopefully keep each other out of trouble.

Late Monday, I got an email from Frank Sinclair asking me to put a tracker on Brittany's car for use when she had the girls. I texted Brett and told him I'd try to do that the next day. The only problem would be if she didn't go anywhere. I couldn't enter the garage to do it.

He did something bold. He called Brittany to see if they could meet to talk about dance lessons the girls were supposedly interested in, and he also wanted to give her a check. He suggested the next morning at ten. She said no, she couldn't possibly. She had a class at a yoga studio at just that time.

Bingo. He gave me the address of the studio, which was in Charlottesville. "It has a large parking lot to the right of the building," he told me. "She'll be driving a dark red Toyota Grand Highlander." Then he gave me the license plate number.

"You've made it easy," I told him.

Our plan was set. The next morning I put on mom clothes

—jeans, tennis shoes, and a great big, oversized sweatshirt that would hide my gun. I put my hair in a loose ponytail, and then, at the last minute, I decided to take Luke with me. Why? For company. Just a mom and her dog, running errands.

We dropped off Mike at Ellie's house. Ellie homeschools her five kids. She says adding one more is no big deal. The older ones take turns playing with Little Mike, and it all works out.

The bright sunshine warmed the left side of my face as I drove south in my mom van toward Charlottesville. The high today was supposed to be fifty-eight degrees, plenty cool enough to leave Luke in the car if I needed to. I did a drive-by past the yoga place. It was last in a line of small shops on a leafy street. As Brett had said, a parking lot sat just to the right side of it. There was also street parking in an adjacent residential neighborhood.

At ten, when Brittany's class was supposed to start, I found a parking place on the street about two blocks away. I decided to leave Luke in the van. He's usually in a crate in the back when we travel. For some reason, I let him ride in the seat this time. Maybe I was a little lonely.

I rolled the windows down a bit to give my dog some air, locked the van, and walked in the opposite direction of the yoga studio to throw off any observers. I took a left at the first street, then another left, then a left on the studio's street. I walked briskly past the front door, the tracker hidden in my right hand.

As I passed the building, the parking lot came into view. I spotted Brittany's dark-red Highlander. It was parked between two other large SUVs. Great cover. I cut diagonally across the lot, as if I were merely taking a shortcut. When I was right next to the back left door of Brittany's car, I crouched down, slid the tracker under the frame, made sure it was attached, and then almost had a heart attack at the sound of a voice behind me.

"You okay, miss?" a man said.

I turned around, my heart pounding, and forced myself to my feet. "Me? Oh, yes, I ... I dropped my key fob."

"Can I reach it for you?"

"No, no. I got it." I fished it out of my pocket and showed him. "It just took me a minute to get up." I thought he was looking at me suspiciously. I rolled my eyes. "My husband says I'm a klutz. Awkward. And you know?" I gestured helplessly. "Maybe I am."

He nodded. Shifted his jaw.

"Well, I'd better get going," I said.

"Right."

"Thanks for checking on me!"

I felt like I was doing a perp walk across the parking lot. I'm sure his eyes were following me. Did he buy my story? Was he going to check under the car? Had he guessed what I was doing? Had he seen the outline of my gun?

My neck and shoulders were so tight I thought I must look like a hunchback. With every step I expected to hear that man's voice calling out to me. But I didn't hear anything.

I got to my van and there was Luke, sitting in the driver's seat, waiting for me. My vigilant guardian. I smiled and opened the door. "Scoot!" I said, and he jumped to the passenger seat. "All the way, buddy!" I gestured toward the back seat, and he complied, releasing a flurry of dog hair. But then, sensing my anxiety, he turned, put his paws on the center console, and licked my ear. I reached back and scratched his neck. "You are a good boy, Luke, a good, good boy." I patted him. "Now, go lie down."

8

AMANDA

After a satisfying day at work, Amanda sat on the front porch of the Main Street house waiting for Henry, playing with the diamond engagement ring on her finger. The spring air smelled sweet. Across the way, the channel flowed smoothly, unruffled by the gentle breeze. The laughing gulls were back after migrating south for the winter. Three of them squawked, fighting over something across the street—maybe a dropped piece of bread?—their black heads poking at it and each other. The sun was sliding down slowly, preparing for its golden farewell to the day.

Henry would stop by whenever he finished with his rounds. Large animal vets didn't keep office hours, because cows and horses always seemed to go into labor at night. Unlike the rest of Henry's generation, he didn't like to text a lot. *I'll be there when I get there*, he always said. By now, she was used to it, but she didn't like it. After all, what if he was in a ditch somewhere? Or broken down on the side of the road?

When should they get married? And where? Her father had offered their farm. It was beautiful, but she couldn't imagine getting married to Henry anywhere other than the beach. As for when? Henry had grinned and said, "Yesterday."

Amanda watched as an old, bent-over man with an ancient dog walked down the street. The dog paused at every light pole, every bush, and sniffed. The man stood, patiently waiting until the dog moved again. She couldn't imagine Henry ever being that old. Or even her dad. What was the point of living if you couldn't, like, *do* things? If even walking was a struggle?

She'd suggested to Henry that they simply elope. Slip away to the courthouse and have a justice of the peace marry them.

He'd said no.

"Why?" she'd asked him. "It'd be so easy!"

Henry had taken her in his arms and said, "Because when we're fifty and boring, I want you to have a beautiful day to look back on. I want you to remember a day when you walked an aisle, looking stunning in a gorgeous white dress with flowers in your hair. A day when, in front of all our family and friends, I looked at you and said I'd love you and care for you forever, for better and for worse, in sickness and in health. I want that for you, Amanda. I want you to have that memory."

Just thinking of him saying that brought tears to her eyes.

Her phone rang. Henry. She answered.

"Hey," he said, "we have a cow in trouble. Not going to make it tonight."

"Okay! Thanks for letting me know."

"I'm sorry. I'll miss you. But I'll make it up to you."

She could hear the grin in his voice. "Oh, really? How's that?"

"I'll let you come with me while I inoculate the herd in a couple of weeks."

She laughed. "Oh, wow, Henry! Would you really? That's so sweet of you."

After they hung up, she went inside and made herself dinner, pasta with sun-dried tomatoes and olives, and good sourdough bread, which she'd been hoarding since their last trip to Salisbury. She studied for a biology course she just started taking, and, just as she was ready for bed, her phone rang. Henry, again. "What's up?"

"Any chance you could come help me?"

An arrow of alarm ran through her. "Where are you? What's going on?" Images of Henry, hurt, Henry in an accident, Henry ... ran through her mind.

"I'm at the clinic. I was on my way back from that farm and I saw something on the edge of the road. I pulled off and, well, it's a dog. It's been hit. Nobody's here, and I could sure use some help. I could call—"

"No, Henry! I'll come. I'll leave now."

AMANDA GRABBED her wallet and some water and protein bars and jumped into her car. The beautiful day had turned into a starlit night, but she kept her eyes on the road. The drive to the clinic would take thirty-five minutes. She wanted to get there sooner.

She arrived at the twenty-nine-minute mark. Good time. Henry had left the door to the clinic unlocked. She walked in and found him in the surgery. Stretched out on the table before him was a thin, black spaniel.

Henry looked up. "Thank you." He nodded toward the sink. "Scrub up."

She laid her wallet and water down and scrubbed her hands and arms, then snapped on gloves. "What's wrong with him?"

"Besides neglect?" Henry barely hid his anger. "He's been hit. His spine is okay. I think he's got a dislocated shoulder and maybe broken ribs. I've got him on oxygen and fluids. I sedated him a little. I want to do X-rays."

"What can I do?"

He nodded toward the dog's head. "Monitor his breathing while I get the X-ray machine ready."

"Will do." Amanda thought of something else. "Was there a microchip?"

"No. And no collar. His pads are worn. He's been on the run for a while. But he's young. That's good. I'd like to keep him lightly sedated. If I need to do surgery, I can take him down deeper."

Henry went into the small room where the X-ray machine was and returned minutes later. The two of them worked together quietly, handling the dog gently, positioning him. Every once in a while, the dog would whimper, but otherwise, he remained still. After they were done, Henry said, "Step out for just a minute so I can get a picture."

Amanda did what he asked, then returned when Henry called her. She stood next to the table, stroking the dog, and talking to him. At one point, the dog turned his head and licked her hand.

Henry came back in. "Okay. Hip is okay, just sore. His shoulder is partially dislocated and he's got a broken rib. No pneumothorax that I can see."

"Pneumo-what?"

"Punctured lung. I'm going to attempt a closed reduction on his shoulder. It'll hurt."

"And what do you do for ribs?"

"Just keep him quiet for a couple of weeks. He'll heal." Henry started pulling things out of drawers. "If you keep talking to him, maybe we can do this without taking him under."

"You're a good boy," she said, rubbing behind the dog's ears, trying to keep his attention. Out of the corner of her eye, she saw Henry put his hands on the dog's leg and shoulder. He moved quickly, the dog yelped, and she flinched.

"Got it," Henry said.

"So that's it?"

"That's it for the shoulder. The rib will heal. And the hip. I'm concerned about his weight, though. He looks like he hasn't eaten in a while. He's got fleas. And his coat is all matted." He shook his head and stroked the dog.

"So what do we do?"

"I should put him in one of the cages and alert the daytime staff. But—"

"But you can't. *We* can't."

"He's such a patient little dude." Henry twisted his mouth.

"Yes."

"He needs to stay quiet. And when a dog is starved like him you have to reintroduce food carefully. A little bit every couple of hours."

Amanda checked her watch. "The daytime staff won't be in for, like, five hours."

"Right." Henry took a deep breath. "I don't like him staying overnight in the clinic. He should be isolated. His immune system is probably low."

"Henry, it sounds like he needs to come home with us."

Henry pressed his lips together and nodded. "Yes. That would be the best thing. Just for a day or two. Until he's a little stronger."

"Great! What should we call him?"

"No names. That's the first step to, well, you know. Let's groom him and give him a bath, and we'll take him home. Temporarily."

9

JESS

Thanks to the tracker I'd put on Brittany's car, for half a day I saw everywhere she traveled around Charlottesville. Then, assured the tracker was working, I set up a geo-fence so it would alert me only if she left that area. I wouldn't monitor her position unless she had the girls with her and left the area. That seemed not only moral, but defensible in court.

She had the girls the next week, beginning on Sunday night. At first, everything seemed normal—the girls were in school all week. Brittany drove around close to home. But early the next Sunday morning, my tracker alerted me. Brittany had taken off up Route 20 toward Orange and Spotsylvania, then she went northbound on Interstate 95.

I got a text from Brett. *Are you getting this?*

Yes, I responded. He was tracking Brittany's travel on his daughter's hidden watch.

It was a weird multitasking morning. I sat on the floor with Mike, playing with his collection of tractors and farm equipment, while watching Brittany's progress on my phone. Where was she going? And was it the same place she'd gone before? My curiosity grew as she drove north.

Scott woke up and came downstairs, saw what I was doing, and said, "Want me to take over with Mike?"

"That would be great," I said. "I can watch this while I make eggs if you want."

"Yes. Thank you."

"And hey, I'm not sure I'm going to be able to go to church."

"Okay."

I stood and gave Scott a good morning kiss, and he took my place on the floor. I went to the kitchen, propped my phone on the counter next to the stove, and scrambled up some eggs. Just as I finished, Brittany's car stopped moving. "Eggs are ready, Scott!"

He came into the kitchen with Mike right behind him and took over. I went upstairs so I could concentrate. My tracker program showed me the address where Brittany had stopped. I opened my laptop and entered it into Google and soon had a Google Earth image. I scanned the neighborhood. Three-story apartment buildings south of Alexandria. They looked familiar. That's when I realized that it was the same Section 8 apartment complex where Jayden Catlett, the missing boy I'd found last year, had lived.

Brett called. "What is that place?" he demanded. By tracking the Apple Watch, he could see the address, but he apparently hadn't checked Google maps to see what was there.

"Section 8 apartments," I said. "I'm familiar with them."

He cursed.

"Let's hang up so I can focus. I'll text you if she moves."

I logged everything. Six minutes later Brittany's car did begin to move, north toward downtown Alexandria. I texted Brett. *Moving north.*

Watch is stationary, he responded.

So either she left the girls at the apartment or Nora wasn't allowed to bring her backpack. My guess? The girls stayed put.

This was getting interesting. I followed Brittany's car up Route 1 into Alexandria. It continued moving north, then stopped. After five minutes, I pronounced her parked.

I was pretty familiar with Alexandria, having been raised in Northern Virginia. Still, I popped the address into Google Earth and browsed around. Brittany's car was in an area of offices and charitable organizations near the river. Interesting. Why was she there? I wanted to know.

"Scott! Scott!" I said, racing downstairs. No answer. Ack! He was out in the barn. I threw on some shoes and ran out there. Luke met me halfway. Scott looked up from the saddle he and Mike were working on. "Scott, I need to run to Alexandria. Can you handle things at home?"

"What's up?"

"She's parked. I know where; now I need to find out why." I paused. "I'll text you the information. And I'll be careful." That should cover it, I thought.

He grimaced. He didn't like it. I was rushing, and that's the way people get in trouble. "Take your gun," he said.

"I will."

"And Jess, slow down. This won't be your only opportunity."

"Right."

"Let me pray for you."

How could I object? I drummed my thumb against my leg. After *amen* I kissed my boys goodbye, told Luke to stay with them, and ran back up to the house. I gathered what I thought I'd need—a hat, small binoculars, my laptop, a camera, my gun, water, a protein bar—and took off in my Jeep.

I love adventures!

. . .

Of course my excitement was dampened once I hit I-95. All that perpetually jammed highway needed was a fender bender to stop traffic for hours. This time the problem was bigger—a tractor trailer hauling pigs had overturned near Springfield and pigs were running all over the place, according to the radio.

Why would a tractor trailer hauling pigs be so close to DC? On a Sunday? I exited as soon as I could and swung over to parallel Route 1. So did everyone else. Around Quantico, still only inching north, I gave up. By the time I got to Alexandria, it would be dark. She could be gone. I turned around and headed south.

I voice-texted Scott and told him I was headed home. I hadn't heard from Brett once, so I texted him again. I kept an eye on my phone. The tracker indicated Brittany's car hadn't moved.

Stuck in traffic again on Routh 3 west, I had an idea. I called my friend, Detective Brad Welsh, in Culver City. We'd worked together last year on the Jayden Catlett case. He said I'd given him hope for some of the other cold cases they'd pretty much given up on.

He answered the phone with his usual, aggressive, "Welsh."

"Hey, Brad. It's Jess Cooper."

His tone immediately softened. "Well, hey, girl! How's my favorite PI?"

We bantered around for a few minutes and then I got to the point. I explained the case I was working on, and said, "Do you happen to know anyone up there that might give me a lead on what she might be doing? What businesses are up there?"

"No, no, Jess, I don't know anybody in Alexandria ... except for my brother!"

"Your brother? He lives there?"

"Better. He's a cop there. The Welsh boys don't know how to do anything but write tickets and chase thugs."

"Works for me! Can you call him?"

"Sure, I'll give him your number. Give me the address you're interested in."

I did that, thanked him, and clicked off.

Traffic finally cleared up, and I started making good time again. I noticed Brittany's car moving. By the time I pulled into my driveway, she was apparently back at the apartment with the girls. I texted Brett to see if he knew that and again didn't get an answer.

Why wasn't Brett responding?

The answer to that question could best be likened to an explosion.

"MOSTLY ALL I DID WAS DRIVE," I told Scott, as we ate dinner together. "It was crazy ridiculous. I thought most livestock transports avoided 95."

"Somebody didn't get the memo," Scott said.

I took a bite of the chicken Scott had grilled. "Brad Welsh's brother is going to send me a list of businesses at that location. He's a cop in Alexandria, can you believe it?"

Scott reached over and took my hand. "I'm just glad you're home."

Just then my phone, which I'd carefully placed in the family room out of sight because we were trying not to use devices during dinner, rang. I glanced at my watch. Frank Sinclair. I looked at Scott. "I'm sorry."

"Go," he said, waving his hand.

"Thank you!"

When I came back, I must have looked stunned, because Scott stopped what he was doing and said, "Are you alright?"

"Brett was arrested."

10

JESS

"Brett was arrested? For what?" my husband asked.

"Assault, attempted kidnapping," my voice cracked, "obstruction of justice."

"Sit down, sit down," Scott said. "Tell me what happened."

Right then Little Mike raised his hands, asking for me to pick him up out of his high chair. That was exactly what I wanted to do. I held him like a security blanket and, praise God, he snuggled against my chest. I took a breath, trying to calm down. "So at my suggestion, Brett gave one of his girls an Apple Watch, which allowed him to track them. This morning, I was tracking Brittany and Brett was following the girls. We both saw them at this apartment building in south Alexandria, the Hybla Valley area. Brett asked me what was at that address, and I told him. I expected him to look it up on Google Earth.

"My tracker indicated when Brittany left, and that's when I jumped in my car to follow her. Apparently, while I was stuck on I-95, Brett decided to drive to that apartment. He used back roads to avoid the traffic I was in. He should have stayed at home. But he didn't. He drove up there, knocked on the door, and demanded his children. The babysitter called the police and Brittany, and well, Brett got arrested. How could he be so stupid!"

"People get emotional when their kids are involved."

"Oh, Scott." I kissed the top of Mike's head. Tears blurred my vision. "All I wanted to do was protect those girls. From what Brett told me, Brittany has gone a little crazy. I just wanted them to be safe! And Brett, he seems like such a nice guy. I felt sorry for him! Now he could lose the whole thing—custody and everything!"

"I don't know what you could have done, other than not suggesting the Apple Watch."

"Well, that's just it, isn't it? I shouldn't have given that idea to him. But then, he'd never given me any reason to think he'd do something like this."

Scott reached over and rubbed my shoulder. "It's not your fault. Brett's responsible for his own actions."

Little Mike looked up at me. Then he lifted a finger and traced a tear running down my cheek. "Mommy sad?"

"Yes, sweetheart. Mommy's sad," I said. "She should have stayed home and played with you and Daddy."

MONDAY WAS AN ABSOLUTELY miserable day for me. I had a long phone conversation with Frank Sinclair. I detailed everything I'd done on the case, and I told him everything I'd discovered. Brett had been released on bail. Oh, and Brittany had announced that, due to Brett's aggressive and abusive behavior, she was moving to Southern California and would take the girls with her. There would be a hearing on Brett's case on Tuesday morning, Frank Sinclair said. It would be really beneficial for me to be there.

My hero husband agreed to switch his in-office days. He'd take care of Mike so I could go.

"Can she just take the girls out of state like that? Without his permission?" I asked Scott.

He shook his head. "Custody laws have changed in the twenty years since Suzanne did that to me. Maybe there are more protections in place now and she's just mouthing off."

"I guess we'll find out," I said. This whole situation felt like a rotten meal in my gut.

"Are you sure you're not in any legal jeopardy for placing the tracking device?"

"I had Brett's lawyer send me an email requesting it. Except for an initial test day, I didn't use it unless she had the kids. So I think I'm okay."

Scott nodded. "Okay, good."

THE NEXT MORNING I dressed in my best skirt suit, navy blue, and added a white silk shirt and heels. I put all my notes in an attaché case and drove my Jeep to the county court where Brett's hearing would be.

He looked bad, like he hadn't slept. His father, James Hudgins, a tall man with gray hair and bright blue eyes, was with him.

Right before the judge came in, I got a text from Brad Welsh's brother. My eyes widened. Quickly, I tapped Frank Sinclair on the shoulder and handed my phone to him. After he read it, he turned and looked sharply at me. And he kept my phone.

The court came to order and the judge took his place. The evidence against Brett was pretty clear. Brett drove to the apartment address and walked through the building, bellowing Nora and Ava's names. The Hispanic woman watching the Hudgins girls flung open the door but felt immediately intimidated by Brett. The girls were not in sight. He demanded to know where they were. She refused to tell him. Meanwhile, they heard his voice and began calling out "Dad! Daddy!" Brett shoved the babysitter aside, then clocked her boyfriend who tried to intervene. Brett took the girls from the apartment and refused to stop until police pulled into the parking lot and blocked his car in. At which point Brittany arrived and began screaming at him.

Brett sat at the defendant's table, his head down. I found myself praying for him silently. I felt so sad for him. When the prosecutor was finished, the judge asked if the defendant had anything to say. Frank and Brett stood up to address the court. Frank started to talk, but Brett touched his arm and began to speak himself. My mouth was dry, my gut tight as he began.

"Your honor, I admit to much of what has been said, but I would like to give context to my actions. I have been concerned about Brittany's behavior when she has custody of the children." He outlined some of his concerns. "At the suggestion of counsel, I provided my daughter Nora with an Apple Watch so I could trace them should I need to. On Sunday, Nora called me through the watch, crying. She was terrified. There was a man in the apartment where Brittany had left them and he was telling them to shut up. Threatening them."

"That's ridiculous," Brittany said.

The judge's gavel went down. "You may not speak at this time."

Brett continued. "Sir, I immediately jumped into my car and drove two and a half hours to their location. I was determined to find them. When the babysitter refused to let me see my children, I did push past her. When her boyfriend, who is a lot bigger than me, tried to stop me, I punched him. I freed my children from a back bedroom and fled. And I would do it again in a heartbeat. Your honor, if you are a father, I hope you will understand. My girls were in danger, and I was determined to save them."

"You're a bully and you have no right," Brittany screamed.

The judge's gavel came down again. "One more outburst, and I will have you removed from the courtroom!"

My heart pounded. No wonder Brett drove to Alexandria! I saw the prosecutor and Brittany's lawyer exchanging looks.

The judge spoke. "How did you know the address of the apartment?"

Brett pressed his lips together. "Because of prior incidents, and Brittany's refusal to tell me where she was going with the girls, and because she has ignored provisions of the court's custody agreement, I was very concerned. On the advice of counsel, I engaged a private investigator, who suggested the watch, which showed me where the girls were. I addition I was able to track the car Brittany drives, which, by the way, I still co-own."

"Was this private investigator licensed?"

"Yes, sir."

"Is he in the courtroom?"

"She is, sir." He turned and gestured toward me. "Ms. Jessica Cooper."

I stood up. The judge asked, "Miss Cooper, are you a private investigator licensed in the Commonwealth of Virginia?"

"Yes, sir."

"And did you attach a tracker to the vehicle in question?"

"Yes, sir. Except for an initial check to make sure it was working, I only monitored it when the children were with Mrs. Hudgins and also away from the Charlottesville area."

"Alright. Thank you. You may sit down."

I was sweaty! It had been a long time since I testified in court.

"Your honor," Frank Sinclair addressed the judge. "I'd like to request a sidebar."

"Is it relevant?"

"Yes, sir, I believe it is."

"Gentlemen, you may come forward."

The prosecutor and Sinclair approached the bench. Sinclair had my phone in his hand. I couldn't quite hear what they were saying but I could guess. Alexandria Police Detective John Welsh had reported that Brittany has been associating with several people currently under investigation for criminal activity involving the distribution of cocaine, methamphetamines, heroin, and fentanyl in Virginia. The location in Alexandria where her SUV was parked on Saturday was associated with this organization, which was also being investigated for manufacturing adult films using underage actors.

"My assistant is on her way to get written confirmation of this," Sinclair said.

Brittany sat forward in her chair. She could tell something was up. "What are they saying?" Brittany said. "I demand to know what they're saying!" A loud stream of profanity followed.

"Bailiff, remove her," the judge said, pounding his gavel. Two uniformed officers escorted Brittany out, screaming all the way. "May I see that?" He gestured toward my phone. Nudging his glasses down, he read the text John Welsh had sent me.

The judge looked up at the prosecutor. "Mr. Radcliff."

Radcliff leaned forward. I don't know exactly what was said, but it was something along the lines of, *Do you really want to proceed with this prosecution?*

The answer was *no, sir.* The judge pounded his gavel and Brett was a free man.

Brett's father, sitting next to me, gave me a huge hug, tears in his eyes. So did Brett. And Frank Sinclair.

Over Frank's shoulder, across the room, I saw a well-dressed, dark-haired man glowering at me. Where had I seen him before?

11

AMANDA

Three weeks after finding him, the black pup lay on Henry's lap in the front porch rocker at Amanda's. The spaniel was well on his way to being healed. He ate well, had gained weight, and he had full range of motion in his formerly dislocated shoulder.

After an attempt to find the pup's owner, Henry decided he'd probably been dumped. He'd texted Amanda and told her he was taking the dog to the shelter. "He's well enough. I'm sure someone will want him."

But when Henry came back that night, the dog was with him. "Couldn't do it," he told Amanda. "I'm not my dad."

Amanda hugged him.

"You're not upset?"

She laughed. "Nope. If you'd turned him into the shelter, I was going to go get him myself."

"You were?"

"Of course! I'd called them once already." She scratched the dog behind his ears. "They said they didn't have any black spaniels. So I was going to try again later. I even sent them a picture!"

Henry blinked.

"Don't worry. I didn't make up a story about my mean boyfriend ..."

"Fiancé."

"... my mean fiancé abducting him. So," she said, tossing her hair, "what's his name?"

He didn't hesitate. "Cash."

"Cash?"

"Yeah. The man in black."

"Wait, like the song?"

"Right. Johnny Cash. A little rough around the edges, but he has a good heart. Also," his voice dropped, "I want to remember that there's hope for alcoholics and drug abusers. Like my brother."

Amanda threw her arms around him. "I love it!"

He shook his head. "Still not sure why we need a dog."

"The universe thinks we do, so I guess that's it. Think of it this way... We have to get married now. We have a child!"

He laughed. "Okay. That works for me!" He continued stroking Cash. "We'll have to work out joint custody until we get married and live together."

"Somedays he goes with you and somedays he stays with me, depending on what we're doing," Amanda suggested.

"Whoever has him in the day gives him up in the evening."

"And no more than two days in a row."

"But the night in between he can stay with the day parent."

Amanda smiled in amusement. "Oh, I get it. Henry Bunting, you are letting him sleep with you!" Even in the dim light she could see the little smile that formed on his face.

He looked up. "So what? You are too."

"How do you know that?"

"I walked in your house the other day to use the bathroom and saw the little set of stairs you bought so he could get in your bed. Quickest way to spoil a dog." He shook his head.

"Maybe those are for me," she protested.

"Yeah. With those long legs of yours? Get real." He shifted his position. "I didn't say anything because I didn't want to shame you. What else do you do," he asked, going on the offensive. "Hand feed him? Buy him little clothes? A raincoat? A Halloween costume?"

The conversation devolved then into a good-natured fight in which Amanda finally claimed victory and Henry claimed a kiss. But Cash was the big winner. He got two homes and two people who loved him.

After that, any day that he could, Henry took him along on his farm visits. Cash soon learned not to chase chickens or roll in poop piles. He followed Henry around, stayed out of the way of hooves, and made friends with many of the farm dogs. On days Amanda had him, she walked him in the morning, came home at lunch, and did not work overtime. When she could, she worked from home.

Together, Amanda and Henry made a life for one little homeless pup.

BY MID-MAY, the weather had warmed, the piping plovers were nesting, and Amanda was spending her days overseeing the interns and hiking with them on the refuge.

"I'm going out tomorrow to inoculate Brady Barlow's cows. You want to come with me?" Henry asked.

Tomorrow was Saturday, and she was off for the first time all month. "Yes!" Amanda said. "Can we take Cash?"

Henry shook his head. "It's going to be hot. Cash would have to stay in the truck with the AC running. He'd be better off here. Let's ask Barbara if she'll come over and let him out midday."

"I'll call her," Amanda said. She smiled at Henry. "You sure know how to arrange a hot date."

He grinned.

THE NEXT MORNING Amanda dressed in farm clothes—a T-shirt, jeans, and boots. Henry said she should prepare to get dirty. At the last minute, she decided to leave her engagement ring at home. She slipped it in its box and buried the box in a drawer.

She heard Henry's truck come into the driveway and went to the side door. Henry stepped out, tanned and smiling. He lifted Cash down from the truck, the little dog's tail wagging nonstop.

"Cash!" she said, bending down to greet the black dog. "Good boy, good boy!"

"Let's let him sniff around a little before we lock him up," Henry said. "What are you bringing?"

"Gloves, water, and some trail mix. Oh, and hand sanitizer."

"Good."

"I told Kate I wouldn't be over until later this afternoon to work with Scarlet."

Henry nodded. "It'll take us an hour or so to do the whole herd. Brady's old. Hopefully, he's gotten someone to help him, and the cows are already in a pen. Then it's just a matter of running them through the chute." He called the dog, and said, "I'll lock him up. You get your stuff."

A few minutes later they were driving across the causeway to the mainland. The bright sun sparkled on the channel waters. Henry pointed out some laughing gulls and herons.

The farm lay about thirty minutes south, down Route 13 and then west a few miles. "What kind of cattle does Brady raise?"

"Beef cattle. Angus, mostly, with a few Hereford mixes. Brady's like a hundred years old and his equipment is old too. I keep waiting for him to give it up. Apparently, his son doesn't want to carry on the business, and Brady, well, he just can't let go of it."

"We had something similar at the ranch," Amanda said, "When Kate rescued Milo. He'd been a family pony. The kids grew up and moved away, the husband died, and the widow couldn't bear to rehome the pony."

"He's the one that needed the farrier so badly," Henry said. His boss, Jim Fuller, had checked him out when Henry was busy on another job.

"Right. Really kind of a mess. He's sweet though. Kate says he'd been alone too much."

"Horses need a herd, even if it's just a goat. And they need to move. I'm sure he's happier at the ranch." Henry pulled into a long lane that ended at a two-story, white farmhouse and an old, almost falling down red barn. A short-coat, gray-and-black cattle dog came toward them barking. Following him was an old man dressed in coveralls. He was limping and carried a walking stick.

"Brady! How's it going?" Henry called out as he began removing the equipment and supplies he'd need from his truck.

"Hello, young man. I see you brought some help."

"Nope. This is my fiancée, Amanda. She just came to watch."

"She's a purty one."

"Don't get any ideas." Henry pulled a cooler from behind the seat. "She does like older men, but she's too tough for you." Amanda rolled her eyes. "Your son coming?" Henry asked. Clearly he hoped the answer was yes. He picked up his medical bag and the cooler, which had two injection guns sticking out of it.

"Tom? No, that boy, he's got something else needs doing. I tell you, he can be worse'n useless. My wife, Martha, she'll lend a hand."

Henry shot Amanda a look. It said something between "unbelievable" and "don't get involved."

"I can help," she said to him in a low voice as they walked toward the small pasture where the cows were clustered.

Henry shook his head. "You're used to horses. Cows are different. A lot less predictable. This is our problem, Brady's and mine. You stay behind that." He nodded toward an old board fence. "I don't want to be worried about you getting hurt."

About forty cows milled around the small pen, lowing or bellowing. On the other side of the pen stood a red chute made of metal pipe. At the end of the chute was a headgate. Beyond that was a large, open field.

Amanda watched as Henry went through into the field and over to the end of the chute. He set down his bag and the cooler, pulled out a clipboard, and set it on a rough-built table. Meanwhile, Brady yelled for his wife. She emerged from the house, an older woman dressed in jeans and a shirt. "I'm comin'!" she hollered. "Don't get your shorts in a wad." She walked over and stood next to Henry. "How are you, Henry? That your girl?" She nodded toward Amanda.

"Yes, ma'am."

"'Bout time you got hitched."

"Yes, ma'am."

Soon the game plan was clear to Amanda. Brady got into the pen and, using what looked like a big flyswatter, he'd move one cow into the chute. He'd close the gate behind her, then move her up toward Henry. The cow would usually balk but then move forward. Martha would pull down on a lever and the cow's head would get captured in the headgate. Henry would give two injections in the cow's neck, spray something along the cow's topline, and then Martha would open the headgate and release her.

The chute and the headgate were old and made clanking

noises as the cows bumped into them. But everything seemed to work. An hour later, they were down to the last three cows.

Henry was hot. Amanda could see him wiping his brow with his sleeve. She wondered if she should take him some more water, but then she saw him pick up a bottle and drink from it. She stayed put and started thinking about where they might go for lunch.

The second-to-the-last cow was black with a white face. She seemed more rambunctious than the rest, and Brady had a hard time getting her into the chute. Finally, she went in and trotted forward. Henry climbed up on the side, his syringe in hand. As Martha started to pull the lever down to capture the cow's head, he leaned over to administer the vaccine. But at the last moment, the cow jerked her head up.

The cow's bony head hit Henry right in the face. He yelled and fell backward. The cow, panicked or angry or both, tried to jump out of the chute, and the old frame broke. The chute and cow collapsed on Henry. His scream of pain sent Amanda catapulting over the fence.

12

AMANDA

When the chute collapsed, Martha fell. Brady started yelling. Amanda ran toward Henry, who was trapped under the chute and the cow. The cow struggled to get to her feet, stepping on him as she did, and ran off. Amanda's heart raced. She tugged at the red metal chute, trying to free Henry, fighting to untangle it.

She pulled the last piece aside and dropped to the ground. "Henry! Henry, are you okay?"

His face told the story. He was white as a ghost, his face twisted in agony. Another shot of adrenaline raced through her. "Where are you hurt?"

He rolled to his right and gestured toward his ribs. Amanda instantly knew what was wrong. He couldn't breathe! He had no air.

Broken ribs. Pneumothorax. Life-threatening!

"Call 911!" she screamed. "Call 911." She tried to remember what Henry had taught her about first aid. ABC. Airway, breathing, circulation.

Airway was clear, but he wasn't breathing. He tried to turn

onto his side. She helped him, sliding her body under his to reposition him. She heard him gasp. It worked!

Circulation. The pulse in his neck felt erratic. She looked around. Martha was on the ground. Brady crouched over her. No one was calling for help. Henry needed it, now. "I'm calling 911, Henry. We'll get help."

She slid her phone out of her back pocket. One bar. Maybe two. She used her thumb to key in 911. Remembering the location was hard. She gave the dispatcher Brady's name. "We're at his farm, and we've got two down, one with trouble breathing.

The dispatcher said they were able to get the coordinates from the phone's location. "Don't hang up!"

"Okay. Henry, help is on the way," she said, setting the phone beside her. She needed to keep him calm. "I've got you." She got a slight nod in response. Then his hand curled around hers. "Medics are on the way. I'm right here. And I won't leave. I've got you, Henry." He squeezed her hand.

In such a rural area first responders might be all volunteers. Many were likely at work. It might take half an hour for an ambulance to get there. Half an hour would feel like half a day.

Martha was sitting up. Apparently, she'd just been knocked down, but she was old enough that even falling could be serious. Brady was talking to her. The cows stood in a semicircle, maybe fifteen feet away, chewing their cuds, staring.

Amanda spoke to Henry. She told him how much she loved him. Said they would get through this. That she would stay with him.

She knew shock was a possibility, a danger, so she just kept talking. Changing his position had allowed him to breathe, but now it seemed he was getting worse. His breathing more shallow. His pulse more erratic. His eyes kept closing.

Then, in the distance, a siren. "They're coming, Henry. I can hear them. Hang on. They're coming."

Flashing lights. The ambulance pulled up. Two first responders came running. They asked what happened. She told them, while the first medic did a quick evaluation. When she used the term "pneumothorax," Henry nodded.

By some miracle, one of the first responders was a paramedic with twenty years in the military. Gray-haired and wise, he knew what to do. "Can you stay right where you are?" he asked Amanda.

She nodded.

"Okay. You might not want to look."

Amanda knew what was about to happen based on what she'd learned. She tightened her jaw, nausea sweeping over her. She squeezed her eyes shut. Heard Henry cry out, then heard the hissing of air escaping from his chest cavity. The medic had used a needle to release the air trapping Henry's collapsed lung. He could breathe. She felt him relax in her arms.

"You okay?" the second medic asked her.

She nodded.

"We can take it from here."

The EMTs put an oxygen mask on Henry, then carefully loaded him onto a gurney and into the ambulance. Amanda secured his medical bag and the cooler in his truck. His keys, she knew, were in the console. His phone too. He always put them there when he was on a farm call.

She climbed in the truck and was about to start the engine when the ambulance driver jogged up, Henry's boots in his hand. "Throw them in the bed," she told him.

The hospital wasn't far. Amanda fought tears as she drove behind the ambulance. Images played in her mind. Henry falling. The sound of his tortured scream. His face, full of fear.

When she got to the parking lot, she forced herself to call Henry's father, using Henry's phone. She'd never even met the man, but it was the right thing to do.

"Hello, son," Professor Henry Bunting II answered automatically. "What's up? I'm right in the middle of something."

"Sir, this is Amanda Cooper, Henry's girlfriend." Why didn't she say fiancée? Frankly, it seemed too familiar. The man didn't deserve to know, not yet. "Henry's been in an accident."

"Accident? What kind of accident? Car crash? He's got insurance, right?"

"No, sir. Not a car accident. A cow fell on him."

The man actually laughed. "A cow?"

"Yes, sir. I think he's got broken ribs. He's been taken to the hospital in Onancock." She read the name off the building. She'd never been there before.

"Okay. Well, look, what does he need? Money? I'll give you my credit card number."

She blinked. "I'm sure he has health insurance. I just thought you'd want to know—"

"Right. Sure. Tell him to call me in a day or two after they've patched him up. I need to run."

Amanda didn't respond. She couldn't respond. She clicked off her phone, tears of anger and frustration welling in her eyes. *What a heartless jerk! Poor Henry.*

She started to get out of the truck. Then she stopped. She had to talk to someone! She took a deep breath and called her dad.

13

JESS

I could hear Scott talking on the phone as I walked downstairs. His serious tone. Short sentences. Was it work? Again? I entered the kitchen just as he hung up.

"Henry's been hurt," he said, frowning.

"Oh no! What happened?" He told me about the cow, the chute, and the pneumothorax.

"That sounds terrible! Was that Amanda?"

"Yes." Scott looked at me. "Do you think I should go?"

"Does she want you to?"

He grimaced. "I asked if she wanted me to come and she said no."

"She may change her mind." I hugged him. "Here's a thought. Clear your desk as much as you can. Maybe pack a bag. And then you can go if she changes her mind."

We were still standing there talking when Scott got a text. "From Amanda," he said. He read it to me. "*I can't do this.*" Scott looked at me. "I think I should go."

I nodded. "Okay, go. But call her and tell her you're coming. How can I help?"

"Could you pack a bag for me while I make some phone calls?"

"Yes." I scooped up Little Mike and the two of us climbed the stairs. "C'mon, buddy. We have to help Daddy." Luke followed close behind. He knew something was wrong.

I assumed the phone calls Scott had to make were work-related and maybe a physical therapy appointment or two. That wasn't all. When he came upstairs a little while later, I found out his travel plans.

"Joe is going to fly me over there."

"What?"

"Joe Nichols. Bureau pilot, retired. He has a light plane at Charlottesville. He'll fly me to the Accomack County Airport. I've arranged for a rental car from there."

"A light plane? Scott, are you sure?"

He laughed. "Sure it's a plane? Yes, I am." He grinned. "It's fine. I've flown with him before." He kissed me. "I just didn't tell you."

"What?"

"It was before we were married."

Twenty minutes later, Mike and I were in the van, driving Scott to Charlottesville. I wasn't even sure he'd fit in that little plane! Mike and I stood outside the hanger and watched him take off in the Cessna, the wings bobbling left and right as it lifted into the sky.

"Da-da bye-bye?"

"Yes," I said to our son. "Daddy's going bye-bye. He'll be back in a couple of days."

Mike waved his little hand. I said a prayer.

14

AMANDA

Amanda walked into the hospital shouldering a sense of dread like she had never felt before. What would she find? Was Henry alive? Dead? Dying?

She had to fight her way past the front-desk clerk. "I'm his fiancée!" The woman automatically looked at Amanda's left hand. She set her jaw. "I left it at home because I was afraid of losing it. I was with him when he got hurt. I need to see him!"

Finally, the woman buzzed the nurse, who appeared at the door seconds later. "Are you Amanda?" she asked.

"Yes."

"Come on. He's been asking for you."

But by the time she hurried back, the cubby that had "Bunting" written on the whiteboard outside was empty. The nurse turned. "What happened to seventeen?" she called out.

"Scans," someone said.

The nurse looked at Amanda. "They've taken him upstairs for scans. They may want to do an MRI in addition to a CT scan. That takes a while. Let me show you where to wait."

Amanda followed her through a maze of hallways and up

one floor in an elevator. They ended up in a large room filled with people staring at their phones or gazing absentmindedly at the walls. "Go over there," the nurse said, "and sign in. Tell them who you're waiting for and they'll call you."

"Thank you." Amanda signed in, writing Henry Bunting in the patient box. She hoped they'd give her information. Was she on his HIPPA list?

In the meantime, she waited, shivers running through her, her stomach tight. She scrolled through her phone and, feeling lonely, decided to text her dad. Then she looked at a magazine and tried to let go of the images haunting her. Henry, his face frozen in fear. Henry, screaming in pain. Henry ... Then those images blurred with the ones of her father when he'd been shot. His face, so gray, his voice so weak, bleeding to death in her car out in the middle of nowhere.

She was staring blindly at a magazine article when the door opened and two guys walked in. Glancing up, she recognized them. Chincoteague. Part of the rescue squad. Her throat closed.

She pretended not to see them. They sat across from her talking in their soft accents, talking about Henry and ribs and collapsed lung, and what were the chances he'd survive. The more they talked, the more her anxiety swelled like a tsunami. Her mouth felt dry. How did they even know? Who told them?

Finally, she couldn't bear it anymore, and she put down the magazine, rose, and quickly walked out of the waiting room.

"Hey, is that Amanda?" she heard one of them say, but she pretended not to hear, and left, tears blurring her eyes. When she reached the hallway, her breath was coming in shallow gasps, like a fish out of water struggling to breathe. She looked left and right. Where could she go? Where could she hide?

A stairwell. She jerked open the door and slid inside just as the panic attack slammed into her. Shaking, she reached for something to hold onto, grasped the handrail, then immediately saw herself hurtling down the flight of stairs.

She shrank against the wall. No ... no. She couldn't breathe! She squeezed her eyes shut and crossed her arms tightly across her chest. Then the door opened.

"Amanda, honey."

Kate. Kate McClellan. Her counselor, her friend.

Amanda collapsed into Kate's arms. "Honey, it's okay. It's okay," Kate murmured. "It's going to be okay."

"How do you know? How do you know that?" Amanda sobbed.

"He's young. He's strong. He'll be okay. It's okay, honey." Kate held her for a few minutes, trying to calm her. Then she said, "Do you remember how to deal with anxiety attacks?"

It had been a while. Amanda shook her head.

"Ground yourself. Feel the floor beneath your feet and grab onto that handrail." Amanda obeyed instinctively. "Now, breathe. In for four, hold for seven, out for eight. Come on, I'll do it with you."

Gradually, the shaking deescalated, first to shivers, then it stopped altogether. "Breathe," Kate said, and she did.

"I'm sorry," she said finally. "I ... I ..."

"Don't be sorry. You've had a shock."

"How did you find out?"

"Word flies fast around here. Jim Fuller was at the ranch when he got a call from the hospital. He's here now, somewhere. I came because, well, because of you. The hospital told him you saved Henry's life. I thought maybe you could use a friend."

"Thank you," Amanda whispered. She swallowed hard. "I ... I was so scared."

Kate hugged her. "Let's go get something to drink. They'll call you when the doctor's ready to update you."

They found their way down to the cafeteria. Kate poured

coffee from a machine into a Styrofoam cup. All Amanda wanted was a bottle of water. "Let's get some crackers for you too," Kate said, putting them on the tray. "You probably need something on your stomach."

They sat down at a table. "Now, tell me what happened," Kate said, and she listened while Amanda went through the story. "How did you know what to do?" she asked when Amanda finished.

"We'd talked about it just a month or so ago when he found the dog that had been hit by a car. Henry was worried about his ribs and especially a pneumothorax. The dog didn't have that, but I knew those steel pipes had hit Henry in the ribs, and when I saw he couldn't breathe, I guessed he had a collapsed lung. I helped him move so he could breathe."

"You did great!"

"Just now, some guys in the waiting room were going on and on about collapsed lungs and it scared me!" Tears came to her eyes again.

"And now?"

"I don't want to go back upstairs!"

"To see him? You don't want to see him?"

Amanda shook her head no.

"Why?"

She waited a long time before responding, and when she did, it was in a whisper. "I realize now I could lose him."

"That is scary."

Kate sat silently for a few minutes, waiting. "Amanda," she said, her eyes soft, "in the past, how have you connected with people you love?"

"I haven't connected. I've either fenced them off so I wouldn't get close, or I've, you know, run away."

"You've protected yourself."

Amanda nodded.

"How has your relationship with Henry been different?"

Amanda's brow furrowed. "He knows the worst things about me and still hangs out with me. Loves me despite my craziness." She sniffed.

"And do you love him?"

Amanda nodded.

"So right now, you have two paths before you—a new path, a path of love, which involves risk, or the path you've always taken, the path of protecting yourself, and being—"

"Alone," Amanda whispered. Her phone signaled a text. The doctor.

"Now is the time to decide which path you're going to take," Kate said.

Amanda stood up. "I need to go."

"Do you want me to come with you?"

"No. I'm fine." But she wasn't.

15

SCOTT

Scott arrived at the hospital less than three hours after Amanda's call. He stepped out of the rental car and looked up at the clear blue skies. The weather had held. Joe would have an easy flight back to Charlottesville. Leaving his duffle bag and backpack in the trunk, Scott locked the car and strode across the parking lot. He adjusted his dark-blue sports jacket, making sure it covered the gun riding on his belt. Old ways died hard. He'd been carrying for over twenty years, prepared. For anything.

He asked at the information desk about Henry, got a room number, and took the elevator to the third floor. When the elevator doors opened, he saw a waiting area of couches and chairs next to a sunny window and a collection of people standing there. He recognized a face.

It took a minute, but then her eyes met his. She excused herself from the conversation she was in and walked toward him. "Mr. Cooper!" she said, extending her hand.

"Good to see you, Dr. McClellan." He shook her hand.

Dressed in boots, jeans, and chambray shirt, Kate McClellan looked like she'd just walked in from Hope Ranch.

"Call me Kate."

"And I'm Scott."

"So good to see you. Was anyone expecting you?"

He shook his head. "Amanda called me earlier. She told me Henry got hurt. Is she back with him?"

Kate took his arm and turned him away from the others, walking him down the hall. "I don't know how much I should tell you, since she's officially still in counseling. What happened was quite a shock." Kate looked at him. "She saved his life."

"But ..."

"She also realized she could lose him. And now—"

"She's scared. Where is she?"

"I don't know. We were having coffee down in the cafeteria. She got a text and said she had to go. I thought she was headed back upstairs, but the doctor hasn't seen her. He told Henry's boss what was going on. Amanda's disappeared."

"And how is Henry?"

"Collapsed lung, a broken rib, a dislocated shoulder, and an awful bruise on his face. They're going to keep him a couple of days in ICU, but they're hoping he won't need surgery. He's young. He'll be okay."

Scott took a deep breath and let it out in relief. "How can I help?"

"Honestly, I don't know."

He paused, tried to think it out. Where would Amanda go? "Could she be at the ranch?"

Kate shook her head. "I tried that. No one's seen her."

Scott's mind ran through the possibilities. They were endless, but he couldn't just stand there. If Kate was still counseling her, she couldn't reveal anything significant. He knew that. He decided to be oblique. "I'm going to go see if I can find her," he said. "Do I need to worry about, I don't know, a car smashed into a tree?" Which was a way of saying *suicide.*

Kate shook her head. She got the message. "No. And she was driving Henry's truck. I saw it in the parking lot when I came in," Kate said.

"Black Toyota Tundra?"

She nodded and told him where it had been parked.

Scott nodded. "That's a pretty big vehicle. Tell you what. Let's exchange cell numbers. Call me if she shows up, and I'll text or call you if I find her."

SCOTT WALKED out of the hospital, verified Henry's truck was no longer where Kate had seen it, and started his rental car. His mind stayed focused on his mission. Find his daughter. That's all that mattered right now.

By nature and by training, his default was left-brain thinking. Logical. Aggressive. In control. That worked pretty well when chasing bad guys and staring death in the face, but not so well when dealing with people he loved. Jess had taught him about standing down from that posture, about accessing his softer side. So had horses, to be honest. Those relationships had to be won and then nurtured, patiently and gently.

Taking a deep breath, he prayed as he drove. "Stop me. Make me fail at this if it's the wrong thing to do, Jesus. Or help me find her. One or the other."

Then, to be sure, he called Jess. He explained what was going on. She listened. And then she said, "You're a man of action, Scott. I can't imagine you sitting passively waiting for her to show up. I'll pray for good results."

He drove first to the Chincoteague house. Amanda's black Rogue was in the driveway. He pulled in behind it and knocked on the door.

No answer. He was returning to his car when a woman came around the back of the house. The neighbor, Barbara. Had to be. He'd heard stories.

"Hi, you must be Barbara." A stocky woman, she had short, curly gray hair, and she limped as she walked. "I'm Scott. Amanda's dad."

Her face softened. "I hear Henry's got hisself hurt."

How'd she know already? "Yes. The doc thinks he'll be okay. Have you seen Amanda?"

"Nope." She shrugged. "I was just comin' to let Cash out."

Cash. The dog. Right. "Where does Henry live? She may have gone there to get Henry extra clothes." *That was a thought.*

"You know. It's that blue one-story over t' Butler Street."

"Do you know the address?"

"Nah. It's the blue one. Can't miss it."

He definitely could miss it because it was green, not blue. Thankfully, a delivery man identified it for him. He knocked on the door. No answer. And the Tundra wasn't there.

Scott entered the address in his contacts, just so he'd have it. And then he got back in his car. Where else could she be? Work? The beach? He decided to take a chance.

The sun beat down on the asphalt and shimmered off the dunes. He drove through the parking lot and then he spotted it: Henry's truck. Scott pulled into a parking spot, locked his gun in the console, and pulled off his sports jacket. Then he walked up to the top of the dunes.

He saw Amanda on the beach, sitting on the sand, arms hugging her knees to her chest. He quickly texted Kate, then silently walked over and sat down next to his daughter. Her eyes widened in surprise, then she dropped her head and buried it in her arms.

The breeze off the ocean felt good, the salt air soft and comforting. Scott tried to relax. The Atlantic waves rolled in one after another after another, curled, crashed, and slid back out. The heartbeat of the sea. He prayed silently, reaching out to the God who'd created all the beauty in front of him, the one who'd fashioned and formed his daughter.

They must have sat in silence together for ten minutes. Maybe fifteen. He wasn't checking his watch. Then she finally spoke. "I feel so stupid."

He let that sit in the air for a minute. "Why?"

"Because."

"Okay. Because why?"

She didn't respond. He wondered if he should press her. Just when he was ready to open his mouth, she did something she'd never done before. She moved close, slipped her arm under his, and rested her head on his shoulder. He turned and kissed the top of her head. "I love you, Amanda."

The bright sun sparkled on the water. A group of large, dark-colored birds flew in formation parallel to the beach, their wings beating the air, and he wanted to ask Amanda what they were. Ahead, right next to the water, little birds ran up and back, just ahead of the incoming waves, pecking at the wet sand as each wave receded. A white-and-gray gull walked over the dry sand toward them, studying them, looking for food. The beach was, he realized, a beautiful place, when you took time to be still and look at it.

Finally she spoke. "How do you do it, Dad? You and Jess?" The question hung in the air like a kite.

"Do what?"

"One of you is getting hurt all the time. Like every other week. How do you handle the idea you could lose each other?"

Scott patted her hand. He thought carefully, rejecting his initial response, which was logical and measured, and went deeper into his heart. "You saw me last year," he said. "I fell apart when I saw Jess in that hospital bed, hooked up to all those monitors, her eyes bandaged." The images came back to him like a nightmare. "I felt a terrible fear. Deep grief. What would I do without her? I was terrified."

Amanda snuggled closer.

"And then I felt a hand on my back, and I heard your voice, and I stood and turned and held on to you." He kissed her head. "That's how you survive. The people who love you come around you and help you. Give you strength. Support you." Scott took a deep breath. How deep did he want to go? "I've tried dealing with loss other ways. When my sister was murdered," he said, his voice catching in his throat, "I decided to fight people like her attacker. I joined the FBI. Became obsessive about it. Eventually I hit a wall. Discovered evil was a far bigger problem than I could handle. My obsession cost me my family. I lost you." He touched her hand and continued.

"Then I tried being aloof. Cold. Logical. Self-sufficient. Independent. I was smart. I could do life on my own, I thought.

"It's a terrible way to live. I did it for years. Then I met Jess. Her combination of spunk and vulnerability attracted me. I tried to resist, but eventually all the barriers I had built up around my heart collapsed.

"Now, I have her, you, Mike, Nate, Kathryn ... I have a real family, real love, and we help each other." A small flock of gulls at the shoreline raised a raucous, fighting over a small piece of food.

"Henry doesn't have a family."

"He has you; that's a start. And if he has you, he has us."

"Even so, what if we all died? All at once?" Amanda asked.

He started to respond logically, to say *the chances of that are* . . .. Then he checked himself. Took a deep breath and said quietly, "Even if everybody died, I'd still have God. And he would be enough." He expected blowback, but Amanda stayed quiet.

They sat in silence for a while, watching the sea roll in,

listening to the sound of the breakers and the squawks of gulls. Unexpectedly, Amanda giggled. "What?" Scott asked.

She raised her head and pointed. "See that?" she whispered.

A nearly transparent crab stood on the hot sand about three feet away, staring at them. Scott could barely pick it out. It was the same color as the sand, all but its black eyes, which bugged out.

"Watch," she whispered. She made a sudden move and the crab skittered down a hole, disappearing. She looked up at her dad, smiling. "That's a ghost crab. And that's also me. I run and hide when I'm scared."

Scott grinned. "You're prettier."

"But just as flaky."

"No." He squeezed her arm. "You just need an anchor." A breeze lifted her hair. He thought again about how beautiful she was, and he prayed for her silently, right there and then.

They seemed to both know when it was time to leave.

"What do you need?" Scott asked. "Food? Coffee?"

"Clean clothes," Amanda responded. "These are filthy from the farm. And then ... and then I think I'd like to go see Henry," she dropped her head. "I'm scared he's mad."

"At you? Why?"

"Because I ran. I'm unreliable."

Scott hugged her. "You were there when he needed you most. He loves you. Besides, I'll bet he's mostly been sleeping. Should we stop by his house and get some clean clothes for him? Sweats, or a button-up shirt, or a big T-shirt in case his arm is in a sling?"

"Yes, Dad. Let's do that."

THEY WORKED to gather what Amanda thought Henry might need. Scott spotted Henry's boots in the back of the truck and washed them off, setting them on the covered back porch to dry.

Leaving Henry's truck parked, they drove to Amanda's house. Scott played with Cash while Amanda showered and put on a pair of clean jeans and a pink top. Then Scott drove her back to the hospital. On the way, Scott said, "Would you tell me what happened?"

So she did. "Dad, he couldn't breathe! His face—" She stopped, her voice catching. She told him about the terror she'd felt and about her anxiety attack later. Scott listened carefully, his eyes fixed on the road.

When she finished speaking, he reached over, squeezed her hand, and said, "Totally understandable. How'd you know how to help him?"

"Our dog. He'd been hit by a car, and Henry checked for broken ribs and a pneumothorax. I asked him what that was, and he explained it. When I saw that metal gate and the steer come crashing down on Henry, I was terrified. I raced to him, and … and when I realized he couldn't breathe, everything he'd told me came back in a flash. I turned him so his good lung was free and held him there while I called 911 with my other hand. I kept talking to him, trying to keep him calm, trying to keep him from going into shock. It was terrifying."

Scott reached over and touched her shoulder. "It's okay. You didn't panic in the moment. You did what you needed to do. You saved his life. I'm so proud of you!"

She was silent for a while. "Dad? I still don't know if I can do this."

"Love is a risk, Amanda. Most things worthwhile are a risk. All I can tell you is that I wouldn't trade what I have now with Jess for anything. My advice is 'take the risk'. It's worth it."

As they walked into the hospital, Amanda reached over and took Scott's hand. "It's alright," he whispered.

Scott hung back as they walked into ICU. Henry was awake,

propped up in bed, a massive bruise covering one side of his face. When his eyes fell on Amanda, he gave her a crooked grin and reached for her. "There's my girl." She took his hand and he pulled her into the best hug they could manage. "You saved my life! Thank you," Henry said. "I love you so much!"

Scott's heart lifted. Henry would be okay. *They* would be okay.

16

JESS

I was about to go crazy wondering what was going on with Scott and Amanda. I mean, for years she'd been a firecracker to deal with, volatile and unpredictable. She and Scott could never seem to connect even when he tried. One or the other of them would say or do something that would set the other off.

This past year things had changed. Now he was with her trying to help her through a hard situation, and I could only imagine what might be going on. Every time my phone signaled a text or a call, I hoped it was him with an update, but he was strangely quiet.

Instead, my phone stayed busy with calls from lawyers wanting my help with cases or with search-and-rescue calls. With Scott gone, I'd volunteered to be the callout coordinator, something I could do from home. The beautiful spring weather was drawing people out into the woods, and a pretty good percentage of them were getting lost. At least it seemed that way. I mean, he'd only been gone for five days, and we'd been called out three times! I was beginning to think we needed to start teaching wilderness navigation skills in schools.

To be honest, I was restless. I could only be a bystander for so long before I needed to jump the fence and get back in the game. Luke, however, was becoming an old man. He'd decided keeping track of Little Mike was his main purpose in life. He followed him around, playing babysitter. He was teaching Mike to play ball by dropping a slobbery tennis ball near the boy every time he got the chance. And he cleaned up around Mike's chair after every meal. Sometimes I caught Mike dropping him food on purpose. The two of them were a team. An insurgency, I called it.

On Friday, nearly a week after Scott had left, he called to say he was coming home. He'd helped Amanda get Henry back to his house; now the young man just had to recover. "The weather's not looking good for flying," Scott said when he called me, "so I'll drive home. Should be there around four."

My weather app predicted thunderstorms for this afternoon. A cold front was dipping down from Canada creating the possibility of some violent storms. So I decided to do as much as I could around the farm so Scott didn't have to worry about slogging through heavy rains to do chores after he got home. I'd rather we spent a quiet evening at home. I was looking forward to some alone time with him. I wanted to hear what happened with Amanda and Henry.

I called the Davidsons to see if one of their boys could come cut the grass. Connor said he could, and now that he was driving, I didn't even have to go get him.

When Connor arrived, he had his sister, Maddie, with him. Maddie, Mike, and I cleaned the barn and took care of the horses. At least Maddie and I did. We mucked out the stalls, refilled the grain bins, and scrubbed out the water buckets. Little Mike played in his stall playroom while Luke watched him.

By noon we were finished. It was amazing how much I could do with a little help. The Davidsons went home, I gave

Mike lunch, and then I put him down for a nap. While he slept, I worked on some of my PI cases—background checks on some potential employees for two different corporations. At two o'clock, my phone signaled a tornado watch for our area until eight tonight. I prayed Scott would be alright on the road.

The alert didn't overly alarm me. Tornado watches in May in my part of Virginia are common. We don't usually get the huge, long-track tornados that rip through middle America, leaving devastation for miles. Still, the smaller ones could do a lot of damage if they ripped through your farm. More common here were the violent thunderstorms that could down trees and tear the roofs off of structures. Over the years, we'd even had a derecho or two, straight-line storms with winds up to seventy miles per hour. Oh, and hurricanes now and then. But May was too early, really, for those. Hurricane season started in June, peaked in August, and ended in November.

I glanced out of the window. The wind had picked up, and clouds were gathering to the west. The horses were out in the field. I wondered if I should bring them in.

I called Scott, told him about the tornado watch, and asked him about the horses. He was still about two hours away. He said not to put them in the barn. They were safer in the field, and their instincts would tell them whether to seek shelter in the woods.

I thought about the terrible, stormy night on Assateague Island so many years ago. I'd been chasing a woman who was having a psychotic break. She'd run into the swampy woods on the island, and just when I had caught up with her and thought she had calmed down, she slipped away. Then she crept up behind me and stabbed me with a knife. I lay in the mud bleeding and trying to breathe, rain beating down and fog surrounding me, watching a herd of wild ponies silently walk by. They were instinctively seeking shelter from the storm, moving to high ground around the Assateague Lighthouse where I had been attacked. It was oddly comforting having those ponies standing all around me.

I shook off that memory. It seemed like a lifetime ago. It practically was.

My phone signaled a call. Ellie Davidson, my friend. "Hey, Ellie! Connor did a great job—"

She interrupted me. "I need you to pray for my sister, Carol."

"Why? What's going on?"

"Her daughter's getting married today at five o'clock up at the winery. It's a garden wedding, outside!"

"Oh, wow. That's today? They don't have an inside option?"

"They have tents. That's it. I told my niece it was a bad idea to plan an outdoor wedding, but her heart was set on it from the moment she got engaged last summer. So here we are."

"Are you going?"

"Me and all the kids. My husband's in Raleigh."

"I will definitely pray."

"Thank you, Jess. These tornado watches hardly ever pan out, but still, wouldn't you know there'd be one today. As if we don't have enough drama!"

I prayed with her on the phone before I hung up. But then I got busy in the kitchen and forgot about the wedding. I wanted a nice relaxing dinner, something I could prep ahead of time so that once Scott got home we could just talk. I finished putting spices on the four boneless chicken breasts in the Crock-Pot, added broth and just a little butter, and set it to cook for four hours. I prepped a salad, saving the dressing for later, and pulled out a couple packages of precooked rice that I could microwave at the last minute.

When Mike woke up from his nap, we played for a while. Scott pulled into the yard at 4:15 p.m. When I opened the front door to greet him, I could hear thunder in the distance, and the wind was blowing hard. Luke and Mike rushed out to greet him. Scott scooped up Mike and walked toward me grinning.

"Welcome home!" I said.

He gave me a big kiss. "I've got to get my duffle bag." He set Mike down, but his son immediately protested.

"I'll get it," I said, laughing. "He missed you!"

"In the back seat," Scott said, picking up Mike again. They disappeared inside.

I pulled his duffle out of the back seat of the small, white foreign rental. That car was so not Scott. When I turned to go back to the house, the sky to the west was almost jet black. As I pushed open the front door and glanced west one more time, lightning flashed.

Scott sat on the floor in our living room playing with Mike. That wouldn't have happened a year ago, I thought. "I'm glad you got home when you did. We're about to get slammed," I said, sitting down next to him.

"The storm?"

"Yes." I pulled my phone out of my back pocket. "Hmm. The tornado watch has been changed to a warning."

"Do we have anything that needs to be put up? Or nailed down?"

I mentally scanned our property. "I don't think so, but I'd better look."

"C'mon, buddy," Scott said, picking up Little Mike. "Let's go check the barn."

Luke followed Scott and Mike. I wasn't offended. Really. Honest.

Okay, I was a little.

We were all back inside in fifteen minutes. A few small items had been stowed or secured. Scott was perpetually concerned about the barn. It was old, and he knew what it would cost to rebuild it—and also it wasn't as essential as our house.

The storm hit hard at 5:00 p.m. The rain pelted the roof, lashed at our windows, and created new streams that flowed down toward the creek. The horses moved up into the woods.

We watched lightning dance in the sky as dark clouds hovered over us. "Boom!" Scott said, each time thunder rumbled. "Boom!" Mike repeated in his little boy's voice.

A thick veil of rain obscured our field. Luke paced, panting. I'd noticed the older he got, the more concerned he was about thunderstorms. Was it because he worried about Mike? I really didn't know. I patted my leg, and he immediately came to me. He put one paw on my foot, like he was holding me down, and he leaned against me. I rubbed his head behind his ear.

The storm continued moving north. The veil of rain thinned. Don't get me wrong, it was still pouring buckets, but our field and woods came back into view. Forty-five minutes later, the violent winds and torrential rain had calmed substantially. But a steady rain continued to fall.

"I'll go finish dinner," I said, leaving Scott and Mike staring out of the large window on the back wall of the house.

I had just put the rice in the microwave and was about to put the dressing on the salad when my phone signaled a text. I looked. A callout! Before I could even process the address and the nature of the callout, Nate phoned me. "Hey," he said. "Scott home yet?"

"Yes, he is. Why?"

"D'you see the callout?"

"I just got it. What's going on?"

"Storm hit hard about fifteen miles away. Pleasant Hills Vineyard. Either a microburst or a tornado."

"Pleasant Hills?" I searched my brain. *Was that Ellie's niece's wedding venue?*

"Flooding. Tents down. A couple of cars washed away. People missing." Nate paused. "Battlefield's the closest SAR group, but we got a lot of people out of town. Only one team responding so far. Any chance you—"

"Yes! I mean, let me check with Scott. I'll get back to you ASAP."

"If you can, I'll come get you. We can ride together."

Scott could tell by the tone of my voice something serious was going on. "What's up?"

I told him. He frowned, his eyes narrowing. He didn't like it. "It's still raining," he said. "You know what these mountains are like. Creeks become rivers real quick."

I knew. Of course I knew. I'd almost died in a mountain flood.

"Scott," I said, keeping my voice even, "I think Ellie's there."

"Ellie?"

"Her niece was getting married at that vineyard or one near there anyway. I want to go. Nate said he'd come get me, and we could go together."

Scott's face visibly relaxed. He took a deep breath, resigned to me leaving. "Alright. But promise me you'll use the Garmin."

"Okay! I will. Dinner's in the Crock-Pot and the microwave, and all you need to do is put the dressing on the salad. Thank you, Scott." I gave him a quick kiss. "I was looking forward to a quiet evening with you."

"Me, too." He shook his head.

"If Ellie or her kids are in danger, I need to go. I'd hate myself if ..."

Scott nodded. "I know. Go!"

17

JESS

By the time I had my search clothes on and my SAR pack ready, Nate drove in to pick me up. He'd brought his black German shepherd, Ember, to stay at our house at Scott's suggestion. "In case your search runs long," is the way he put it. I thought that was kind of Scott.

On the way I told Nate about Ellie's phone call. "Could be this place," Nate responded. "They said they had a weddin' goin' on."

I tried calling Ellie while Nate drove, but I got no response. In fact, the call sounded weird, like maybe it didn't even go through.

"Could be a cell tower got hit," Nate said. "Lot of lightning in that storm."

It was still raining, although the timing between the thunder and the lightning indicated the storm had moved farther away. Conducting searches in the rain was not my favorite thing to do. Also, heavy clouds blocked the daylight, making it much darker than it should have been at five-thirty. I knew this search wouldn't be easy.

Nate turned into the long driveway, leading up to the vineyard. In the flashing lights of the emergency vehicles, I could see there was a house on top of the hill, totally dark, like it had lost power. Below it on the slope lay a lot of white patches, which I realized were collapsed tents.

We were the first SAR team there, although Battlefield's coordinator, Tom, arrived right behind us. We had crossed the county line, but we knew the sheriff and he was glad to see us. He briefed the three of us, using topographic maps he'd printed out.

"Our biggest concern is this creek. It rose up and swamped some cars, swept away a tent or two. And you can see," he pointed to the map, "the woods beyond it. Are people there? Are they in the cars? Are they hurt? We're checking these tents to see if there are people under them, and I got swift-water rescue team coming out for the cars in the creek. But anything you can do for us would help."

The three of us huddled and worked out a plan. With first responders checking the tents and the creek still rising, we needed to see if we could cross it to check the woods on the other side for any cars or people we could help. Nate and I decided we'd stick together, rather than work with a deputy as a walker. We told the sheriff our plan, and he agreed to it.

"There's a place a little way up you might be able to cross," he said, pointing up the hill. "Look here on the map." He tapped parallel lines, indicating a bridge across the stream.

When we got to that spot, we saw a decorative stone bridge span overwhelmed by the rushing water and clogged with tree debris. Nate and I scanned it with flashlights. "Think we can make it?" I asked.

He nodded. "I think we can."

Just as we were about to cross, I heard my name.

"Jess! Oh, Jess!"

I turned to see Ellie, soaking wet in a nice dress, racing toward me with her son Connor right behind her. "Ellie!"

She grabbed me. "It's Jamie and Maddie. We can't find them. They may be over there," she said, pointing across the creek.

"Mom, let me go! I can find them," Connor said.

"No! You're not going over there!"

I grabbed Ellie's arms to steady her. "We're going across."

"Let me go with you." Connor was amped up.

"No, stay with your mom. If the kids are over there, we'll find them. Your mom needs you."

"She's right, son," I heard Nate say.

Panicked, Ellie kept looking across the creek for any sign of her missing kids.

"Go, Ellie! We got this."

I could imagine what had happened. Six-year-old Jamie had gotten restless, and sweet Maddie had volunteered to take him over to the woods to play. Then the storm hit, and they got stuck ... or washed away. I didn't want to think about that.

I also did not want to cross that bridge! With the water rushing around it and all the debris piled up, it looked fragile, more decorative than sturdy, even though it was made of stone. If we were going to cross, it had better be now.

"Let's go!" I yelled to Nate, and he nodded. I kept Luke on a loose leash and my dog led us, picking his way across branches and mud and other debris while the stream roared beneath us and lightning flashed.

We finally made it. Now, the question was, would I have the courage to unleash my dog and let him work? He'd fallen into a swollen creek once before and gotten lost. He was gone nearly a month. It almost killed me.

But Jamie and Maddie were missing ...

I looked at Nate. He knew exactly what I was thinking. His jaw was set. He nodded slightly. I bent down and unclipped

Luke's leash. Then I put him in a heel position, leaned over, and said, "Seek, Luke! Seek!"

He took off. I could tell he was happy to be working, to be using his muscles, brain, and nose to do what he was trained for—find any person in the area.

We walked upstream parallel to the creek first. We saw a lot of leafy branches, tumbled rocks, and tree limbs, but nothing suggesting a person was in the creek. So we turned and walked downstream. Luke ranged ahead, back and forth, eagerly sniffing.

At one point he stopped, looked toward the creek, and barked repeatedly. A car floated in the creek, pressed up against a large rock. Nate and I shined our flashlights into the interior but didn't see anybody. "Wait here and hold Luke," Nate said, and he crawled out over a rain-slick, downed tree and out onto the rock. Then he scooched back.

"Window's down and there's stuff in there. Looks like presents, clothes. Not sure whether someone got out, or if the car was empty when the creek took it. No people in it now, anyways."

"Okay," I said. "Let's reset." Nate nodded his agreement. The rain was letting up, but the creek was still rising. I brought Luke to my left side in the heel position. I spoke to him gently, drawing his attention, then I extended my arm downstream and slightly to the north, and said, "Seek! Seek, Luke!"

We trudged on. I was happy the rain had slowed but was concerned about the rising water. About ten minutes after we'd restarted, I heard Luke barking, but he didn't come back to me. I wondered what was going on and quickened my pace, leaving Nate behind. I finally saw Luke lying near the creek, his tail wagging.

That was his cadaver indication. His sign that he'd found the scent of a dead human. My heart dropped. "Nate!" I really didn't want to see one of those kids dead. No. Not Ellie's children. Not any child.

I gritted my teeth and pushed on toward Luke. And there, caught in a thicket by rushing water, was the body. It wasn't a child. It was a woman in a blue dress. "Nate!"

He caught up to me, slightly out of breath. "Take care of the dog. I'll call it in."

I took Luke a little way away and played with him. That was his big reward, and he loved retrieving his special Kong toy. Then I went back to where Nate stood.

"What are you doing?" I asked him. He was unzipping his field khakis, turning the pants into shorts.

"I got to secure the body," he said, "but this leg don't do good in water."

The electronics in his expensive artificial leg would get ruined. So he was going to what? Take it off and hop out there on his one good leg? No. That was ridiculous.

"I'll do it. I'll go in there," I said.

"No. It's too dangerous."

"Don't be ridiculous. I can do it." I didn't want to, but I could. I pulled blue medical gloves out of my pack and put them on. "She's not that far."

"You promised Scott you'd stay out of swift-water rescues!"

"This isn't a rescue, it's a recovery. And besides, that's when I was pregnant."

Nate scowled. "Something happens to you, Scott's gonna kill me." But he knew I was right. He zipped the pants leg back on.

I pulled a length of rope off my pack. "Nothing's going to happen. The force of the stream is way out there." I told Luke to stay and put the rope in my teeth, then I waded into the water, careful to hold onto the bushes and trees. Luke whined. He wasn't happy with me putting myself in danger either.

She was in her fifties, I guessed, a woman with bleached

blonde hair in a blue dress, and wearing diamond studded rings. Her face was already swollen. Definitely a wedding guest.

Dead weight is heavy, but a dead body is easier to pull out of the water than a drowning person who's fighting you. I looped the rope around her body and pulled her to the edge of the creek. Then Nate and I moved her to higher ground. Just to be double sure nothing would happen, we tied the rope to a tree.

"I reckon she was in that car," Nate said. We pulled off our gloves and both used hand sanitizer. "Sheriff said they'd be here soon as they could. May have to come 'round the back way."

I nodded, out of breath. Then I noticed my dog was gone. "Where's Luke?"

Nate frowned. "Don't know. He was right here. I was watchin' you."

"Luke! Luke," I called.

He came running back, hard. He grabbed the sopping wet tug on my belt and took off again.

"Nate! He's found somebody."

"Let's go!"

I swung my pack on and followed my dog. The pack felt like it weighed a hundred pounds, but that's just because I was tired. My mind raced faster than I could walk. I saw Luke again, barreling toward me. He barely touched my tug before taking off again. We pushed our way through the trees and bushes.

"Help! Help!"

"The kids!" I yelled over my shoulder. Their little voices propelled me faster. Finally, I saw them, Ellie's kids, Maddie and Jamie. They'd climbed up into some trees that looked like crape myrtles, thin trees, lots of branches close down, about twenty feet out in the overflowing creek. The water was just a foot or so below them and still rising. Maddie was hanging onto Jamie with one arm and clinging to the tree with the other.

"We're coming! We'll get you!" I said.

Nate caught up to me as I dropped my pack on the ground. Just then Luke jumped into the water, swimming toward the kids, and my panic soared. "No, Luke! Come, come!" I could envision him being swept away by the current just like a few years ago. "Come! Luke, come!" He turned and paddled back. "Down! Stay," I told him when he'd climbed out of the water.

Then I turned to Nate. "I'm going out to get them."

"No. Rescue squad's comin'."

"How long will that be? Half an hour? Look at those kids, Nate. They're barely hanging on."

"Jess, no. You cain't do that. The current's too strong."

I could taste fear in my throat. But these were Ellie's children. Little Jamie. My sweet Maddie. "I can't just stand here, Nate. I can't!"

"I'll go," he said.

"No! You'll ruin your leg."

"I'll take it off."

"And hop out there? No. I'm going. Now you can help me, or I'll figure out a way to do it myself."

"Oh Lord, have mercy! Why'd I ever teach you anything?" He spat the words out, angry. "Hold on." He pulled a climbing rope off his pack and tied it around me, high, under my armpits. "Get them one at a time! Hear me? Don't you go tryin' to bring 'em both back at once." His words were fierce.

"Okay, Nate. I got this." I grinned.

Maddie screamed. Jamie's foot had slipped off the branch he stood on.

"I've got to go!" I waded out. The water was over my waist. "I'm coming for you! Hang on." Maddie's face looked frozen, her eyes bugging out, her mouth in an O.

The cold current pressed hard against my legs. I kept losing my footing. What was I walking on? Rocks? Flattened bushes? A tree stump? It was part of the land currently swamped by this flood. Who knows what was under my feet?

I worked my way out to the kids. The water was almost to my chest. One wrong step and I'd be swept away. I knew it. I could hear Luke whining.

I grabbed onto the trees the kids had climbed into. I couldn't quite reach Jamie. "Jamie, jump! I'll catch you." But he was too scared. "Come on, just like at the pool!" I said. "Maddie let go. Let him jump. I'll catch him. I promise."

Finally, she released her grip on her brother. He fell. I caught him, nearly losing my balance. The splash of his fall sloshed water over my face. I couldn't see. Suddenly, I heard a scream. I saw a blur and heard a splash. Maddie! Instinctively, I turned and grabbed and caught her dress. Nate yelled. I pulled with all my might. I would not let the flood take her!

I felt the rope tighten around me, like an anchor. I gripped Jamie with my left arm and tugged Maddie's dress with my right. My heart pounded as I fought the current. I gulped for air and heard a huge splash. Nate? I tossed my head to clear my vision and saw something brown and black. Luke! Luke was in the water swimming toward me.

"No, Luke!"

My dog ignored me, just like I'd ignored Nate. He paddled right past me and grabbed Maddie's arm, then turned back toward Nate.

Luke had her, but I couldn't let go of her dress. I was afraid of losing her, but Luke was pulling most of her weight. I felt the rope tugging me, pulling me steadily back to land. Jamie had a death grip on my neck, wailing in my ear. At least he was breathing. Luke paddled next to me. My legs were about to give out when I realized we were close to Nate. One more push, and he took the boy. Then I turned and pulled Maddie up out of the water.

For a moment I thought she had drowned. I held her and pounded her back. Then she coughed. Luke crawled out, shook off, and stood near me, panting.

Nate came back for Maddie. I climbed out and collapsed to my knees in the mud, gasping for breath. I was so cold, so exhausted, I couldn't untie the rope around my chest.

I looked up. Jamie sat shivering, his body visibly shaking. His lips and the skin around his mouth had turned blue. Hypothermia. I crawled to my pack and pulled out an emergency blanket, wrapped it around him, and hugged him. Nearby, Nate had Maddie on her side, helping her get the water out of her lungs and gut. I threw Nate my other emergency blanket, and he wrapped it around her.

He was muttering something, and it took me a minute to figure out what he was saying. He was praying, actually, as he worked, a Scripture verse. *When you pass through the waters, I'll be with you.* He recited it over and over.

When he could, he came to me. I was still holding Jamie, both of us shaking like a leaf. Nate looked at me, his eyes sharp. "Get up. I'll take him."

I hesitated. Nate untied the rope around my chest. Then he unzipped my pack and found my spare clothes. "Get up. Get these on. Jump around if you have to. You got to warm up." He held out his hand and pulled me to my feet.

I was shaking so hard I could barely strip my clothes off. Somehow I managed to change behind a thick row of bushes. Then, to warm up, I started jumping around. I heard a giggle. Nate had both kids in his lap, trying to use his body heat to warm them. Jamie was laughing at me.

Twenty-five minutes later, emergency responders showed up. They had dry blankets and warmers. They told us the bridge we'd crossed was now impassable and said they'd take the kids to the hospital. "She needs to go too," Nate said, pointing to me, but I refused.

"Take care of the kids. I'll be okay."

Nate rolled his eyes.

The EMTs chose to believe me. They stowed the kids in a basket stretcher and carried them away while I tried to find enough strength to walk out.

Nate had called the sheriff and made arrangements for us to be picked up back where the ambulance had been. We packed up our gear. I gave Luke water and a protein treat and ate something myself, then we walked out, stumbled really, Luke and Nate and I, going slower than I ever had before. By the time we were at our pickup point, I was soaked and muddy again.

We got a lift back to the vineyard where we discovered SAR was no longer needed. Everyone had been found, dead and alive. Muddy, exhausted, and chilled to the bone, we climbed into Nate's Tahoe and drove home.

I think I dozed off. Nate must have called Scott, because my wonderful husband met us in the driveway. He didn't complain about two muddy people and one muddy dog traipsing into the house so late. He helped me shower in our first-floor bathroom while Nate washed off Luke. Then Scott brought me warm, dry sweat pants and an oversized T-shirt and made me hot tea with lots of sugar while Nate showered and changed clothes.

I found out later the wedding never happened … and that Ellie's sister had been wearing a blue dress.

18

JESS

Scott had talked Nate into spending the night. "He felt really bad," he told me that morning in bed, "that you had to go in the water to get the kids."

"He couldn't because of his leg."

"He said he wished he'd sacrificed the leg."

I grimaced. "I was fine. He had me on a rope. He was watching out for me. I was scared for the kids, not myself." A partial truth at best.

Later, we were all downstairs talking. Mike was playing with his toys. A car pulled up in our driveway. "It's a dark SUV," Scott said, looking out of the window. "Wait. I think it's Ellie's husband."

I jumped up and looked. "Yes! It's Paul." Scott had only met him once and the same was true for Nate.

We welcomed him inside. He had flowers in his hand and a box of Milk-Bones for Luke. Paul asked us to tell him the whole story because Ellie just had a few facts. He had driven through the night to get back when he learned what happened.

So we told him, Nate and I alternating and adding details

the other forgot. Scott didn't make eye contact with either one of us the whole time. His gaze was fixed across the room where Mike was playing with his trucks. I wondered if he was angry. *How much had we told him last night?* I couldn't remember, but I knew he was getting the whole story now.

"We can't thank you enough," Paul said. "We are so grateful. You saved their lives." His eyes glistened.

"We were glad we could help," I said. "How are they doing?"

"The doctors say they'll be fine. They kept them overnight in the hospital. Something about dry drowning."

I knew about dry drowning. It's when someone has inhaled water and, even after they seem safe, they can develop trouble breathing. They need to be watched for at least twenty-four hours.

He continued. "Ellie stayed with them. I'm going there now to bring everyone home." He paused, his voice catching. "Connor's still angry because Ellie wouldn't let him go search for Maddie and Jamie. She was really afraid for him to cross that bridge."

Nate spoke up. "Unless he'd had a rope and a second person, I don't think he could have saved them. Mighta drowned hisself."

Paul nodded. "I'm so grateful you were there." He hugged me and shook hands with Nate and Scott and then left.

I went out in the kitchen to find a vase for the flowers. I was standing in front of the counter arranging them when Scott came up behind me. He put his arms around me and pulled me close.

I stopped what I was doing and turned, embracing him. "I'm sorry if that scared you."

He squeezed me gently. "I love you so much."

"I couldn't ... I couldn't ..."

"I know." He kissed me. "There's no way you could see those kids in that tree without trying to get to them. It was dangerous, he said, "but you had to do it and I love you for it. Even if it terrifies me." He shook his head. "It's crazy. I just had this conversation with Amanda."

"What conversation?"

"She asked me how we coped with the reality we could lose each other."

"Because of Henry's accident?"

"Right." He rubbed my back. "It scared her. I told her … I said I would be devastated if I lost you, but loving you was worth the risk. That love makes life rich." He kissed my head. "I told her if something happened other friends and other family members would come around me and support me. Help me get through it." He smiled. "Of course, she argued. She asked me what would happen if you and all my friends died, how I'd cope with that."

"Did you tell her the likelihood of that is slim and none?"

He shook his head. "I said even if that happened, I'd still have God."

I pulled back and looked at him. "And?"

"She didn't say a word."

"No eruption? Scorn? Anger?"

"No."

I put my head back down on my husband's chest. I could hear Nate playing with Mike in the front room. "Good for you." I squeezed him and looked up. "I want to know more about your trip. Let's go in the living room so Nate can hear."

They found Nate sitting on a small chair playing trucks with Mike. He looked up when they came in. "I thought you might want to hear about Scott's trip to the Eastern Shore," I said.

"You bet," Nate said.

"Here, let me play with him. You go relax." I knew he'd be stiff sitting on that chair for so long, so I took his place and Scott gestured for him to take the recliner. My husband sat down on the couch and told us all about Henry's accident and how Amanda saved his life. He told us about their conversation on the beach and helping get Henry home.

"Oh, by the way," Scott said suddenly. "You're going to see a big charge on the Visa bill. Sorry about that. I bought Henry a recliner."

"A recliner?"

"Like ours. I remember how much it helped when I was hurt to be able to sleep without lying flat in a bed. I asked him if it would be okay. He didn't want me to at first, but I think that he just didn't want me to spend the money on him. But Amanda talked him into it." He grinned. "I didn't think you'd mind."

"I'll take it out of your steak budget," I joked. "I'm glad we could help him."

Nate listened intently. Suddenly, he lowered the footrest on the recliner and sat forward. "You know," he said, "this is nothin' but the grace of God. Start to finish. It's God's grace." His blue eyes were shining.

"Meaning?" Scott asked.

"Look at it." Nate gestured with his hands. "She goes with Henry to the farm. She don't always do that, the way I understand it. So she's there when he gets hurt. It just so happens that a month ago she learns about pneumothorax because of the dog. She recognizes it, knows what's happening, knows he needs help pronto, and in the meantime, gets him in a position he can breathe.

"The help that comes ain't no normal ambulance crew. It just happens to have a paramedic with military experience on board. Doubtful a regular EMT could do a pneumothorax decompression. I seen a Marine die of one in the war when his vehicle overturned and there weren't no medic around. Believe me, it's terrifying. Alls we could do was hold his hand." He closed his eyes and put both hands over his mouth and nose for a minute, breathing into the triangle as he processed the memory.

"Anyways, Henry gets just the right help. Scott, you make a bold move, goin' over there. Your pilot buddy is available and the weather is good. Not only are you there when she needs steadyin', but you're able to witness to her on the beach. And she don't spit in your face. She listens. You talk about faith and she don't flip out! Glory!"

Nate was so intense I noticed Mike had stopped playing and was staring at him, wide-eyed.

"Good gravy!" Nate said, continuing. "How long we been praying for that girl? Five years? Six? Would you have even guessed at any of this a year ago? No! God is workin'!" He took a deep breath. "I don't know 'bout you, but I got to pray!"

And so we did. Right there. All of us.

WHENEVER NATE GOES off like that I always wonder why I didn't think that way. Why don't I see the hand of God so readily? Be so quick to praise him?

So much gets by me. I mean, I get the big stuff. God has pulled me out of the miry pit many times, literally and figuratively. He gave me Luke. And Nate and Scott and definitely Mike. Saved my life just last year and maybe yesterday. Healed a lot of wounds, physical and emotional. But day-to-day? My eyes are on the laundry, the grocery list, the little boy and the husband and the dog and the horses and ... well, you get it.

I sometimes see God at work, but Nate, he just breathes God in and out 24/7.

19

JESS

Mike cried when Nate and Ember left about noon. Scott promised his son he'd take him for a ride on Ace after his nap. We got him settled in his high chair, eating lunch, with Luke watching attentively.

"By the way," Scott said as he made sandwiches for the two of us, "the coolest thing. Amanda took me by Hope Ranch and showed me what she's been doing with the horses."

"Like what?"

"Kate has her on track to be a mentor, to start working with kids who come there for help."

"Impressive. She must be doing well." I put more cut up, slightly cooked carrots on Mike's tray.

"I guess so." Scott laid a stacked turkey and cheese sandwich in front of me and sat down. "Some of what they're doing is like the natural horsemanship my uncle taught me, but more. Very low key, very gentle. Creates a calm, trusting relationship with the horse. When you bring a troubled kid in, the kid learns how to trust and relate, first to the horse, then to people.

Kate told me the ultimate aim is to help them learn to relate to God." He took a bite of his own sandwich.

I added bits of turkey to Mike's tray. "Do you think she—"

Mike interrupted me, reaching for my food. Apparently, my sandwich looked better to him than his food.

Scott picked up the conversation. "Is Kate talking to Amanda about God? I think Kate has to walk a fine line. In counseling, she really can't. When it comes to the horses, I don't know what the rules are. At any rate, Kate knows Amanda well enough to be smart about what she shares with her. And Amanda really loves her."

A quarter of my sandwich, now deconstructed, was on Mike's tray. He was fingerpainting with the mustard. Luke had his eye on the turkey.

Scott went on. "Amanda showed me the red mare she's been working with. Remember? She told us about her last year. Now, that horse is much calmer, much more stable, and she's even able to be out with at least one other horse. Amanda was able to walk right into the paddock with her. She's done an amazing job."

I smiled. "You must have felt so proud."

"I was proud. And I told her so." He finished his sandwich and took a big drink of water. "I think … I think actually working with the horses is part of what has stabilized her. Because she has to regulate her emotions and stay calm so she doesn't trigger them."

"Henry's played a part."

"Yes, Henry for sure. And Kate."

I took Scott's hand and smiled. "And the grace of God."

WE SPENT the rest of the weekend relaxing and recovering from our adventures. Scott checked in with Amanda every day.

Henry was doing well. Ellie called me on Sunday to thank me and tell me they were home.

"How are the kids?" I asked.

"Jamie acts like it never happened. But Maddie? I don't know. She's very quiet."

"She's old enough to comprehend what could have happened," I suggested. "Plus, her aunt died."

"Yes."

On Monday, Scott went into his office at Quantico, and I got the strangest phone call from Brett Hudgins. He called to see if I could meet him for coffee because he had some questions to ask me. About the case, he said.

Funny. I thought that PI case was closed. I'd just deposited the check. I wondered what this was all about. So, I told him I could meet him on Wednesday in Charlottesville.

I didn't have a lot of time to think about it, honestly, between my child, my dog, the house, and other things I had to do, plus working on my PI business while Mike napped, and then making dinner for all of us. Plus, I was still tired from the weekend.

I checked in with Ellie when I had a chance. She told me things were the same. Jamie was running around as usual, but Maddie was still quiet.

"Give her time," I advised.

I left early on Wednesday morning and drove to Charlottesville to meet Brett Hudgins, still wondering what in the world he wanted. I walked into Serein, the café where we'd met previously. He was there already and had a black coffee waiting for me at a table away from the other patrons.

"So, what's up?" I asked him.

He cradled his mug in his hands. I noticed his knuckles were bruised, but before I could ask him about it, he started talking. "I'm worried about my wife. I … I mean my ex-wife."

"Brittany? Why? What's going on?"

He paused, staring into his mug. I noticed a little more gray in his hair, gray that hadn't been there before. His face looked strained. Finally, he looked up at me, his blue eyes clear and imploring.

"This isn't her. I mean, all this craziness. The screaming, the connection with … with this group in Alexandria. Drugs. I mean, it's not like her. Something's happened to her. I don't know what. But she's … she's not like she was before. She's not like the woman I married."

What am I, a counselor? I groped for my role in this soap opera. "Brett, you're divorced. So why do you care?"

His face reddened. "She's the mother of my children and … and I still love her."

Oh, good grief.

"I think I always will," he said. "I feel protective, like I need to help her, but …"

Words like enmeshed and codependent flashed through my mind.

"…but I don't know how."

I took a drink of my coffee, trying to regroup. "I'm not sure why you called me," I said.

"I'd like to hire you to keep track of her for me. Just for a while. Just until I know she's okay."

My stomach clenched.

"My name's still on that car registration. It should be legal. I'd just like to know she's not falling into dangerous hands, that she's getting the help she needs."

I measured my words carefully. "Brett, I feel for you. I really do. What you've been through is hard. But I can't just follow somebody without cause. It's not ethical, not in my book anyway."

"There is cause! I mean, she's being entrapped by somebody, some gang. I know it. And she needs help!" His hands shook. "I'll pay you well. I promise you I can pay whatever you want."

"Money isn't the issue, Brett. The problem is I wouldn't be trying to identify the facts for a divorce proceeding. Or child custody. There is no purpose beyond you wanting to know what she's up to. You're asking me to be a paid stalker, and I just can't do it." I kept my voice soft. I liked the guy. I felt sorry for him. I just couldn't do what he wanted.

He looked crestfallen. "Okay, well, do you know any other PIs who might do it?"

"No. You need to drop your plan. Trust me. For the sake of your children. It's up to Brittany to make her own decisions. You can't save her. She has to walk away on her own from whatever she's into. If you try to interfere, you could get in trouble. And how would that be for your girls?"

He stared at the table. I'm sure he was trying to come up with another argument. Finally, he gave it up. He looked at me with sad eyes. "Well, thank you for meeting with me anyway."

"You're welcome," I said. "And thanks for the coffee." I started to rise, stopped, and put a hand on Brett's arm. "Take care of your girls, Brett. They need you more than ever."

He nodded silently.

WHEN I GOT HOME, Scott asked me what Brett had wanted. I told him, and I also told him my response.

"Good. Stay out of that mess."

"I fully intend to." Case closed, I thought.

He was quiet for a few minutes, then he continued. "I do

understand him, though. After Suzanne and I divorced, after all the arguments and accusations and crazy making, when I saw her making bad decisions, my gut instinct was still to protect her."

His tone was almost confessional. No, not almost. It *was* confessional. "What did you do?"

"I made suggestions a couple of times. Questioned what she was doing. You know, when I was picking up or dropping off Amanda. Just little things." He shook his head. "That door slammed in my face so hard. She threatened me. I was afraid I'd lose what little contact with Amanda I had, so I shut up. But the instinct was there."

I wondered what Brett would do next.

20

AMANDA

Amanda slept on Henry's couch at night, just as her dad had done before he went home. Cash lay curled at her feet, while Henry slept in the recliner. She wanted to be there for him in case he needed something—more meds or help getting up from the recliner or ice. Anything.

Henry was still sleeping a lot, which he attributed to the opioids he'd been prescribed. He made it clear he didn't like taking them, but Scott had told him how important it was to stay ahead of the pain. Still, Henry insisted the drugs stay out of reach and in his bedroom. Amanda laughed and called him quirky.

Her boss was understanding. She could work from home for a week or so to take care of Henry. She could come in for partial days when she needed to do something with the interns or check the plovers.

Amanda had no worries about him being alone when she did have to leave for a few hours. He had a constant parade of visitors. She couldn't keep track of them. Fire department members, pony people, folks he'd gone to high school with. His boss. Even *her* boss. Some people brought food, others gift cards. Everybody seemed to know Henry and liked him.

She teased Henry about it. "No wonder you always want to hang out on my porch," she said. "You're escaping all this traffic!"

One day, after she'd taken Cash for a walk, she entered the house to find someone new sitting in the visitor's chair. He looked older and rough around the edges. Dark hair. Tall and a little gaunt. In front of him, on the wooden coffee table, was a six-pack of beer with two cans removed. One was in his hand. The other was on the table next to Henry.

"Amanda," Henry said, a hesitation in his voice, "this is my brother, Cal."

Cal. His older brother. Worked on an oil rig. Another disconnected family member.

Henry went on. "This is my fiancée, Amanda."

"Fiancée? Well, Dad didn't tell me that!" Cal rose and started to hug her. She offered her hand. "When's the big day?" he asked.

Amanda fumbled for an answer. Henry said, "Soon."

"She is beautiful," Cal said. "How'd you get a hot girl like that?"

Amanda started to retort, but thought better of it. No need to start something between the two brothers. Instead, she went out to the kitchen where she could make lunch and listen at the same time.

"How'd you find out I was hurt?" she heard Henry say.

"Dad told me. He said your girlfriend called him. Is that the same girl?"

"I've only got one," Henry responded. "So you've seen Dad?"

"Yeah."

There was a long pause. "How's your job going?" Henry asked.

Cal laughed. "Ah, I needed a break. It's stressful out there, you know. On the salt. Isolating. It's hard on your body."

Harder than having a cow crash down on you? Break your ribs? Amanda jerked a pot out of the cabinet, put it on the stove, and dumped a large can of chicken noodle soup in it.

She heard Henry ask Cal, "So, are you on a break? From your job?"

Cal laughed. "A break? Yeah. A long one."

"Did you quit?"

"More or less. I got tired of it. Most of the time, it wasn't too bad except if storms came up. Fishing was good. Rough though. We had a guy get his hand caught in the machinery. That was a bloody sight."

"Not you, though? You didn't get hurt?"

"Nah. I just needed a break."

They talked more, their voices low enough that she couldn't quite hear what they were saying, so she quit trying. She was just about to go out and ask if Cal would like some soup when she heard him say, "Okay, look, I gotta go, man. Mind if I use your bathroom?"

"Go ahead," Henry said.

Amanda heard footsteps heading back to the bathroom. She was ladling soup into two big mugs when she heard him coming back down the hall. Cal stuck his head into the kitchen. "Bye, Amanda. Can you give your brother-in-law a hug?"

"*Future* brother-in-law," she said as he put his arms around her and squeezed her.

"Take care of my bro'!" he said, and before she could dodge it, he gave her a quick kiss. On the lips.

Ugh! She nearly slapped him. But he grinned, turned, and left.

She had to calm down before taking the mugs out to the living room. "Here you go," she said, to Henry, forcing a smile. *Should she tell him?* She didn't want to upset him.

"Thank you."

"Want to take a pill with that?" Amanda asked.

"How many are left, do you know?"

She raised her eyebrows, then frowned. "Oxycodone? You have five left."

"Okay."

She walked back to the bedroom, found the bottle, and out of curiosity, opened the lid. Two. There were only two pills in there! Her jaw tight, anger flushing her face, she walked back to Henry. "Now we know why he came to visit!" She showed him the bottle. "Henry there were five in there. Five! I can't believe he stole from his own brother."

"Amanda—"

"How could he? What a jerk! You need to call the police. Right now. Report it."

Henry looked at her. "Yeah. I should. But I won't. Could you get me some crackers? And some more water?"

She blinked. Henry. Patient Henry. "Yeah, sure." She started toward the kitchen, then turned back. "It's not right, Henry. You don't deserve that."

"I know. Crackers?"

She turned, went into the kitchen, and got the crackers and water. When she came back into the living room, she said, "Really, Henry. You need to report it. It's theft." She picked up his phone and handed it to him.

He took the phone and tucked it next to him. "He's my brother."

"So what?"

"He's my brother."

She sat down, still agitated. "Well, if you won't call the police, are you going to call your doctor? Get some replacements? I mean, you'll have to explain it but—"

He shrugged. "I'm about to the point I don't need it."

"So you're going to sit there and suffer because of your stupid brother? Henry, that is so not fair! Why should you—"

"Amanda—"

"—make up for his—"

"Amanda!"

His raised voice stopped her.

He reached out and took her hand. "Thank you. You're right. It's not fair. But Amanda, he's about all the family I've got."

She was about to make a retort when she caught the look in Henry's eyes. She fought to calm down. "I'm so sorry, Henry. Really, I am. You deserve better." She squeezed his hand. "I'll hide the rest of them."

"Put the bottle in the pocket of my navy sports coat."

"Your what?"

"You've never seen me wear it." He grinned. "It's in my closet, trust me."

LATER THAT NIGHT, she rehearsed in her head what she'd do if Cal came back, how she'd confront him. Force him to face what he'd done. *What a total jerk!* Henry should have kicked his butt out. Was he afraid of him? Why was he so passive?

She could imagine what her dad would say. He'd be really angry. He'd say you have to take a hard line with drug addicts. Pretty soon he'd be mansplaining the evils of opioid abuse, probably with statistics and a report on the latest FBI Task Force trying to stop it. He'd agree with her. He'd know what to do.

She looked across the room. Henry was sound asleep. Impulsively, Amanda pulled her phone out of her back pocket, walked to the back bedroom, and called her dad. Told him about Cal. Waited for his heated response.

Instead of giving her instant support, her dad listened quietly. Then he asked a couple of questions and finally, gave her his opinion. "I'm sorry, Amanda. Henry's in a tough position. It's hard when a family member is feeding an addiction. Very hard to know what to do. I'm glad you're there to support him."

What?

A few minutes later, after some mindless chatter, she hung up, mystified. Then it hit her. Hard. Images from her out-of-control drinking days raced through her mind. Calling her dad when she was plastered, her words slurring. Drinking beer after beer every time he took her out. Walking out to the car afterward unsteady on her feet. Her dad had been through it—with her!

He'd set boundaries, she remembered. Refused to have alcohol in his home. Told her if she got a DUI he was taking back his car. But he never gave up on her. He never quit loving her. He always offered her a safe place to land.

Her face got hot. Finally, she understood.

She heard Henry call her. He looked up as she entered the living room. "You okay?"

She walked over and kissed him. "I get it. He's your brother."

A look of relief flooded his face, and he lowered the footrest of the recliner and pulled her into his lap. "Thank you. I love you," he said, kissing her.

Amanda relaxed. She nestled her head under his jaw, felt the stubble of his beard and the warmth of his arms. Her breathing slowed. Her heart settled. Henry.

21

JESS

I went over to see Ellie and the kids several times in the weeks following the flood. I thought seeing me, Little Mike, and Luke would bring a sense of normalcy to them, like waking up after a nightmare to see that your nightstand and lamp are still where they're supposed to be, your dresser is steady, and the stuffies you sleep with are still gathered around you in solidarity.

By our third visit, Jamie was fine. Connor had gotten over his anger. But Maddie? She remained too quiet, lost in her thoughts, and Ellie was worried.

"Maddie and I have always had a good relationship. Maybe I could draw her out," I suggested. Ellie told me to give it a try.

I prayed as I walked up to the bedroom Maddie and her sister shared. I found her crammed in a corner, sitting on the floor, reading a book. "Hey, Maddie! What are you reading?" I'd brought Luke up with me, and he sniffed Maddie and tried to lie down near her. She shoved him away. To be fair, she was in a small space, but still, I was surprised.

"What's the book?" I repeated.

Instead of answering, she turned the cover so I could read it. *The Silver Creek Ranch Mysteries, Book 3.* I could tell she wasn't far into it. "Have you read the first two in the series?"

She shook her head no.

I paused, trying to find a way into her heart. "How are you feeling, Maddie?"

She shrugged.

"Are your lungs all cleared up?"

She nodded yes.

"Hey, you know, I could use some help around the farm, with Little Mike and all. Any chance you want to come hang out with me for a while?"

"I can't," she responded.

At least I got words. "Why not?"

She shrugged.

"You could bring your book."

No response.

I let the silence ride for a while, and then I said, "That flood really scared you, didn't it?"

She drew up her knees and buried her face in her arms. "Oh, Maddie," I said, reaching down to rub her back. "You were so brave. You got through it and so did Jamie. He's fine. You worked so hard to save him, didn't you? I am so proud of you."

She did not look up.

I groped for what to say next. Her silence rendered her out of reach, and I didn't know what to do. Toddlers are easier, I thought, than preadolescent girls.

I sat in silence for a time, and then I did the only other thing I could think of. I prayed for Maddie, out loud, with my hand on her back. I asked the Lord to heal her completely, to instill in her the knowledge that she was loved, that she was his child, and that she was safe in his sovereign grace. I went on until I ran out of words. And then I said, "Amen."

When I opened my eyes, I saw Luke's head was on my foot and his eyes were fixed on mine. At least my dog was listening.

LITTLE MIKE and I went home, and because it was such a beautiful day, we gave Luke a bath outside. Mike loved the hose, like all toddlers, and I let him rinse Luke off, except for his face. I was working the shampoo out of his coat when I noticed a lump on Luke's side, right behind his last rib. My heart clenched. No!

Luke was nine years old. How long did German shepherds live? I wondered. Standing right there in the back yard, my dog dripping wet, I Googled it. *Nine to thirteen years.* Panic gripped me.

I heard Mike giggle. I looked up. He was holding the hose and Luke was biting the water. I realized I'd only rinsed off one side of my dog. Still, my anxiety forced my fingers to call our vet.

I couldn't get an appointment for two days. My hand shaking, I called Nate. Nate would know what to do.

He must have been out cutting grass. His phone went to voicemail. I turned around to see Mike squirting the house and Luke rolling in the grass, completely undoing the bath I'd just given him. I started to end the chaos ... and that's when I thought of Henry.

Henry was a large animal vet. Still, Henry would know.

I called him, forcing myself to adopt a calm voice, fake as it might be. I remembered to ask Henry how he was first, and I was genuinely pleased to learn he was up and moving around. Next week, he said, he was going back to work, but first at the clinic with small animals for just a few hours a day.

"Speaking of which," I said, and I told him about the lump I'd found on Luke's side. To my chagrin, my voice caught.

"Is it moveable?" he asked me.

"Maybe. I don't know."

"Is he near you?"

"Yes."

"Try it. Gently.

I called Luke, who got up from his mud spa treatments, and came to me, wet, filthy, grassy, and grinning. The picture of health. "Stand," I told him, and then I inspected the lump. "Yes," I said to Henry. "It's moveable. Is that good or bad?"

"Probably good," he said. "How old is he?"

"Nine." *Already nine? Why don't dogs live forever?* My heart drummed.

"Okay. It's most likely a lipoma, a benign, fatty tumor some dogs get when they get older."

A glimmer of hope. "Will he have to have surgery?"

"Probably not. The vet will most likely aspirate a little fluid and confirm that's what it is. Then they'll just watch it. As long as it doesn't grow a lot or invade the surrounding tissue, they'll just leave it alone."

Relief flooded through me. "Thank you, Henry."

"Yep. Glad to help."

As I clicked off the phone, Little Mike sprayed water in my face.

THAT NIGHT, I told Scott about finding the lump. Tears filled my eyes, and I turned away, hoping he didn't see them. But I know he did, because he came over and wrapped his arms around me and whispered in my ear. "Maybe you should think about getting a second dog."

"What?" I turned around. *Another dog? Inconceivable!*

"It might be good for him to have a buddy."

"I can't imagine ..." My words trailed off.

"Jess, there will never be another Luke," he said. "We all know that. You don't even have to get another shepherd. We have enough land for like, a border collie. They do well in search and rescue, right? Or a Lab. A German shorthaired pointer. Lots of breeds. Maybe an Aussie, like your first dog."

Finn. The dog my uncle gave me after my dad died.

Scott continued. "Think about it. Are you really going to put Luke through those mountain searches four or five years from now? Maybe you should start a young dog, like Nate did with Ember, or get a puppy! Of course, it'll take three years or so to get him to where he can search."

"Luke was two."

"But then, Luke is special."

I smiled at my husband's kindness. "You know what Nate says? He says the reason why God gave dogs such short lives is because if they lived as long as we do, we'd decide we didn't need people."

Scott laughed. "I know! I'm living on the edge every day." He grinned and hugged me. "You'll figure it out. Just know that I'm open to another dog whenever you want one."

THE LUMP DID TURN out to be a benign lipoma, just as Henry had guessed. Luke likely had years ahead of him, the vet said. But Scott in his kindness had planted the seed of the idea of a second dog in my head. Maybe. Someday. It was something to consider. Sort of.

Battlefield had three searches shortly after that, and in each one our team had a frustrating circumstance. That's not totally unusual. We had a debriefing where people aired their complaints, everything from "law enforcement waited four hours to call us out" and "they called off the search at nightfall" to "the subject was evasive" to "the subject's family gave wrong information" and finally, "a car was coming, and my dog was so focused on scent he almost got hit."

We can't control law enforcement decisions, as frustrating

as that might be sometimes. Good questions might reveal improper information from a subject's family, but some of those other things could be improved with training.

"Can I work with the newer dogs this time?" I asked Nate, the training director.

"Sure." His searchlight blue eyes asked the next logical question, *why,* so I told him what Scott had said. "That ain't a bad idea," he responded. "In fact, sounds wise to me, if you want to keep going in SAR."

"Yes!" I said. "Of course!"

He nodded. "Then let's pray about it."

Pray about a new dog? Yes. Of course. Why didn't I think of that?

ON THE DAY of our training, Scott took Little Mike to Northern Virginia to see my mother, which I thought was really sweet of him. He knew Mike would go crazy with all the dogs on the farm. He didn't want him interfering with what we were doing. So it was off to Grandma's house. My mom was very pleased.

We had sixteen handlers and eighteen dogs show up. Nate and I had come up with three goals:

1. Reinforcing the emergency stop
2. Teaching the evasive subject
3. Persisting when there is more than one subject

All of these were responses to frustrating problems we'd had recently. The first issue, the emergency stop, we set as a goal because one of Battlefield's dogs nearly got hit crossing a road. SAR is more complicated than it seems because you *want* the dog to be intent on the scent, right? If I call him, but he's on a scent, he needs to ignore me. On the other hand, if he's hot on a scent but racing toward danger, he needs to listen to my command.

Part of the solution is learning to read your dog better so you can tell if he's got a scent or not. Part is training a separate "Stop!" command rather than using a simple recall. *Stop!* means you're about to get hit by a car. Or fall over a cliff. Or enter a field with an angry bull. Dogs can get hyper-focused on a task, just like people. *Stop!* wakes them up.

The second teaching point originated with a search I wasn't on—a callout to search for a despondent teenager. The fifteen-year-old boy had been missing for fourteen hours. One of our handlers reported her dog, a Lab, had given strong signals he was on the boy's scent in a wooded, mountainous area. After following him for a while, the handler thought he'd lost the scent. He kept coming back and sniffing one area.

Then law enforcement called off the search. It was nearly 9:30 p.m. The boy was found the next day by a drone not far away. Talk about frustrating! The boy told police he'd dodged a dog that was following him by dropping down into a twelve-foot ditch. He didn't want to be found.

The third scenario we wanted to work on was a search in which there is more than one subject. The dog finds one person, gets a reward, and thinks that's it. How do you teach him to keep looking?

I mean, not to brag, but Luke would. We had a situation where an older couple had gone for what they thought was an easy hike in the woods. They'd missed a turn, got lost, and then the wife turned her ankle. The husband went for help. So both were lost, but separately.

Did Luke find them both? Well, no, but he did find the husband and eagerly went searching again for the wife when I told him to "seek!" But not all dogs will. Some will just look at you, confused.

. . .

THE WEATHER TURNED out to be perfect for training, sunny and not too hot. Scott had cleaned out a water trough and added fresh water to use as a dog swimming pool in case we needed it. We also placed lots of water in buckets all around and filled a large cooler with bottles of water for the handlers.

It was a great day. Honestly, people paid attention. I saw progress in some of the teams, and a general air of camaraderie prevailed. We had ordered pizza delivery for lunch, and afterward, we split up. Nate took the experienced dogs, and I took the newer ones. Truth was, I wanted to revisit training a new dog since I was considering getting one. Would I have the patience? I was so used to my old man!

We ended the day at four o'clock, with everyone tired and happy and ready to continue training on their own. Nate stayed. Scott and Mike came home, and I put a casserole in the oven for dinner. It was such a beautiful day we sat on the front porch in rockers talking. Luke was tired, sleeping like an old man at my feet. Nate had put his dog Ember inside.

Nate was just telling Scott about one of the problems he'd put the handlers through when two things happened at once. I suddenly realized I didn't know where Mike was. He'd been playing with his trucks in the garden just off the porch. And Luke jumped to his feet from a dead sleep and began racing around toward the back of the house.

"Where's Mike?" I said, leaving the porch. My feet followed Luke. The two men jumped up as well.

"Mike? Mike!" Scott called, urgency in his voice.

I turned the corner of the house, ran down the side, and turned the last corner. I saw my son teetering on the edge of the horse trough, reaching down toward the water, his face inches away. "Mike, no!" I yelled, racing faster toward him.

Luke grabbed his shoe. That was more effective. He tugged, and Mike tumbled back onto the ground. Immediately, he began crying, and Luke started licking his face.

I picked up my son and dropped to the ground, holding him. "It's okay, it's okay. You're fine." My heart beat a thousand miles an hour. "Mommy's got you. You're okay."

Scott ran his hand over Mike's head, as if he were checking to see if he was really okay.

Nate immediately let the plug out on the downhill side to empty the trough.

All of us praised Luke.

"How'd he know?" I heard Scott say to Nate as I blinked away tears.

"Grace," Nate responded.

Yes, Jesus. Thank you.

Life can change in a heartbeat

22

AMANDA

Three weeks after Henry's accident he got a package. "What's that?" Amanda asked, as she walked in from work.

He opened it and pulled out a padded black sleeveless vest. "Football players use these," he said, holding it up, "to protect their ribs."

A shimmer of fear ran through her. "Why do you need that? What are you doing?"

"I'm going back to work Monday. They need me at the clinic."

"Henry!"

"It'll be fine! When I saw my doc two days ago I talked to him about it. He cleared me. Suggested I wear this for a few weeks." He smiled and gently touched her jawline. "I'll be fine. I'm not doing large animals. Just dogs and cats and an occasional parrot. I'll handle the clinic while Jim does the farm work. Oh, and by the way, Brady sold all his cows last week at auction."

"Really?"

"Yeah, his wife made him. Said enough was enough. So that white-faced cow will soon be hamburger."

"Still, Henry ..."

Henry grimaced as he slipped on the vest. "See, feel it. It protects me."

Amanda felt the padded vest, then Henry pulled her into an embrace.

"It's amazing," he said. "We can even hug now."

She gently pulled away. "I don't think you should. I mean, I wish you wouldn't ..."

"Wish I wouldn't what? Get back to my life?"

"I mean, I just don't want you to get hurt."

"I know." His voice was gentle. "I'll be fine."

LATER THAT NIGHT, they sat together on the couch with his arm around her, and she leaned against his good side.

"Henry," she said softly as the evening shadows darkened the room. "This feels so good, being here with you. Why don't I just move my stuff over here?"

He kissed her ear. "No."

"Why?"

"I like my space."

She sat up and looked at him. He was grinning. "What are you going to do when we're married? Confine me to the back room?"

"Maybe."

She jumped up. "Henry Bunting, you are not!"

He grinned more broadly. "Okay."

"Then why not just let me move in? Save the rent at the other house."

"Because."

"Because *why*?"

He took a deep breath. “For the same reason you don’t name a stray dog.”

“I’m not a stray dog!”

He laughed. “No, no you most certainly are not.” He pressed his lips together, then said, “I’ll be honest. I’d like nothing more than to have you here with me all the time. To sleep together. For you to *be* here with me. Here’s the problem: If you moved in, I wouldn’t be able to resist making mad, passionate love with you. It’s hard enough as it is.”

“I’ve been here three weeks and you’ve managed!”

“Only because I was in so much pain the thought of mad passionate anything brought tears to my eyes.”

“Oh, Henry!”

He continued. “Look, I’ve made a promise to myself and to you that I will not make love to you until we’re married. Legally. Officially. Married.”

“That is ridiculous.” She raised her hand toward him in a formal salute. “I absolve you of that promise.”

“But I don’t absolve myself of it.”

Her eyes widened. “You are so old!”

“Yes, I am.”

“I don’t know anybody who thinks that way. What is this? 1890?”

He held up his hand. “It’s important. To me. That’s all.”

“Henry … I’m going to start calling you Pops.”

He sighed. “Look, I’m not judging anybody. People can do what they want. This is a conviction I’ve had since I was fourteen. It’s a way to honor my mother.”

“She died forever ago! Do you really think she’d care?”

He winced and looked away.

Guilt took a stab at her, but she kept going. “You are crazy. I might as well leave tonight.” She walked out of the room angry, her heart pounding.

She returned with her backpack, scooped up Cash, and left. Henry was on the phone.

Her anger only lasted a couple of hours. Alone in the Main Street house, she started thinking. What if he needed something? Shouldn't he be taking a pill? What if he fell?

She wrestled with what to do, trying to distract herself with Netflix. It didn't work.

Finally, she got up, left the house, and made her way back to Henry's. She opened the front door and put Cash down. The lights were still on. And Henry smiled and held out his hand.

Amanda dropped her backpack. "You need to take Advil," she said.

"I need you." He motioned for her to come close, and he moved over and pulled her onto the recliner with him."

"I'm sorry," she whispered.

He kissed her head, and they snuggled together. After a while, Henry said, "You know, I meant to ask you, what do you do when Scarlet throws a fit? Stomps her feet and all?"

"Why are you asking?"

He shrugged. "I get horses like that sometimes."

"But you'll just be doing dogs, right? And cats?"

"And the occasional parrot. But someday I'll get back to large animals. So I was wondering what you do."

Amanda considered the question. "First of all, I stay calm myself. That's the most important thing. I wait for Scarlet to blow off steam, as long as she's being safe. Then, after she's thrown her fit, I start again doing what we did before." She yawned.

Henry stayed silent, and then he said, "So how'd I do?"

"What?"

"When you were throwing that fit? Did I do it right?"

Amanda jumped up and glared at him. "Are you saying ..."

Henry gripped his side, laughing.

"Well," she said, tossing her head, "if I'm like Scarlet, that makes you Milo."

Henry sat up. "That fat, gray pony? No, I'm more like Ajax, or Ryder. Riptide, maybe." He flexed his muscles.

"Nope. Milo." She tossed her head. "And you definitely need meds."

LIKE IT OR NOT, Henry went back to the clinic. On Monday afternoon, Amanda got home a little early. She wanted to make him a nice dinner. She'd splurged and bought some steaks. mixed up a salad, and had rolls to pop in the oven.

Work had gone well. Five new plovers had hatched. The oyster catchers were thriving. The interns were intrepid about finding them and cataloguing their nesting progress. Her boss had been doing a long-term study of water levels and duck populations and Amanda was able to help her compile the statistics. Everything was going well.

She heard the front door open. "In here, Henry!" she called out. She smiled as she turned to greet him but ... but it wasn't Henry. It was Cal. And he'd been drinking. Correction. He was drunk. His eyes were bloodshot. He gripped the doorjamb. He had a leer on his face that sent chills down her spine.

"He'll be here any minute, Cal. Why don't you wait for him—"

"Right here." He lurched toward her. "With you, right? That's what you were going to say."

"Stay away from me!" she said. "Cal, stay back."

"You don't mean that." He grabbed her wrist.

She tried to twist away. Fear filled her mouth. Her throat tightened. "Let go, Cal," she said, forcing an unnatural calm. "You're drunk. You don't know what you're doing. Just let go of me and ... and I'll get you some coffee. Please, Cal ..."

"Oh, I know what I'm doing. I know exactly what I'm

doing." He pulled her close and wrapped his other arm around her, pinning her to himself, her back against the counter. "Why should he have you? Him of all people." He leaned down to kiss her. She bit him and raised her knee to hit him in the crotch. He blocked that. "Oh, you are a feisty one." He pressed himself against her harder, and then he started groping her.

Amanda grew dizzy. She couldn't breathe!

"You love this, don't you? You will love this!"

Suddenly, she was on a dark street in Charlottesville and a man was all over her and she couldn't stop him, couldn't ...

And then there was a sound, a yell, more like a roar, and Cal was jerked away, sent crashing into the table, salad flying everywhere. She forced her eyes open and it was Henry, enraged, yelling his brother's name. She saw him pick Cal up by his shirt and smash his fist into Cal's face and do it again and again, slamming his brother against the wall and into the cabinets. Then they were fighting, throwing punches, and knocking each other around. She heard a crash as Henry pushed Cal into the living room."

"Out!" she heard Henry yell. "Never come back. You hear me, Cal? Never! You are not allowed in my house." The front door slammed shut and the lock engaged.

Then he came to her, his face red, his nose bleeding. She was on the floor, crying, her blouse buttons ripped off, her cheek bruised.

"Amanda, Amanda." He slipped to the floor and held her. "Manda. I'm so sorry, baby, I'm so sorry."

She tucked her face into his shirt and wept.

THEY FORGOT about dinner and sat on the couch for hours, holding each other while the sun set and the dark shadows of evening crept into the room. He tried to talk her into reporting it. Attempted rape. Assault. Drunk and disorderly.

She refused.

"I don't care if it is my brother," he said.

"No," she responded, "I won't do it.

After all, Amanda thought, what was the evidence? Her messed up hair? Her torn blouse? Cal's father would hire a fancy lawyer, and it would be the worst kind of he-said, she-said trial, ripping apart whatever was left of Henry's family, making him the bad guy once and for all.

No. She wouldn't do it.

"Did you get hurt?" Amanda asked Henry when she finally felt stable enough to think.

"What?"

"Your ribs. Did you get hurt? When you were fighting?"

Henry blew it off. "I'm alright. Just angry."

"Thank you. For defending me."

He gave her a long kiss.

23

HENRY

They were still cuddled on the couch at three in the morning when there was a loud pounding on the door. "Henry!" a voice called out. "Henry!"

Cal.

Henry jumped up. He moved some books aside on the top shelf of his bookcase and pulled out a gun. He checked to see that it was loaded and put it in his waistband at the small of his back. "Go back in the bedroom," he told Amanda. "Stay out of sight." They both could hear Cal outside, yelling.

She did what he asked. Then he opened the door, stepped quickly onto the porch, and closed the door behind him. "What do you want, Cal?"

Cal stood halfway down the front sidewalk. "I'm sorry, brother," he said, his words slurred. "I was just playin', you know? Just playin'. I wouldn't really hurt her."

"You assaulted her. She could have you arrested."

"I know. I'm no good. No good to anyone."

"You're not allowed here. Go away."

"I'm sorry, brother."

"You need help, Cal. Real help. And you need to stick with it."

"It's jus'... jus' too much, bro. I tried. I can't do it. I'm not like you."

In the dim light, Henry could see Cal had something in his left hand and a liquor bottle in his right. "It's not too late, Cal. You can do it. You know dad will help you."

"Nah, man. It's too late ..."

Cal raised his left hand, put something in his mouth, then lifted the whiskey bottle and glugged down all that was left. Seconds later, he collapsed.

Henry stood frozen, waiting to see what Cal would do next. Swing the bottle as Henry got close? Kick him? Jump up and laugh?

Nothing happened. Cautiously, Henry moved forward. Cal's arm was stretched out, his hand relaxed; the bottle had fallen nearby. His eyes were closed, his mouth slightly open.

In a flash, Henry went from caution to panic. "Cal!" he yelled. "Cal!"

He ran and slid down beside him. Shallow breath. Pinpoint pupils. Weak pulse. Overdose!

Henry shook his brother. Shouted his name. No response.

The front door opened. He turned and saw Amanda silhouetted in the doorway. "Call 911," he yelled, then he raced inside, pulled open a drawer, and dug out two Narcan blister packs.

He ran back to Cal. He could hear Amanda on the phone talking to the dispatcher. He ripped a blister pack open and fought to remember the Narcan directions. *Pull off the tab. Insert the tip into one nostril all the way. Now, plunge it!*

He removed the device and turned Cal onto his side in the recovery position. "Cal, wake up, come on!" He called, he cursed, he yelled. He heard sirens in the distance.

Henry checked his watch. After two minutes, he rolled Cal onto his back, gave him a second dose, then rolled him back onto his side. "Cal! Come on, man! Cal!" Three minutes later, Henry started CPR.

The ambulance rolled up, siren blaring, lights flashing. The EMTs poured out. "We've got him," one said.

Henry stepped back. Under a cloudless, black sky, he watched them administer more Narcan. Watched them provide oxygen. Watched them do CPR. Watched until he could no longer watch.

He dropped his head and turned away. He ran his hand through his hair. *Cal, you idiot! Cal...* Tears came to his eyes.

Amanda came to him and put her arms around him. "He's gone," Henry whispered in her ear. The rumble of the ambulance engine and its flashing lights faded into the background. *What was the point? What really was the point of Cal's life?*

"Henry?"

A voice he knew. He turned. A cop, Sonny Carter.

"You doing okay?"

Henry nodded. Actually, he was having trouble breathing. His ribs hurt, and he thought he was going to throw up.

"Can we go inside? I'd like to hear what happened."

"Sure." He started to move, then stopped. "I have a gun in my waistband at my back."

Sonny took a step away. "Keep your hands up, where I can see them."

"Yes, sir." He raised his hands high and felt the cop lift the gun out of his waistband.

"You have a concealed carry permit?"

"Yes, sir."

"Do you have any other weapons on you?"

"No."

"Why'd you have the gun with you?"

Henry shook his head. "I didn't know what he was going to do."

The cop nodded and called to a fellow officer. Handing her the gun, he said, “Log that for Henry Bunting.”

“The Third,” Henry said. “My father has the same name.”

“Henry Bunting III,” the cop called out. Then he said to Henry, “You’ll get that back in a few days. Let’s go in.”

Henry glanced back. He saw the EMTs standing around.

“They’ve called the medical examiner,” Carter said.

Henry shook his head and turned away. He didn’t need to see Cal’s body zipped into a bag, didn’t need to watch the medical examiner’s van drive silently away. His brother was dead. Dead! Cal was dead.

His hand shook as he opened the front door. “Come on in,” he said. Sonny followed him, his duty belt creaking as he moved. Henry walked to the couch and sat down. Cash jumped up next to him.

“What can I get you?” Amanda said. “Water, tea, soda?”

Henry started to say *nothing*, then he realized how thick his throat felt, and how dry. “Tea,” he said, “hot tea. Lots of sugar.” He looked at Sonny. “Want anything?”

“No, I’m good.” Sonny was mid-thirties, burly, with light-brown hair cut short. Henry had gone to school with his younger brother, Ben. Before Sonny sat down, he spotted the family portrait hanging on the wall and stopped to look at it. “Just the four of you?” he asked.

“Yeah.”

“And Cal was older?”

“Right. By four years.”

“Your mom died.”

“Right.”

“You moved down with your grandparents and went to high school here. But Cal never did live here.”

“Right.”

Sonny sat down. He pulled out a small notebook. “So tell me, Henry, what happened here tonight?”

Henry started in, his hand automatically stroking Cash, the feel of the dog's soft coat and the repetitive motion calming him. The dog turned his head and licked Henry's hand.

He began with Cal pounding on the door at 3:00 a.m. "He was wasted. I could tell." He went on to talk about Cal's addictions, his drug use and alcoholism. "Twice that I know of, he went through rehab," he said. "It just didn't stick."

"What was he on?"

"He'd take anything. Oxy, fentanyl, meth, anything he could get ahold of."

Amanda came in and put Henry's tea down on the end table next to him. "He even stole from Henry," she said, as she sat down.

Henry took her hand and squeezed it. He hoped the cop didn't see it.

Sonny raised his eyebrows. "Yeah?"

Henry downplayed it. "I got hurt a while back. Broke some ribs and dislocated a shoulder."

"Yeah, I heard about that," the cop said.

"The doc prescribed Oxy. I had it on my night table in the bedroom. Cal showed up. I didn't expect him. Didn't think about the drugs back there. Sure enough, he spotted the bottle and took three pills."

"Stole from his own hurt brother!" Amanda said.

Henry squeezed her hand again.

"How long ago was that?" Sonny asked.

Henry glanced at Amanda. "Two weeks?"

She nodded.

Sonny went on asking questions. Where was Cal's home? How often did he come to Chincoteague? Did he mention any names of his contacts on the island? What was his place of employment? Who was next of kin?

Henry answered as best he could, his neck growing tighter and tighter. Amanda leaned on his shoulder, her body warm against his. Cash lay on his lap. Still, he felt chilly, and he drank the hot tea down all at once as soon as it was cool enough.

Finally, Sonny was finished. He rose to leave. "Don't get up," he said to Henry and Amanda. "You've had a rough night."

Henry nodded. "What happens next?"

"We'll notify your dad. The medical examiner will probably do an autopsy, then the body will be released. After that, it's up to the next of kin. You pick the funeral home you want and go from there."

"Okay, thank you."

Sonny started to leave and then turned back around. "Your brother's face looks like he got into it with somebody recently. He must have had contact with some rough people."

Henry applied constant pressure to Amanda's hand. "I'm sure he did."

"Yes, sir. Drug dealers don't mess around." Sonny left, and once again the house was quiet.

"HENRY, why didn't you tell him?" Amanda asked after the cop left.

"Tell him what?"

"About the fight you had."

"He didn't ask."

"But Henry..."

His heart drummed. How could he explain it? "Amanda, when you're talking to a cop, you answer the questions they ask. Honestly. If you start adding extra stuff, they may start thinking of you as a suspect in whatever happened. Misinterpreting things. I know I didn't do anything wrong. If he calls me down to the station and starts questioning me, I'll answer clearly and honestly, but I may have a lawyer with me, just in case."

"You were justified! Defending me when you hit him!"

"Yeah, and if that part of the story gets around somebody

might say you led him on or you were flirting with him and it wasn't really his fault. I don't want your reputation debated. Gossiped about. It's a small town, Amanda, and I love that, but people can talk."

She was silent for a while, and then Amanda said, "I didn't know you had a gun."

"You didn't need to know. I don't usually carry it. But if I need it, I have it."

She shivered. "Why do you think he OD'd here? Do you think that was intentional?"

"Absolutely."

"Why?"

"Drama. Self-centeredness. He knew it would hurt me." Frustration and anger welled up in him. "Why didn't I react sooner! Why'd I wait?"

"What do you mean? You were right there. You had that … stuff …"

"Narcan."

"You had the Narcan on hand. You knew what to do. How could you have reacted sooner?"

Henry sagged down on the couch and held his head in his hands. "I waited. I didn't know what he was doing. Maybe he was faking it. Maybe he'd hit me with that bottle. Maybe he'd start fighting me again." He raised his hands in frustration. "I should have moved! Right away. And he'd still be alive."

"Henry! Stop! You're blaming yourself for something he did." Amanda wrapped her arms around him. "Stop beating yourself up."

He shook his head and got quiet. "Now comes the hard part."

"What's that?"

"Calling my dad."

24

HENRY

Henry tightened his jaw and tapped his father's phone number in his contact list. Henry Bunting II, PhD. He paced, bracing himself, as the phone rang, one, two, three, four, and then voicemail clicked in. "Dad, it's Henry. Call me please, soon. It's urgent." He clicked off the phone and looked at Amanda, who was watching him, her face a picture of anxiety. He shrugged. "Now, we wait." He slid the phone into his pocket. "I'll try again in half an hour. If he sees multiple calls from me, he may actually call back."

Amanda moved toward him, and he wrapped his arms around her. "I'm so sorry, Henry."

"I hate that Cal hurt you, that he had the nerve to ... to do that to you. Amanda, I'm so, so sorry." His heart pounded as he thought of it, of what might have happened if he hadn't come home right at that time. He looked at her. Hand shaking, he traced her jawline and touched her hair. Then he pulled her close again. "I love you, Amanda, so much."

She squeezed him and stepped back. "You got home just in time. I've never seen you so angry."

He shook his head. "How can you love somebody and hate them at the same time?"

THEY SPENT the rest of the night puttering, cleaning up the kitchen, throwing out the ignored and uncooked steaks, then straightening up around the house while Cash watched, confused by all the overnight activity. Henry called his father every half hour. No answer.

Neither one of them could sleep. As the sky began to lighten, Amanda made scrambled eggs. They had just finished eating when pounding on the door made them both jump. Henry leaped to his feet. "Stay back," he said, and he went to the front door and opened it a crack.

His father stood on the porch, unshaven, his gray hair disheveled, his eyes red.

Henry swung the door open. "Dad! Come in. I've been trying to call you."

"Why didn't you help him?" His anger was like an assault wave.

His heart racing, Henry stepped back and gestured an invitation. "Come on in, Dad."

He was tall and thin, like Cal, but suntanned and fit from years in the field as an archeologist. He was wearing khaki cargo pants and a navy-blue field shirt. The skin around his gray eyes was tight, his jaw set. "Who's this?" He glared at Amanda.

"Amanda Cooper, my fiancée. Amanda, my dad, Henry Bunting II."

"I'm sorry for your loss, Dr. Bunting," Amanda said.

The professor said nothing. He turned back to Henry. "How could you let this happen, Henry? How could you let him die?"

Henry took a step back, his heart rate soaring. He breathed in slowly, trying to calm down.

"He came to you. He needed help. Why didn't you do something?"

"I tried, Dad. I tried so many times."

"You tried." Disgust filled his voice. "And then you just let him die. Right here. Right in front of you."

"I did all I could, Dad."

"Which was what? Stand by and watch it happen?"

"He was already wasted when he got here, and—"

"You're a medical person. You knew he had a problem. Why didn't you do something?"

"I did!"

"Like what?"

Henry told him the whole story. "Why do you think I had Narcan on hand, Dad? Because I knew he was doing drugs, and I wanted be able to help him if he OD'd. And I tried. It just ... just didn't work. He was too far gone; he had too many drugs in his system."

His father looked away. "Your mother always coddled you. Treated you as her favorite. Pushed him away. No wonder Cal got into drugs."

"My mother did nothing to hurt him. She loved him. He chose to do drugs. And he decided to leave home. On his own."

"You were always her favorite. It was always Henry this and Henry that."

"How do you know that?"

"Oh, he told me."

"And you believed him?"

"Yes! Why would he lie? What did he ever do to hurt you?"

Images of Cal assaulting Amanda flashed in Henry's mind. He kept silent.

"Poor Cal felt so ... unloved."

"You were never home, Dad! You weren't there, not for Cal, not for me, not even for Mom. You were lost in your own world. So, how do you know anything about how our family worked?"

"He told me about it. You were the golden boy. He said he couldn't compete with you." He shook his head. "Poor Cal."

"Poor Cal nothing! He started smoking cigarettes at twelve, took up pot at fourteen. Mom didn't know what to do about it. She tried. He refused to listen to her. You gave him a car at sixteen so he could be 'free' you said. He used that car to meet his dealers. At eighteen, he left. Just took off. Do you know why? Mom was diagnosed with cancer and he couldn't handle it. Is that why you stayed away, Dad? Because you needed a world you could control? That's its own addiction, Dad, did you know that?"

"Don't psychoanalyze me."

"Well somebody needs to. You gave him money whenever he showed up. You know what he did with that money, Dad? He bought drugs. Every time he quit a job you had some excuse ready. Poor Cal. When he dropped out of the rehab you paid for—twice—you blamed the doctors. You couldn't say no to him even when you saw him self-destructing.

"For crying out loud, Dad. You told him I'd been hurt, and you know what? He came here, not to see me, but to steal my pain pills."

"That's ridiculous."

"It's not—he took three Oxycodone. I think on some level you knew he might do that. I think you thought that might help him get through until you could arrange the next counselor, the next rehab, the next ... whatever." Henry threw up his hands in disgust.

"So it's my fault, Henry? Is that what you're saying?"

"I'm saying don't blame Mom. Or me. This is on Cal."

"I loved him." He suddenly looked like an old man, broken and discouraged.

Henry's voice softened. "I know you did, Dad. He looked like you. Talked like you. Had the same sense of adventure as you. But he had a wild streak that nobody knew what to do with, not even Cal himself. You've lost your son. I've lost a brother. And I am so sorry."

They were quiet for a minute, then his father looked at him, his eyes narrowed. "And now you get it all."

"What does that mean?" A hot rush of anger raced through Henry.

"You get the Bunting house. You get the estate. You're the designated survivor. You even got the Henry Bunting name."

"Who's fault was that?"

"Cal said you stole his birthright."

"*You* named him! And me!"

"Still. He felt ... disinherited."

"He manipulated you, Dad! Can't you see that? He was a master manipulator."

Henry II raised his head. "He was my son. My firstborn. Don't disrespect him."

"It's not disrespect, Dad. It's the truth."

"If your mother hadn't ..."

"Leave Mom out of it!" Henry exploded. "She loved us both and even loved you, though I have no idea why!"

"I'll not have you talk to me that way, Henry!"

"Then maybe we shouldn't talk at all."

"Fine." His father turned and walked out. Halfway down the front walk, Henry II turned and pointed toward his son. "I thought we were a family, Henry! Family members take care of each other."

Henry slammed the front door, anger and frustration seizing him, consuming every bit of his energy. His eyes fell on the mug on the end table, the one that had contained his tea, the one that carried the Bunting label. He strode toward it, picked it up, opened the front door, and hurled it down onto the sidewalk, just at the place his father last stood, right where Cal took his own life. It shattered into pieces. The handle bounced into the grass.

He stepped back inside, closed the door, and leaned his head against it. Amanda stood looking at him, wide-eyed. "I didn't even *want* the name," he said. "I am *nothing* like my father. Nothing."

He brushed past her and walked into the bedroom. When he came back out, he had on swim trunks and a T-shirt and a beach towel hung over his shoulder.

"What are you doing?" she asked him.

"What does it look like? I'm going surfing."

"Henry, you can't!"

"Yes," he said, "I can." He grabbed his keys.

"Wait, I'm coming with you."

"I'm leaving now."

"I'll be right out."

"I'm not waiting."

She raced back to the bedroom, threw on some shorts, and got to the truck just as he got the board into the bed. Wordlessly, she climbed into the passenger seat.

They rode in silence the whole way to the beach. The day was chilly and cloudy with a stiff wind that blurred the edges of the sand. A storm out in the Atlantic was churning up waves, according to the weather app. Coastal flooding possible, riptides and dangerous surf.

The ocean looked angry. A cold blue. A stiff wind whipped up the breakers and sent spray flying. Henry threw his board down on the sand, wincing. Then he sat down next to it, resting his arms on his bent knees. The wind ruffled his brown hair. His eyes stayed focused on the horizon, while waves of trembling went through him.

Amanda sat down next to him, silently watching the breakers roll in, feeling Henry shaking beside her. Ahead, a dozen or more sanderlings raced back and forth with the wave action, catching the tiny invertebrates carried in with the tide. A herring gull stood on one leg. The clouds well out to the east were dark blue, almost purple. A solitary brown pelican dove into the ocean and came up with a fish.

After half an hour, Henry reached over and took her hand. “I’m sorry,” he said. “You didn’t need to see all that.”

“It’s alright.”

He raised her hand and kissed it. “You’re right. I can’t surf. It’s too rough, and my ribs aren’t ready.”

She squeezed his hand. “Surfing is how you process your emotions,” she said.

He nodded. “One way.”

“Maybe let’s try talking.”

So they did, the good, the bad, and the ugly. The love, the hate, the hurt, the regret. The anger. The sorrow. The grief.

And afterward, she helped him carry the board back to the truck, helped him load it, and he let her drive home, because he really was hurting.

Once they were home, he cleaned up the shattered mug on the front walk so Cash wouldn’t cut his feet. They let Cash out in the back yard and fed him. She called both of their bosses and said they’d had a family emergency and would be in at noon. And then they went to sleep.

25

JESS

When Scott called me from work Tuesday afternoon and told me what had happened in Chincoteague, my heart broke for Henry and Amanda. He got hurt, she got triggered, and Henry's father! How horrible! What a dysfunctional family.

Not that mine was much better. My parents were teetering on divorce when 9/11 stole my NYPD father from me. My mom remarried way too soon. I was angry and alienated for a long time, until I got Luke and found Nate and, through him, the love of Jesus began seeping into my life. Eventually, I learned to forgive my mom. We are all broken people.

After an hour mulling over what Scott told me, I called him back. "If they have a funeral, we need to go."

"What?"

"We need to go, Scott. To be there for Henry. And Amanda."

"Alright," he replied. "We can do that. Can you text Amanda and ask her to let us know when it is? I'm tied up with something today."

"Yes, of course."

I called Nate first to tell him what happened, and also

because there is no one better to talk to than Nate when bad things happen. He said he'd like to come too. "We can all fit in the van," I said. "We just have to board the dogs somewhere."

"We do have to board the dogs, but I'll drive separate," he said.

"Are you sure? We have room."

"I may want to stay longer."

I tried puzzling that out but couldn't, so I called Amanda. "Honey, I'm so, so sorry.

She answered me in a halting, teary voice.

"Your dad and I would like to come down for the funeral or memorial service if they have one. Will you let us know when and where it is?"

"If his dad lets us know. Things are pretty bad between them."

"Well, let's hope he cools off for everyone's sake. We can get a hotel or something, so don't worry. Nate may be coming too."

Silence. "Henry's been talking to him."

"Really? I had no idea."

"Their families had similar dynamics." Amanda sighed. "Thanks, Jess. I'll let you know when we find out what's going on. It'll be a few days because they'll most likely do an autopsy. I'll let you know."

Then, to my surprise, she opened up to me. "Henry told me this morning he wanted to get married, like right now. Go to the courthouse, get the license, and find a justice of the peace."

"What did you tell him?" I asked, curiosity surging.

Amanda hesitated. "I told him no."

"No? Why?"

She sighed. "Because when I wanted to do that, he said no, because he wanted me to have a special day, a beautiful dress, a ceremony with family and friends, and a reception afterward. He wanted me to have something I could always look back on and remember.

"So, I reminded him of that. I told him he was reacting to grief and anger, and I wanted our wedding to be a time when we were filled with love. I told him how much I loved him, how I admired him, and that as soon as we got past this ... this horrible time, we could set a date and plan for it."

"Oh, Amanda! That was so wise of you. Good for you!"

I told Scott later his daughter was growing up.

I FOUND the obituary online a week later. It read, "Calvert Quinn Bunting was survived by his father, Henry Bunting II, PhD, distinguished professor of history at Salisbury University, and other relatives."

Other relatives. That's it. No mention of Henry III, "our Henry" as I called him when I told Scott and Nate. Just "other relatives." A memorial service was scheduled for next Saturday.

Scott called Henry and gently told him. "We'd like to come down," he said, "if that wouldn't cause more problems."

Henry thought about it for a couple of days, then called Scott back and said he'd like it if we came down. We could stay with Amanda in the Main Street house, and Nate could stay with him.

Perfect.

THE SERVICE WOULD BE at a funeral home in Salisbury, the same one, Amanda told me, where Henry's mother's funeral had been. We made the long drive over on Friday, beating most of the beach traffic and arriving by two o'clock. Amanda wouldn't be home until after six, she said, but she left the house open for us.

It was Mike's first long trip, and for an active boy, he did pretty well. Once we got our suitcases and everything inside, we explored the house and the large yard, and then we took him over to a really neat playground Amanda had told us about. It's a "sensory" playground, with all the normal equipment plus things you could play music on or drum. He loved it.

We picked up dinner for everyone at a restaurant Amanda had recommended. When she got home, she said we shouldn't wait for Henry—he had a late shift at the clinic. So we had dinner, talked, then played in the living room with Mike until it was time for him to go to bed. While I was still upstairs with him, Scott texted me to say Henry was tired and had gone straight home. Amanda was taking him dinner. And he, Scott, was going to read for a while and then he'd be up.

The next morning we got up, had breakfast, and then Scott took Mike out to a playground to run some energy off of him. The service was at eleven and it was an hour away, so we needed to leave around nine thirty. Amanda wanted to ride with Henry. "He's nervous," she told me. "He doesn't know what his father is going to do when he shows up." Turns out his dad had never called Henry to invite him to the funeral, never mentioned what the arrangements would be. It was like he was disinheriting him already.

I asked Amanda if that's what she thought was going to happen, that Henry would be disinherited. "I don't know," she replied. "I think he'd be disappointed and hurt if his father won't acknowledge him. And if he's disinherited, it'll bother him if he doesn't get the Bunting house, where he lived with his grandparents, but as for the rest of it," she said, shrugging, "he's making his own way. It's mostly the emotional estrangement," she said. "He didn't want that."

"The conflicts I had with Dad," she went on to say, "were mostly about his rules and my resistance. On some level, I knew he wouldn't reject me completely."

"No, he really loves you," I said.

"I mean, he almost died for me!" Amanda responded.

I didn't respond. Nate would have been all over that, like a hawk on a rabbit. Me? I'm more of a flighty little sparrow that hides in the bushes rather than press my case.

We arrived at the funeral, Scott looking so handsome in his black suit. I wore a basic black dress with, *ugh*, heels. There were just a few people there, so we decided to wait outside for Henry and Amanda. Finally, their truck pulled up and parked. Little Mike saw Henry get out, and he pulled away from Scott. "'Ree! 'Ree!" he said, truncating Henry's name. Scott caught him just before he got to the curb.

When Henry, dressed in a sharp-looking black suit and a white shirt, reached the sidewalk, Scott let Mike go and our son ran to him and wrapped his arms around his legs. "'Ree!"

Henry bent down. "Hey, little man!" he said, and he smiled. I wondered if it was the first time he'd smiled in weeks. "How are you, buddy?"

Then Mike spotted Nate. "Naa!"

Someday, he'd get their names all the way out, I thought. Someday.

The rest of us greeted Henry. Mike ran to Nate, arms raised, and Nate picked him up. I realized the only time I ever saw my friend in a suit was at a funeral.

"Where would you like us to sit?" Scott asked.

"I have no idea. I don't know where I'll be. Next to Amanda, that's all I know." He was holding her hand. She looked stunning in her black dress, her long blonde hair flowing over her shoulders. She really could be a model, I thought.

"How 'bout we sit behind you," Nate said, and we all agreed and went inside.

I recognized Henry II immediately. Tall. Thin. Gray-haired. Good-looking in a different way. He was standing next to someone who looked official at the front, the funeral director or a pastor. There was no casket, just a small wooden box next to a large, framed picture of his older son. I presumed he'd had Cal's body cremated. When his eyes fell on Henry, he visibly stiffened.

We walked down the aisle on a rich, burgundy-red carpet. The room had church-like pews. Henry guided Amanda into the second row on the right and whispered something to her. We all filed into the third row as Amanda sat down, and Henry walked up to his father and extended his hand. For a minute, it looked like Henry II would refuse to take it, but then he relented. Henry introduced himself to the other man, and they shook hands. Then he came and sat down, a pained expression on his face. Nate, right behind Henry, touched his shoulder.

What can I say about a funeral service where no one believes anything? Honestly, it was as dry as a desert, as thin as a skim of ice on a not-quite frozen pond. I was so uncomfortable. Henry's father got up and spoke about his son, recounting stories from his childhood and praising his adventurous spirit, his love for his family, and his work on the oil rigs, "a difficult job, only for the most hardy," is the way he described it.

A string trio of what looked like college students played some classical music. Then the official-looking man stood up. He was a minister of sorts, but he talked in platitudes, saying Cal "departed this life" and was now "on his greatest adventure." God was not mentioned, nor was Jesus, and it became very clear he wasn't going to even allude to faith of any kind. There was no comfort, no talk of eternity, and no hope. Nothing.

That morning, Scott and I had been worried about Little Mike being quiet in the service, but I was the one who could barely get through it. I think I could have handled a Buddhist service better. At least they believe something.

I did manage to keep still, but just barely. Finally, it was over, and the official escorted Henry's father down the aisle and out the back door. We rose to go, and I was surprised at how many people had filled in the pews behind us. I met Henry's boss, and Amanda's, half of the fire department, and a couple dozen members of Henry's Chincoteague High School class. If you took away all the people who came because of Henry, I think there were fewer than a dozen others present.

There was no reception or lunch or anything afterward. As we were walking toward our cars, Henry broke away and walked back toward his father. Their body language told me their conversation was stiff. Then Henry walked to his truck, his face looking weary.

We all drove home, changed clothes, and Scott went out and got some really good fried chicken, coleslaw, potato salad, rolls, and baked beans. Comfort food. We ate at Amanda's house. I was hoping to get Mike down for a nap, but clearly, with 'Ree and Naa' around, that wasn't going to happen.

What the service had lacked in spiritual depth, Nate made up for as he said grace, asking the Lord to comfort those who were grieving, have mercy on those who found it difficult to love, to open the eyes of the blind, and set the prisoners free. Then he thanked God for the food.

Toward the end of the meal, Amanda said, "Henry suggested I take you all to the ranch so you can see what we're doing there."

We all agreed that would be a good thing to do. Henry, meanwhile, stood near the front door, his phone to his ear. He finished his call, slid his phone into his back pocket, and walked toward us.

"The guys have a pony they want me to look at," he said to Amanda. "Southern herd."

"What's wrong?"

"She's limping." He turned toward Nate. "Want to come along?"

I knew at that moment Henry needed to talk.

"Sure," Nate said. "I can limp along with the best of 'em."

"Why don't you all go on to the ranch," Henry said. "Depending on how quick this is, we'll either catch up with you or meet you back here for dinner. Tomorrow looks like a good beach day," he added. "We can do that if you like. I could use some time out there."

26

HENRY

Henry made a phone call as he and Nate walked out to his truck. He unlocked it and checked to make sure his medical bag was behind the driver's seat. The toolbox lid in his truck bed felt secure. He'd straightened that up after it was broken into as soon as he could stand to bend over to do it. There was nothing in there but bandages, splints, dental tools, a twitch, hoof files, and some topical medicines. Everything an addict might want he carried in his bag.

Still, whoever had broken into the box, and he presumed it was Cal, had made a mess of it. Some of the bandages had to be thrown away. The lock, which was built into the box, was broken. Henry thought he might just leave it that way.

He really didn't need to go out on this call. He could have told the boys to watch the mare and let him know if she was still limping on Monday. Or he could have asked them to bring her into the carnival grounds. But he had to get away from town. He wanted to work and he wanted to talk. *Needed* to talk. And Nate was the only one he wanted to talk to.

Henry started the engine, blew out a deep breath, and

wiped his hands down his thighs. Then he reached over and pulled his seatbelt across his body. "What a day." He backed carefully out of the driveway and turned north on Main Street.

"How're you feelin'?" Nate asked.

"Exhausted. Angry." He eased the truck through town.

"Well, you did good."

"With my father?"

"Right."

Henry turned right. "I don't know how I could be his son," he said, shaking his head. "He is so mean and so blind. I wanted to hit him."

"Prob'ly was good you didn't."

"All that stuff he said about my brother was a lie. Cal barely tolerated us. He cut free the moment he could. His sense of adventure mostly involved trying new drugs."

"Born to trouble."

"I tried so many times to help him get straight. My father put him through rehab twice, that I know of, at sixty thousand a pop. At the same time, Dad enabled him! He never held him accountable. He kept giving him money. He excused every rotten thing he did."

"Do you think your father felt guilty about how he turned out?"

Henry gestured in frustration. "I don't know. Honestly. It makes me so mad. Cal wasted his life! He didn't have to. He was smart but so incredibly stupid."

"It's hard to deal with someone who's addicted. That's all they can think about. Gettin' their next fix."

"But then he got malicious."

"Stealin' your meds?"

"Not just that." Henry took a deep breath. "I wasn't going to say anything about this, but I am still so angry."

"Whatever you say stays with me. It don't go nowhere."

Henry pulled into a parking place near the pens on

Assateague. And then, with his hands clenched, he told Nate about coming home, finding Cal assaulting Amanda, about beating him up, and then throwing him out of the house. "I could have killed him," Henry said. "I was so angry."

"I cain't say I blame you."

"I threw him out the front door and told him not to come back." Henry wiped his hands on his pants. "Later that night he OD'd."

"That weren't your fault," Nate said.

Henry looked at him sharply, gauging his expression.

"It was his choice," Nate said, continuing, "to take drugs to begin with, and keep usin' right up until he died."

"They say it's a disease."

"It's true. It does take hold of you. But it was Cal's choice to start and Cal's choice to keep usin' until he couldn't stop. Not you, Henry. Don't take that on yourself."

"The police told Dad it looked like Cal had been in a fight. He had bruises on his face and swelling. If my dad knew it was me—"

"In his eyes, Cal's death would be your fault too."

"Absolutely."

Nate reached over and gripped Henry's shoulder. "Then he would be an unjust judge. Cal's problems ain't your responsibility. None of it. Not Cal's drug use and not his death." Nate let go of him. "Scott and me, we talk about stuff like that, like when is it legal to shoot somebody and when it's not. 'In defense of self and others' is the phrase he uses. You were defending Amanda. You stopped the threat by throwing Cal out of the house. You acted justly, with restraint even." He paused. "Don't carry the burden of his death, Henry. It ain't yours to bear."

There was a sound outside. Henry sat back in his seat. He unbuckled his seat belt. "Here's our ride." He glanced over. "Thanks, Nate."

"I love you, son. I'm proud of you."

His words stopped Henry short. Like he had never heard them before.

The Polaris, which looked like a cross between a four-wheeler and a pickup, pulled up with a burly guy driving it. Henry pulled his bag and some other equipment out of his truck and locked it up.

"Jake," he said, "this is my friend Nate. He's coming along for the ride. Nate, you sit in the second seat, I'll ride on the back."

The ride through the woods and deeper into the marsh was rougher than Henry had anticipated, and it hurt his still-healing ribs. He probably would have walked in if he'd come out alone, but conscious of Nate's artificial leg, he'd asked for the Polaris.

They arrived to see three other members of the pony committee, standing and holding a solid, dark-chestnut mare with a flaxen mane. Treasure.

Henry winced as he hopped off the back of the Polaris. He grabbed his bag and walked toward the mare. "What do we have here?"

"Right front leg," one of the men said.

"Walk her a little." Henry was aware of Nate, standing just to his left. The sun was hot and the humidity—and the mosquitos—were thick. Still, he was glad to be out on the refuge in the real world, the world he understood. He narrowed his eyes as the man holding the lead rope walked Treasure away. The ponies were wild, feral really, but used to the minimal handling required to keep them healthy. Treasure was one of the gentler ones.

Yes, there was the limp. "Hold up," Henry said.

The man leading Treasure had turned her, so Henry had to walk around the pony to get to the leg in question. As he did,

Nate said, "Watch it!" and Henry moved away just as Treasure kicked.

He looked at Nate and nodded his thanks. "She got a wild eye," Nate said.

Henry looked at the pony crew. "Y'all didn't see that? My friend had to warn me?" He was joking, and they knew it.

"Aw, Henry, you're the doc. We thought you knew horses."

"He's been working with dogs and cats. Forgot what he knows about horses."

"Billy, you set me up, turning her like that so I had to go behind her. Were you trying to get my ribs broke again?"

"I thought you wanted to see her move!"

The jesting continued for a few more rounds. Henry put his hand on the mare's side and moved toward her injured leg. She must be hurting a lot, he thought, or she wouldn't have kicked. "Hold her now." He positioned himself so if she kicked forward, he'd be out of reach. He ran his hand down the leg, his mind cataloguing the parts as he did. *Proximal phalanx, middle phalanx, distal phalanx.*

As he approached the hoof, he felt heat. Using his shoulder, he shifted the mare's weight to her other leg, and picked up the injured one, straddling it like a farrier. Using a brush, he cleaned off her hoof as best he could. "Jake, hand me the hoof tester." He held out his hand.

Jake found the tong-like instrument in Henry's bag and handed it to him. Henry used it to apply gentle pressure all around the edge of the hoof. When he hit the sore spot, the mare threw up her head, snorted, and tried to pull away.

"Hoof abscess," Henry said. He handed the hoof tester back to Jake, pulled the brush out of his pocket, and cleaned the hoof again. "Hand me the bottle that's in there. I'll need the knife too." He took the bottle, squirted a liquid antiseptic over the hoof, and then traded it for the knife Jake was holding. Then he said, "Hang on!" He made a quick move, lancing the abscess. The pony jerked her head, and Henry released the foot and moved quickly away.

"That'll help her," Henry said, wiping off the knife.

"Whoa, mare. Whoa," the man holding her tried to calm the pony down.

"Take her in. I'll finish up there."

"Thanks, doc," Jake said.

Henry nodded. "Absolutely."

"Hoof abscesses," Henry explained to Nate as they drove back to Chincoteague, "are common. They step on who knows what and it pierces into the hoof or around it. An infection starts and it's very painful. They go from fine to lame in one day. I kind of figured that's what it was when they called me. Now, they'll take her back to the carnival grounds and I'll dress it."

"You got healing hands," Nate said.

Henry looked over, surprised.

"The way you were around her, the way you touched her, your energy. You're a healer."

Henry frowned a little. "I hope so. I always wanted to be. Ever since ..." His throat tightened. He stopped.

"Your mom?" Nate guessed.

Henry nodded. "I was giving her Neulasta shots at fourteen. Monitoring her meds. Helping with her pain."

"That kind of thing makes you grow up quick." Nate paused. "You didn't want to be a doctor?"

He shrugged. "I like animals better than people."

Nate laughed, reached over, and slapped Henry on the shoulder. "A man after my own heart."

They crossed over the bridge back to Chincoteague. Terns were lined up on it like a black-and-white bird honor guard. Henry looked down at the familiar waters of the Assateague

Channel and the marsh stretching out from it. He thought about the next bit of work he would do for the mare.

"You know what's amazing?" Henry said.

"What?"

"A hoof. It looks fairly simple, right? Like an exaggerated fingernail or a claw. But it's actually very complex. There are over a dozen structures in a hoof. Bone, muscle, tendon, cartilage, blood vessels—all kinds of things. When I learned that in vet school it blew me away."

"There's a lot to it."

"Right. And it's all important to the horse. I've seen a three-legged dog or even a two-legged dog do okay, but a horse? They need all four legs, and every hoof needs to be in good working order."

"She gonna be okay?"

"Yes. This mare will heal. We got to her in time. I need to pack her hoof, then change her dressing over in a couple of days. One of the guys, Bobby, is a farrier. I'll have him check on her, too, once he gets back after the weekend."

They swung through the circle on Maddox. "How're your ribs feelin' with all that bendin' over?"

Henry smiled softly. "I hadn't planned on a pony call. I should've stopped by my house and picked up my rib protector. I forgot." He shook his head. "They'll quiet down after a bit."

"That cow did a number on you."

"You got that right." Henry stayed silent as he wound through the streets toward the carnival grounds. He pulled up near the corral and turned off his truck. The trailer with the mare wasn't there yet. Ahead of him was the empty fairgrounds, booths, the frame of the Ferris wheel, pavilions—all familiar, all standing since his childhood. Those were big times, visiting his grandparents during Pony Penning.

His thoughts shifted. "When that cow hit me," he told Nate, "I jerked up and fell backward. The gate collapsed on me, then the cow." He swallowed, tasting the fear again. "I couldn't breathe. My vision darkened. I could see death coming for me, right there."

"Must've been terrifyin'."

"It was." He glanced at Nate. "I wasn't ready to die. I was too young, I thought, and I still had too many questions. Things I wanted to do." He took a deep breath. "Amanda saved my life. She really did."

"Praise God," Nate said.

"That's one reason Cal's death is bothering me so much. I know what death is like. I saw Cal was dying. And I couldn't save him."

Nate paused and then said, "You loved your brother."

Henry looked at him quickly.

"He was a pain in the butt, but you loved him," Nate continued. "You would have done anything to save him. Because he was your brother. Same flesh, same bone, same blood. Frustrating as he was, down deep you loved him."

"Yes, I did," Henry said, his voice cracking. "I didn't want him to die." He sniffed.

Nate rubbed his shoulder again.

The truck towing the horse trailer pulled up just then. Henry swallowed his pain, pulled his keys out of the ignition, dropped them in the cupholder, and opened his door.

27

HENRY

Packing the pony's hoof took Henry no time at all. Jake held the mare, who was cooperating, and kept up a running conversation about his kids and his wife and their new puppy. Nate watched from outside the fence. Soon Treasure was free of her halter, walking without pain, and munching hay with the handful of other ponies.

They walked out of the corral and Jake locked it up. "I'll check her tomorrow," Henry said, shaking Jake's hand. "Thanks for your help."

"Yes, sir. Oh, and sorry about your brother."

Henry acknowledged his comment with a nod as he turned to walk back to his truck. His brother. He cursed silently.

Henry got back in the truck and looked at Nate. "I need to rest a little. You want me to take you to the ranch, or do you want to come back to my house with me?"

"I'll hang with you," Nate said.

"I'll stop by and pick up Cash first."

. . .

Back at the house, Henry immediately headed for the recliner. Cash jumped up into his lap.

"What are you doing for pain these days?" Nate asked him. "I'll get you some."

"Just ibuprofen. In the kitchen on the counter."

Nate went out and returned a while later with the bottle of ibuprofen and two glasses of water. Henry was lying back in the recliner, his eyes closed, stroking Cash.

"Here you go," Nate said.

Henry opened his eyes, sat up a little, and took the meds. "Thanks."

"What are you thinking about?" Nate said after awhile.

"My brother."

"What about him?"

"How frustrating he was." Henry took a deep breath. "He had everything he needed to succeed in life. An intact family. A home. Good food. Parents who loved him. He was smart too. He got along with people. And yet he self-destructed. Why? It's such a waste of life."

"They got a lot of theories about addiction."

"Oh, I know the science behind it. The drugs basically hijack the reward circuit of the brain. After a while, it's hard to feel pleasure without that extra jolt. The brain's neural pathways are changed, and even if you want to stop using, you can't, without a lot of help."

"That goes for a lot of things, not just drugs."

"Yeah, I know. Alcohol, tobacco..."

Nate continued the list. "Gambling. Porn."

Henry looked at him, eyebrows raised.

"Those things may not have the same direct chemical effect, but even respectable things, like work or shopping, entertainment, food, can become almost like an addiction. We all got problems in some way or another."

"You make it sound like we're not supposed to enjoy anything."

"Oh no. God gives us richly all things to enjoy. He also gives us boundaries on 'em. Otherwise, they get a grip on us and the next thing you know, we cain't let go."

Henry shook his head. "Everything is so messed up. My brother, my father, the world ..."

Nate laughed. "Son, you just flung a door wide open, invitin' me to charge right in."

Henry smiled. "As soon as those words were out of my mouth I realized what I'd done. Trouble is, Nate, you can't prove any of that stuff. You can't prove Adam and Eve and the snake ever existed. Or even God. There's no proof! I'm a scientist. I need proof." He settled back down.

"Alright. Where's your proof that, that horse's hoof evolved over millions of years?"

"Well, it's true, evolution is just a theory, but it's accepted because it makes sense."

"Makes sense? Show me one thing in this world that gets more organized, more advanced, on its own." Nate paused. "You cain't. There's even a law about that, right? The second law of thermodynamics? Everything moves toward disorder, not order."

Henry shrugged. "They're working on that."

"On the other hand, there ain't nothing makes more sense than the doctrine of sin. That proof is all around us! We just don't like to admit it."

Henry shook his head. "I got to go with science."

Nate paused, regrouping. He looked over at Henry, whose hand continually stroked Cash. "You know, science can tell you all kinds of things about that little dog of yours, about its bones and blood vessels and organs, how to fix him when he gets sick. But can science tell you why he loves you?"

"Sure! Cash loves me because when I rub behind his ears it

releases endorphins in his body. He feels good so he keeps coming back for more. We interpret that as love."

Nate leveled his blue eyes at Henry. He unbuttoned his shirt and pulled it open. The left side of his chest was covered with thick, ropey burn scars. His right side and his belly were smooth and clear. "You see this? I guarantee you, my dog Rock wasn't floatin' on endorphins when he threw his body across mine to protect me from the RPG that hit us in Afghanistan. Ain't nothin' felt good about what he did. You'll never convince me it was anything but love that drove him to protect me."

He continued to keep eye contact with Henry while he rebuttoned his shirt. "Love, beauty, and goodness, those things come straight from the character of God, who created this world and everything in it. He loves you, Henry, and so do I, and I'm praying one day he'll help you see that."

Henry was quiet for a few minutes, then he smiled. "You make good arguments."

"Well, arguin' is good entertainment, but it ain't arguin' that brings people to Christ. It's God himself opening their eyes."

"I think in my case it's going to take a miracle," Henry said, grinning. "I'm pretty stubborn."

Nate leaned forward. "A miracle? Would you know one if you even saw one? Or would your mind suppress the truth?" He rested back. "You're a good man, Henry. I enjoy talkin' with you. Now, you probably need to rest. Or at least I do."

28

JESS

As I walked the path toward the fences and paddocks and barns at Hope Ranch, I automatically noted the enormity of the operation. I could scarcely imagine what it took to run it. Of course, I'd been there before, but now that I was living with horses and caring for them, I was even more impressed.

Kate McClellan showed us around. The two big, green barns were set up well for horses, with wide aisles and large, solid-built stalls on each side. The high ceilings were studded with lights, and fans gave the barns an airy feel. And they were clean. I wondered how Kate did it all.

Of course, she didn't do it alone. She had volunteers, an army of them, and also some paid staff. Still, I was impressed.

Amanda brought Scarlet out, and we watched as she worked with her in a paddock. The horse looked calm and cooperative to me, but Kate explained how violent she'd been a year ago, before Amanda started working with her.

"Even today," Kate said, "she's high-spirited and prone to getting rattled when something new happens. But she's so much better. She allows us to handle her, Amanda can ride her, and one day we hope she'll be helping kids as part of our program."

As we walked through the paddock area, Kate pointed out a young girl off in the distance. She was far enough away we wouldn't be able to recognize her, but we could see what she was doing. With an adult mentor beside her, the girl was learning to gently and calmly lead the horse around a simple obstacle course in the paddock.

"That young lady was in a terrible accident almost a year ago. Her mom was driving their family van. They were sitting in a left-turn lane, waiting for traffic to clear, and a dump truck rear-ended them. They never saw it coming. Air bags deployed and they were shoved into a grassy median. They both were injured, and both spent time in the hospital. The girl, who I'll call Julie, was traumatized by it. Such a sudden shock! She developed severe anxiety.

"After trying a series of meds and counseling, her mom heard about Hope Ranch and decided to give us a try. She's been with us about three months now. Shadow, the horse she's working with, was in a horse-trailer accident. Julie identifies with him. She says he gets her. He's calm, easygoing, and she benefits from that energy.

"The root of her anxiety was a fear of losing control, which is completely understandable considering what happened. Horses are prey animals. They can be jumpy and ready to run at a moment's notice. Traumatized people are like that too. In our program, we are trying to teach trust, communication, boundaries, and leadership in progressive steps. The bottom line is, we're about building relationships. The traumatized child learns to trust the horse, then people, and finally, because we are faith-based, we hope they'll also learn to trust God."

I thought about how Luke helped stabilize me when I'd gone through trauma. He wasn't calm—he was wired and crazy —but in learning to channel that energy, a bond developed between us that helped me heal emotionally. Horses, I realized, could do that too.

Little Mike spent the whole time at Hope Ranch in his daddy's arms, reaching for every horse he saw. When we were almost done, Kate took us to a sweet pony named Sunny that Mike could pet. She told Scott he could put Mike on Sunny's back as long as he held onto him. So he did, and Mike instantly grasped Sunny's mane, like he knew what he was doing. And then he leaned forward and hugged her neck.

"He loves horses," Scott said, not just a little proud.

Kate smiled. "Why am I not surprised?"

Later I found out that all the time we were listening to Kate, Scott and I were having the same thought. Could bonding with a horse help our sweet Maddie get over the trauma of the flood?

We spent the next day at the beach. Henry and Amanda drove over early so they could catch low tide and surf. We went over at about eight thirty. We found Henry's truck and parked next to it, then we walked over the dunes, hauling a blanket, towels, snacks, an umbrella, and a huge tote bag of sand toys. We crossed the dunes and suddenly, this Long Island-raised girl was home.

I inhaled the salt air. Felt the onshore breeze. Curled my toes in the sand, still cool from the night. "I've missed this," I said to Scott.

He nodded, his eyes fixed on the ocean, where Amanda was catching a wave, balancing, staying up, and then jumping off her board, laughing. Henry, it turns out, had decided not to surf, but he was out there coaching Amanda anyway.

After the tensions of the funeral the day before, our time at the beach relaxed us. Little Mike was at first annoyed with the life jacket I made him wear and intimidated by the ocean waves crashing on the shore. When Henry swam in, he saved the day, taking Mike down to the waves and playing a game he called Sandy Pants, which involved sitting down on the beach and letting the waves wash over your legs and laughing.

"He's really good with kids," I said to Scott, watching them. Then I had a thought. "Hey, as long as Henry's with him, I think I'll go for a swim."

"Go for it," my husband said.

So I entered the Atlantic, diving through an arching wave.

It had been years since I'd been in the ocean, but the feelings all came back. The refreshing water, the tug of the waves, the salty taste in my mouth. I swam parallel to shore, fighting the littoral current as I went north, then drifting back easily. Memories of swimming with my dad off Long Island, and sailing with him on Long Island Sound, came flooding into my mind. They were bittersweet, these memories, the joy of having known his love mixed with the pain of losing him. I turned onto my back and whispered to the sky, "Jesus, will you tell my dad about Little Mike? He's named for him. He's going to love him."

When I'd had enough, I swam ashore, pretending to be a shark that would "get" Little Mike. He giggled, and Henry "saved" him.

"I've missed this," I told Scott as I dried off. "I want Mike to know the ocean and the beach, too, not just mountains."

Scott nodded. "We can come here on vacation," he said, "if either one of us can learn to take one."

WE LEFT Chincoteague at one o'clock, hoping Little Mike would sleep on the way home. Nate decided to stay an extra day.

Soon Mike, tired from the beach, fell asleep in his car seat, giving Scott and I lots of time to talk. I pretended not to notice him checking his phone every time we stopped. He pretended the same for me when I got and answered texts.

The texts were from Brett Hudgins and Battlefield. Brett still worried about his wife. Apparently, he still thought I was his counselor. And Battlefield had been called out to do a search on Monday in Appomattox County, well south of our home. It would be a recovery, not a rescue, they said, a search for a person who was now likely deceased. I looked down at the beautiful Chesapeake Bay as we crossed the bridge and wondered how I could possibly respond. Monday was Scott's day to go to Quantico, my day to watch Mike.

Juggling priorities. Back to real life.

I HAD to let that callout go by. The next morning Scott's truck wouldn't start. He asked if he could use my Jeep to get to work.

"Of course," I told him, giving up any chance of responding to the callout. Something was making him anxious to get to Quantico. I wondered if it had to do with the texts he'd been getting.

It was a good thing I didn't know what was ahead.

29

SCOTT

Scott texted his boss on the way to Quantico, giving his ETA. Justin Barnes could have used him over the weekend, but there was no way Scott was going to pull his family back from that trip and drive home. Henry needed them, and maybe so did Amanda, and that took priority this time.

Still, he was anxious to hear what the street agents had found out about the second young man who'd targeted a suburban Cleveland high school. Was he a lone wolf? Was it a coincidence with the other incident? Or were these two young men part of a larger group being radicalized online?

The FBI Academy, where Scott was going, is located in the middle of the Quantico Marine Corps base. Anyone going to the academy had to pass through a Marine Corps checkpoint in addition to the academy's own security gate.

He was only half-thinking when he pulled up at the checkpoint. He rolled down his window, said good morning to the young marine guard and held up his creds.

A second guard was checking the underside of Scott's Jeep with a mirror. Scott saw him stand up suddenly and gesture.

"Step out of your car, sir," the first guard said.

"What? I've got a meeting," Scott said, checking his watch, "in six minutes."

"Step out, sir."

Irritated, Scott complied.

"Put your hands on your car, sir," the guard said.

What?

To Scott's shock, the guard frisked him, removing his gun, handing it off, and checking for a backup weapon.

"What the ...." Scott protested. "What's going on? I'm an agent!"

"Come with me, sir," the second guard said, gesturing.

Frustration and anger fueling him, Scott followed the guard up into the small office.

The guard gestured toward an office with an empty desk and two chairs. "Have a seat, sir."

"I want my phones," Scott said, "both of them."

"Yes, sir. My supervisor will be right with you, sir."

What was going on? Scott hadn't done anything! Not speeding, not anything. Furious, he couldn't sit down. He paced, anger stiffening him.

They'd taken his phones. He voice-texted Jess through his Apple Watch. *Call Quantico. Ask to speak to my boss. Tell him I got stopped by the marines. Currently in the guard shack.*

Five minutes later the door opened and a sergeant Scott recognized walked in. *Finally!* "What's going on?" Scott said, coloring his question with a mild curse word.

"Sit down, sir."

Scott reluctantly complied.

"Is that the car you usually drive?"

"No. It's my wife's."

The sergeant nodded. "Okay..."

The door burst open and Scott's boss walked in. His language was more colorful than Scott's. "What do you want with him? We've got headquarters on the line waiting for us."

"The sergeant's eyes flicked toward Justin, then looked straight at Scott. "My guards found a tracking device on the undercarriage of your car."

"A what?" Scott said, incredulous.

"A tracking device. Any reason why it should be on there?"

"No!"

"You said it's your wife's car. Were you tracking her?"

"Me? No. Of course not." His mind raced. *Who could've...*

The sergeant was asking him a question. "Does she work outside the home?"

"She is a private investigator. She has her own company. She's a former Fairfax County homicide detective."

"Any reason to think she's associated with a person under investigation by the government?"

"No, absolutely not. She wouldn't do that."

"How often do you drive that Jeep?"

"Rarely. I haven't driven it for six months. She does K-9 search and rescue. The Jeep is outfitted for that."

"Well, somebody is tracking her. We will impound the car and remove the device."

Scott's boss interrupted. "Let the FBI motor pool come and get it. They'll work it over, in case Scott is the target."

"Okay. In the meantime, if she was my wife, I'd get her out of Dodge for a while." The sergeant stood. "Here are your phones, sir, and your gun."

Scott stared at the phones for a second before taking them. One was personal, the other an encrypted Bureau phone. *Surreal. This is so weird.*

"C'mon, Scott," his boss said. "Let's go. You can call your wife on the way."

30

JESS

When Scott called me and told me about the tracker on my Jeep, I thought it was a joke. Seriously. Who in the world would do that? And why? And were they tracking me or him? Because my husband gets wrapped up in some gnarly stuff, believe me.

I rarely used the Jeep. Scott uses it even less. Most of the time it's parked in the yard at the farm. Would somebody come onto the farm to attach the tracker? That's creepy!

He went on. "Lock the doors. Set the alarm system. Keep your gun nearby, especially if you go out. As soon as you can, send me a list of the places you've driven that Jeep over the last twelve months."

"Twelve months! Scott, I can barely remember last week."

"Just do the best you can. I'm calling the county sheriff to see if he'll have their mechanics take a look under the van."

"Don't forget your truck!"

"I'll look under the truck when I get home. Look, Jess, I've got to run. Please take this seriously. The head of security said if it were his wife he'd want her to leave town."

"Leave town? And go where? Scott—"

"Got to run, Jess. We can talk more later."

I hung up the phone. Scott's anxiety was giving me ulcers. I thought about what we needed to do today. First, pick up Luke from the boarding kennel. Should I take the van? I mean ... what if ...?

Wait, I told myself. I'm not helpless. Little Mike was playing quietly in the living room. I grabbed a flashlight. "Mike, I've got to go out to the van for a second. Stay right there, okay?"

Was I being stupid? I didn't know. The baby gate was up. It would confine him to the living room. I had to chance it.

I opened the front door, bounded off the porch, ran to the van, threw myself on the ground, and shined the flashlight over the undercarriage. I felt with my hand under the side panels on both sides. Then I raced back inside. Mike stood at the baby gate, throwing his trucks into the foyer. He grinned at me.

"Okay, buddy. Want to go get Luke?"

Of course he did. I was pretty sure the van was clear. However, I put Mike in his car seat, buckled him in, then checked for a smaller device, like an Apple Air Tag, under the front and back bumpers.

Nada.

So we drove to pick up Luke, who was absolutely ecstatic to be sprung from that jail where he had no access to his loved ones, and no way to patrol the perimeter, and no ability to make the other dogs *be quiet* and *behave*. Poor Luke.

Thank goodness dogs live in the moment. He was soon over whatever angst he'd felt. As a treat, I let him ride in the back seat next to Mike's car seat. I saw a lot of happy hand licking going on in the baby-view mirror.

When we got home, I decided to check the barn. The horses were in the pasture, heads down, grazing. The Davidson boys had taken care of them over the weekend. I wanted to make sure the barn was in good order. Halfway there, with Mike in tow, I realized I didn't have my gun, which was in my purse, which I'd laid on the front porch.

I decided to chance it. After all, what are the odds?

Stepping into the barn, though, I realized how many places there were for someone to hide. The loft, for example. Behind hay bales. In each of the four stalls. In the tack room. Inside the large tack trunk. Outside around every corner.

Thinking about Little Mike had my nerves on edge. If someone attacked us, I'd have a hard time defending him without my gun. I decided everything looked great in the barn. I picked up Mike and headed for the house.

It wasn't as hard to figure out where I'd driven the Jeep as I thought it might be. While Mike played with his special puzzles and trucks near me in my office, I checked my records. I had to keep track of mileage for my PI work, as a business expense, and also for SAR. Almost all of those times I was driving the Jeep. So without too much trouble, I came up with a list of most of the places I'd driven it over the last year.

As I loaded all those locations into an Excel spreadsheet, one place jumped out at me, the courthouse from the day I drove to testify at Brett Hudgins's hearing after he was arrested for assault. I'd parked the Jeep in a large, public parking lot. All kinds of people had access to it.

And then I remembered the guy with dark eyes, who glowered at me from across the room as charges against Brett were dismissed.

Who was he? Why was he there? Why was he staring at me? Could he, or one of his associates, have put the tracker on my car? Why would he?

I'd never told Scott about that guy. I mean, why would I? All he did was stare.

Maybe I did want to answer Brett Hudgins's text. Maybe I

did want to talk to him again. Because maybe then I'd find out who was tracking me.

I DROPPED off Mike at Ellie's after lunch. He was beginning to give up his afternoon nap on some days, and I decided to take a chance. Ellie said she didn't care; she'd watch him whether he napped or not.

"When my kids were his age, some days they'd fall asleep on the couch or on the floor. What difference does it make? If he's tired, he'll sleep. If not, we'll play."

I wasn't quite that relaxed about things, but I guess if it worked for Ellie, Mike would survive.

I didn't tell Ellie where I was going, just that I had a meeting with a client. Brett Hudgins was that client.

We met at our usual coffee shop, Serein. He looked tired and worn out.

"What's up, Brett?" I asked as I sat down at his table. He'd ordered my usual, black coffee, and it sat in front of me in one of the café's exquisite, hand-thrown pottery mugs. I wondered if they sold them. Not that I needed another mug.

"It's my wi ... uh, ex-wife."

"What's going on with Brittany?" I asked, as if I couldn't guess.

He held his coffee mug in midair, like he was trying to decide whether to take a sip or not. His hand shook. He put it down and cupped both hands around it.

"I've been seeing her, well, taking the girls to see her."

"You have full custody, right?"

"I do. But the girls, they miss their mom. And so I've ... I've been meeting up with her, with the girls, in a park or a restaurant, somewhere they can spend time together."

"You stay with them," I suggested. I certainly hoped so.

He nodded. "We spend a couple of hours together. We talk.

She fixes the girls' hair. Sometimes we all go shopping together ... for the girls. Or we have a meal." He stared at his mug. "She isn't well, Jessica. I can tell. She's lost weight, a lot of weight, and she looks pale. I think ... I think she's using drugs."

"Her prescribed drugs?"

He shook his head no. "Did you ever see that show, *Breaking Bad*?"

"I know of it. I didn't watch it."

"She reminds me of that guy. She looks thin, gaunt even, nervous all the time. I saw a sore on her arm, and when I mentioned it, she said it was nothing and quickly pulled down her sleeve."

I nodded. Meth. That's what he was talking about.

He went on. "Once when she was pulling a tissue out of her coat pocket, a little plastic bag fell out. She grabbed it—fast. I couldn't see what it was, but it seemed suspicious."

"Does she seem high?"

"Not when she's with us. We were leaving one time though, and I looked over at her in her car, and she was taking something."

"By mouth?"

He nodded.

"Brett," I said, "where is she living?"

He shrugged. "Northern Virginia, that's all I know."

"Is she living with somebody?"

"I don't know."

"You don't know the names of any of the people she hangs out with?"

He shook his head.

"Have you talked to her about the drugs?"

"I don't want to bring it up in front of the girls."

"What else are you concerned about? Besides the drugs."

He shifted in his seat, obviously uncomfortable. Then he took a deep breath. "I think that someone is using her. Whether for sex, or, well, I don't know. She's mentioned movies. What kind of movies is the question. And something about a website."

We were dipping into some dark areas. I took a long drink of coffee. My mug had a design that looked like the universe—planets, stars, a swirl of light.

I looked at my former client. "Brett, why do you care?"

"She's my daughters's mother and ... and I still have feelings for her."

Oh, Brett. You idiot. "Maybe you should see a counselor."

He shook his head vigorously. "No. Not gonna happen. If my boss found out..."

I sighed. "Brett, what do you want me to do for you? Why did you call me?"

He looked at me, his eyes full of sincerity. "I'm willing to pay you a large fee to meet with her. Talk to her."

"Me? Why?"

"Because you're sensible. You're a woman. You've been a cop. You know she's gone off the rails, and maybe you can help her get back on. And also because you care about our children."

He was right about that. I did care about their daughters. But the rest of it—so many red flags popped up I thought my eyes were bleeding.

He read my hesitation. "Think about it. What I'm asking is that you meet with her in a public place, so no risk. Implore her to consider the girls. I'm willing to pay for rehab. I've found a place that I think could help her. I've already talked to them. They could take her. All I need is for someone to offer it to her. Explain it. Give her hope."

"I'm not a social worker, Brett."

"But you care. You do care. I can tell. You care about justice and you care about people. Most of all, you care about kids." He paused. "Look, if Brittany and I never get back together, well, it wasn't meant to be. But she needs help and hope. If anyone can give that to her, it's you. I will pay you, whether or not she agrees to the rehab, just for talking to her."

All the correct responses ran through my head: *No.* Or, *That's not what I do.* Or, *I know you care about her, but....*

What came out of my mouth was, "Let me think about it."

I kicked myself all the way back to Ellie's house. "It went fine," I told her when she asked about the meeting with my client. The truth was I had given Brett false hope, because the minute I walked out of the coffee shop, I knew there was no way, no possible way, that I could talk to Brittany Hudgins.

Little Mike did not take a nap at Ellie's, so by the time six o'clock rolled around, he was tired and grouchy and it was all I could do to get dinner into him. We fed the horses, I gave Mike a bath, and by seven thirty he was in bed, asleep.

Scott rolled in at eight o'clock as tense as a boxer just entering the ring. Apparently, I was the other boxer. It was a match I hadn't signed up for.

"Did you make that list?" Those were the first words out of his mouth.

I could tell he was tired. And probably hungry. "Do you want to eat first?"

"Give me the list. I'll look over it while I eat."

I dished up two plates of the meal I'd made earlier—a beautiful salad and my go-to fake beef stroganoff. Ground beef, frozen vegetables, and cream of chicken soup. With noodles. A quick, easy dinner. My working mother used to make it all the time. I added bread for Scott and made it a feast.

I said grace, and we began eating. Scott shoveled food in his mouth while staring at the printout. He spotted the threat right away. "You drove the Jeep to the courthouse when you testified in that case?"

"Yes."

"Who had access to it?"

"The Jeep? Everybody. It was in a large, public parking lot."

"So anybody could have attached the tracker to it."

"Right. Plus, they could have gotten the wrong Jeep. It could also be mistaken identity." His tension slammed into me like waves.

"Who was at that hearing?"

"My client, Brett. His ex-wife. His lawyer, her lawyer, the normal courtroom staff. Oh, and a few spectators."

"What's her name? The ex?"

"Brittany."

"Who were the spectators?"

"Brett's dad and some people who seemed to know Brittany." *Including the dark-eyed man who stared me down.* Only I didn't mention him.

"Okay, so Brett and Brittany Hudgins, right?" He typed them into a note on his phone. "I need you to send me those contacts, and I need more names. Like the lawyers, the name of the judge—"

"Wait, why?"

"Because it's likely somebody connected with that case put a tracker on your car."

"And ..."

"I'm going to find out who it is!"

"Whoa, whoa, don't go all cowboy on me!"

"I'm not! You're my wife, and—"

"And I carry a gun and used to be a cop and—"

"And you run around with my son in your car!"

Boom.

I swallowed hard, forcing myself to calm down. I hate arguing with Scott. "Mike is never in the Jeep. And I checked the van. There's nothing under the van. No tracker, no Air Tag. I'm not a helpless woman, Scott. And I'm as protective of Mike as you are, if not more."

He shifted his jaw, trying to release his own tension. "How about if you and Mike go stay with your mom for a while."

I shook my head. "No. Why should we?"

"Just until I get this straightened out."

"*You* get this straightened out. Are you serious?"

"Yes, I'm serious!"

"It's my car. I'm the one being tracked. It was my case, whatever it was. And I'll be the one to solve it. Brett told me today—"

"What? You spoke to him today?" He pushed his chair back.

"I saw him. In Charlottesville. At that coffee shop."

He stood up, paced away, and then turned to face me. "You went there in person. In the van. So anyone who saw you now knows you drive that van. Was Mike with you?"

"No, of course not."

"Did you tell this guy we found the tracker?"

"No, Scott."

"Did he ask you? Because how do we know he's not the one who attached it?"

"For crying out loud, Scott! Just calm down. He asked to see me because he's concerned his wife is using drugs. He wants me to talk to her—"

"No! Absolutely not." He pointed his index finger at me. "Do not go anywhere near her. With or without Little Mike. Do you hear me?"

My heartbeat pounded in my ears. My face felt hot. Flashes of adrenalin shot through my body. "If I remember," I said coolly, rising to my feet, "you controlling where I go and who I see was not in our marriage vows." And I walked away, fighting tears of anger.

In my fury, I forgot to deactivate the alarm before I opened the front door. The alarm went off. Luke barked. Mike woke up and started screaming.

I stepped outside and pulled the door shut behind me.

31

AMANDA

"Give me a date in October," Henry said. He and Amanda were sitting on the front porch of the Main Street house, watching night fall on the channel, regrouping from the weekend, from Cal's funeral, their visiting guests, and his father's intransigence. He stroked Cash. The black spaniel sat in his lap, quietly licking Henry's hand.

"A date? What are you talking about?" Amanda responded. "Like a movie date? October's like four months away. Why are we talking about this now?"

Amanda's questions felt like shotgun pellets. He smiled. Her fire was one of the things that attracted him to her. "Just give me a date. You won't get married now, so give me a date in October," he said.

"To get married? Why October?"

"Weather's nice. And it'll be after the fall roundup." Fall roundup was a busy time for him. The Saltwater Cowboys would bring the wild ponies into pens, where the ponies would be vet-checked, inoculated, and some of them dewormed. The fall pickups, foals sold at the summer auction, needed to be examined and documented so their new owners could take them. It would be several very active days for him, hopefully without collapsing gates or unplanned hospital visits.

His ribs felt a little sore after all the activity of the weekend. He shouldn't have gone out in the ocean, but he needed to. Something about being out there in the salt gave him peace. And when Amanda came with him, well, it made time on the waves complete.

"I love your parents," he said suddenly.

"What? My parents? You mean Dad and Jess?"

"I feel comfortable with them."

"Of course you do. They love you, Henry! You may be their favorite."

He laughed.

"But truthfully, anybody who would take me off Dad's hands would qualify. The bar is pretty low."

He grinned. "There's something ... I don't know, settled about them. Stable. Yet they do the most interesting things. FBI. SAR. And Nate! Oh my gosh, he's like a walking contradiction. The way he speaks is ignorant but the words he speaks are wise. It's crazy. You feel like you're talking to a hick, and then he says something that strikes you as smarter than anything any professor had ever told you."

Amanda agreed. "You were great with Little Mike. 'Sandy Pants'? How in the world did you come up with that game?"

He shrugged. "I wanted him to get over his fear of the waves. That worked. I'll have him on a board in no time."

They were quiet for a while, then Amanda said. "You want to have kids, don't you."

"Yeah, I guess so. Eventually."

She took a deep breath. "I'm not sure how I'm going to feel about, you know, getting pregnant again."

"Because of Mia?"

She nodded. The baby she lost was never far from her mind.

He reached over and took her hand. "Let's worry about that when the time comes." He looked at her. "It wasn't your fault," he reminded her.

She looked away quickly.

"Things just happen in nature. Trust me. I know about this stuff. I'm a professional." He squeezed her hand gently.

"You're a horse doctor," she said, recovering her composure. "What can you possibly know about women?"

"Oh, I know a thing or two! Like, when you ask them to give you a date, they'll change the subject. Wander all over the place! So you have to press them." He got up, put Cash on the floor, and got down on one knee and took her hand. "My dearest Amanda, would you please give me a date in October when we can get married?"

"Henry, I ..."

He rose abruptly. "That's it, I'm calling it." He pulled out his phone and looked at the calendar app. "October 11. That's when we're getting married." His thumbs started working. "I'm texting your dad and Jess and Nate." He looked up. "There. Settled."

"But Henry, what if ..."

"No what ifs about it. The date is set." He slid his phone into his back pocket. "Everything else will work out." He sat back down in his rocker. Cash jumped into his lap.

"Henry Bunting!"

"The Third," he said. "Henry Bunting the Third. That's important."

"Henry Bunting the Third, you are crazy!"

"Yes, probably. And also, I'm crazy in love with you. I don't want to be apart anymore. I want to create a life with you, a new life, our life, and a new family. Cash has a broken home. We need to fix that.

"I can wait 'til October. That's it. That ought to give you time to find a dress, pick a place for the reception, and send invitations. The piping plovers will have flown south, the fall pickup ponies will have been delivered, the refuge will survive for a few days without us, and I will take you to an incredible, magical place for our honeymoon."

She smirked at him. "Where? Wallops Island?"

"I was thinking Cape Charles."

She swatted him.

"Ow!" He laughed. "I'm kidding. Okay—maybe as far as Virginia Beach." He stood up and stretched. "I've got to go. I have work tomorrow, and I'm beat."

She stood and hugged him, gently because of his ribs. "I love you, Henry Bunting the Third."

He kissed her and looked deeply into her eyes. "Thank you for being there for me these past couple of weeks. It's been a tough ride."

She cocked her head. "You're in a good mood, though."

"Not really. I'm happy here with you. Watching my brother die and then my father—my father going off on me—letting go of all that is going to take some time."

"Stay here with me."

He kissed her. "I love you. So, no, I won't do that."

"You are such an old man!"

32

JESS

I sat in the rocker on our front porch, watching the full moon rise in the eastern sky, trying to let go of the argument I'd just had with Scott. The moon was a lovely pearl, a shining disc, a shimmering circle of light, eclipsing nearby stars with its glory, so beautiful I could understand why some ancient people worshipped it.

Its beauty is but a reflection of the greater light's glory.

Where did that come from? I could not process it.

I propped my knees up and wrapped my arms around them, giving myself a whole-body hug. My stomach hurt. The dinner I'd just eaten wouldn't settle.

In the night, a whippoorwill called its mate. Good luck with that, I thought, a little bitterly. The cool evening chilled the hot tears streaking my cheeks, and a thousand thoughts flew like bats through my mind.

Why was he so bullheaded? Why did he have to come on so strong? Why was he treating me like a helpless airhead? He was so controlling!

I should have told him I was going to meet Brett.

But he was so anxious to get to work this morning! I knew he was on something hot. And then there was that mess with the Jeep at the gate. Plus, I didn't know what Brett wanted.

Why did I get so angry? Isn't protecting me part of his role as a husband? Was I trying to usurp that? What does it mean to be "submissive" in this context? I'm a terrible wife! Oh, God, help me! Help us!

I unfolded my legs and let the tears flow, soaking them up now and then with the sleeve of my T-shirt. I rocked and thought and rocked and thought until my brain was a tangled mess. I wanted to call Nate, but I knew what he'd say. He told me when I got married that when Scott and I fought, if I asked him for advice, he wouldn't take my side or Scott's, he would advocate for the marriage. In the long run, he'd said, that was what was most important.

It seemed to be a given to him that Scott and I would fight.

Good call.

I'd been out on the porch for a long time, probably an hour, thinking and praying and rocking, when I heard the front door quietly open. Luke slipped out, came to me, licked my face, and laid down near me. Then Scott emerged, baby monitor in hand, and closed the door behind him.

He walked over to me and gave me a soft kiss on my cheek. In the moonlight, I saw him press his lips together. He must have tasted my salty tears.

He moved the other rocker closer and sat down. Then he took my hand. "Jess, I am so sorry."

Good Scott was speaking. Kind, gentle Scott who loved me despite me ... being me.

"I came home hot," he said.

No kidding.

"It's no excuse but there was that ... that stuff at the gate this morning. Then we had a case go bad. A shooter, mishandled, who ended up killing a cop and killing himself. I was angry and upset. I laid that on you. And I never, ever should have done that." He gently squeezed my hand.

"You came onto me like a charging bull," I said, sniffing.

Scott handed me a fresh tissue. "I know. I'm sorry."

I blew my nose. My shoulders started to relax. The moonlight was so bright it penetrated the woods next to our lane and cast shadows of the trees. An owl called, *whoo-hoo-hoo, whoo-hoo*. A great horned owl. Nate had taught me that call, sitting on his porch one evening when I wasn't sure I wanted to keep living. I'd already met Scott, but he seemed cold, closed off, and so was I.

Now, life looked so different.

I squeezed my husband's hand. "I'm sorry too, Scottie," I said, using the pet name reserved for special times. "I violated our agreement. We said we'd tell each other when we were meeting someone, so we could have each other's back. I didn't do that, and I am sorry."

"I jumped on you with both feet. I don't blame you for being angry." He settled back in his chair.

I swallowed. "I resented your protective impulses. I saw your words as demeaning. I got angry."

"I spoke to you like you were a child. It did sound demeaning. I'm sorry. You are fully capable of defending yourself, as we've seen so many times. But ... but it's an honor to be your husband, Jess, and protecting you is part of that."

"I know," I said. We rocked some more, our rockers moving in unison. "I'm sorry about your case."

"They were texting me about it all weekend when they first learned about the threat. I thought it would wait until today, that it was just a tip. But it blew up quicker than I thought it would. The local cops got anxious and moved too soon. Then *boom*! That was it."

"Where was it?"

"Ohio."

"I'm sorry, Scott."

"I shouldn't bring that stuff home. I try not to, but sometimes ..."

"It's okay." I heard a rustle in the woods. I wondered if it was a fox or a deer. Maybe a possum. They eat ticks, so I like having them around, even if they are ugly. I heard a train far away. We must be ten miles at least from the tracks, but I could hear that whistle. It's odd how far noise can travel at night when the air is clear.

When the air is clear.

"Scott?"

"Yeah."

"I need to tell you something else."

"What's that?"

I told him about the dark-eyed man in the courtroom, who glowered at me. "I don't know his name, and it may be nothing—"

"Or it could be a lead," he said. "Do you want to follow up or do you want me to do it?" His words were gentle.

"I will. I'll start with the clerk of the court. They may have security footage of the courtroom. Then I'll go to John Welsh, Alexandria police, and see if he knows who he is."

"Sounds good. If you have any trouble, I'll apply some FBI weight."

"I'll let you know."

"I love you, Jess." He rose, leaned over me, and kissed me.

"I love you, too, Scottie." I stood up. "I'll tell Brett I won't meet with his wife."

Scott started to agree, then stopped and said, "Why don't you hold off on that? If your lead develops, it might be a useful way to follow through."

He was right. "Good idea."

"Just not alone, okay? You have to have backup."

"Right. I agree."

"Let's go inside."

"Sounds good."

We moved toward the door. Luke rose and followed us. Scott put his hand on the knob to open the door for me.

The knob didn't turn. He tried again. The door was locked.

We looked at each other. We'd locked ourselves out of the house! We started to laugh.

"Back door?" he asked.

"Securely locked," I responded, "just like you wanted."

He shook his head and backed down off the porch, staring up at the darkened house.

"If you break a window, the alarm will go off," I said, standing next to him. "Wait, look! The small window up there for the hall bathroom. It's open, isn't it?"

He squinted. "Yeah, I think so. I'll get the ladder."

"Boost me up," I said. "I can get there from the porch roof."

"What? No!"

"Boost me up, Scottie!" I said, laughing. "Trust me. I can do this."

"It's no wonder I've got gray hair," he muttered, but he smiled at the same time.

He did what I asked. I scrambled onto the roof of the porch, carefully walked over to the bathroom window, pried the screen off with my pocketknife, hoisted the window up the rest of the way, and climbed in. "Be right down!" I called out to him.

Fifteen minutes later we were finally in bed. Together. Still laughing.

What a relief. What a day.

On Tuesday, we regrouped. Scott drove into Quantico to what I suspected would be a tense debriefing with both the bureau higher-ups and the local police in Ohio. I fed the horses, played with Mike, and had a long phone conversation with Ellie about Maddie. I invited her over to the house for tea and to talk more.

Ellie came over, dressed in jeans and a flowery peasant blouse. She'd brought Jamie, and he and Mike played with Duplo in the living room while Luke supervised.

I made tea and we sat at our farm table. For the first time since I'd known her, Ellie seemed discouraged, almost despondent. She'd taken Maddie to their doctor and a counselor she told me. They recommended anti-anxiety meds, an anathema to my whole-foods, fresh-air, homeschooling friend.

"The counselor made me feel like an incompetent, ignorant mom when I questioned the need for meds," Ellie told me.

"You're not, Ellie. You're not incompetent and you're certainly not ignorant. You're a wonderful mom."

"But when the professionals say—"

I blew that off with a wave. "You know your kid. What's more, you know the Lord. You and Paul need to pray it out and then do what you think is best. God's going to redeem this somehow, Ellie. I just know it."

Her shoulders sagged a little more. "Paul thinks we should go with the meds."

Oh no! Here we go again. Follow your husband's lead or fight him? *Why is this so hard, Lord?*

I reached over and touched Ellie's hand. "Trying the meds is not an irreversible decision. If you've talked it out, and if Paul has listened to your point of view, maybe you should try it."

Tears gathered in Ellie's eyes. I wondered if she thought I was betraying her.

"He's worried about suicide," she explained.

Maddie? At age eleven? Still, kids these days ...

"He reads too much."

"He loves her," I said. "Look, meds or no meds, why don't I

invite Maddie over to help with the horses? Or play with Mike? Maybe a little time away from her room would help."

Ellie agreed and said she'd ask Maddie. We settled on Friday, when Scott would be at the farm.

After lunch while Mike napped, I called the courthouse where Brett Hudgins's arraignment had taken place. I talked to someone in the clerk's office, who said I needed to talk to security, who said no, the clerk needed to authorize it, and around I went, until I finally got someone to agree to let me look at footage from the courthouse on that day.

On Wednesday, I got dressed in a business suit. Scott grinned and said I looked "hot." I accused him of sexual harassment.

I drove to the courthouse, found the clerk's office, got the authorization I needed, and found the head of security's office. A deputy helped me scroll through the security camera's videos and boom! There he was, the Glowering Man, standing near the window on the east side of the courtroom just after the judge had dismissed the charges against Brett.

"Do you know him?" I asked the deputy.

"No."

"Can we print that frame?"

We could and we did. I had him make multiple copies.

Because I wasn't far from Alexandria, I called Detective John Welsh. I told him what I was doing and asked if I could see him.

He said he'd be at the office for two more hours, so I drove up to Alexandria, went into the office, and asked for him.

"You look like your brother!" I said, as the fifty-something detective walked out to greet me. I'd worked with Brad Welsh on a cold case last year.

"I should! Coincidentally, we have the same parents," he joked. "Come on back."

We walked through gray-painted halls to his office, which was painted a light, pleasant green.

He saw me looking around. "My wife and I painted this one weekend. This color isn't on the approved list, but I thought if I had to live in a gray office I was going to go mad. I felt like Gandalf as it was!"

"That was nice of your wife," I said.

He shrugged. "Thirty-one years of marriage. We get each other."

I gave him one of the prints and he studied the picture.

"Yeah, I don't know him."

"You said you all were targeting that location where Mrs. Hudgins's van was parked. What for?"

"Initially, we thought it was a drug operation. However," he paused, "we think something else is happening there."

"What?"

"Adult films, Internet videos, some involving children."

Oh no!

"The FBI is on the case. They're not ready to bust it open. We're providing support."

"Do you know the names of any of the agents assigned to it?"

"Don't remember. I'm not on it directly. I'll see if I can find out and let you know."

"Would you mind just keeping that," I said, nodding toward the print, "and showing it around?"

"Not at all. Oh, and my brother says hi."

"He's a good guy," I said.

"Yep. Stayin' on the right side of the bars," John said, joking.

. . .

I DROVE HOME SATISFIED. When I told Scott the FBI was involved in the Alexandria case and showed him the printout, he got excited. "They can run facial recognition on this," he said. "I'll find out whose case this is and see if we can get some help."

The agent fraternity, I knew, was about to spring into action.

33

JESS

All those shows that depict FBI cases being solved in forty-seven minutes are lying to you. In real life, it can take days or even weeks to get the answers needed to solve crimes. Sometimes it's even longer.

To try to identify the Glowering Man, Scott had to meet with the case agent handling the Alexandria investigation. That took a week. Then the agent had to agree to take the photo and submit it to the facial recognition program in Charleston, West Virginia, which would compare the security camera photo to mugshots collected from around the country. If the image was good enough.

At CJIS, the Criminal Justice Information Services Division, the photo had to get in line behind a lot of other requests because there were no exigent circumstances—that is, no one's life was being immediately threatened.

Scott had a different view but then, he's just one agent among many.

In the meantime, life went on.

Maddie did not come over on Friday. She went to the

doctor's instead. And Scott soon got distracted by the seven other potential mass shooting cases he was currently working.

I did call Amanda over the weekend to see how they were doing.

She told me Henry seemed to be okay. "He's more quiet than he usually is," she said. "Sometimes I catch him staring into space. But he's back to working the large animal cases, which he loves. Cash goes with him most of the time."

"It's going to take a while to process what he's been through," I suggested.

"I guess so. Especially his stupid father."

I didn't respond, even though I had to agree. I changed the subject. I told Amanda a little more about Maddie and asked for advice. "Is there any way we could help her ourselves? I mean, your ranch is too far to travel."

Amanda hesitated. I could tell she was thinking. "I mean," she said, finally, "the problem is your horses are a little hot for the kind of work we do. Abby, especially. She's built for barrel racing. I don't know. Maybe somebody in your area has an old pony hanging out in the field that would work."

"What would I look for?" I asked her.

"Steadiness. An even temperament. No biting. Not prone to kicking. A pony who likes people," she said.

"I'll look around. Maybe I can find something. Thanks, Amanda."

"I'll send you some basic information about our process," she said. Before we hung up she told me about October 11.

"Is that it!" I said. "Henry's text just said we should save that date and plan to come over there. So you're getting married that day?"

"He said, 'Give me a date in October.' I mean, I hesitated, right? And he just picked it! He is crazy."

"Sounds like he wants to get married."

"I think it's weird. He refuses to let me move in or ... or anything. He insists we get married before anything happens."

I smiled, thankful we weren't FaceTiming.

She went on. "It's something his mom talked to him about, apparently. He's really stubborn about it."

"Well, Amanda, I am very happy for you!" I said. "Your dad and I will help however we can, money, or if you want to come up here, we can go dress shopping. I could meet you in Northern Virginia. Whatever you want, we'll help out. We love you both!"

"I'll let you know," she replied, and I knew from the tone of her voice she was hesitant about something.

A red flag popped up in my head. *Oh, Amanda, don't mess this up! Henry's a good guy.* Somehow I kept my mouth shut.

We said goodbye and I clicked off my phone. I still had so many questions. *Where are you getting married? Will you have a reception? Where? How many people do you think you'll invite? And most of all, will you invite your mother?*

As far as I knew, Amanda hadn't had contact with Suzanne since she'd left her mother's California home at age sixteen. She'd flown by herself to DC and took an Uber to Scott's house in Manassas, surprising him. I'd certainly never met Suzanne and Scott didn't talk about her.

This wedding could be interesting.

NATE and I were on tap to run SAR recertification tests the next Saturday, but that got cancelled by a callout we got Friday night at 11:00 p.m. An eighty-one-year-old man had "gone for a walk" that evening in the thickly wooded mountainous area where he lived. No one could find him, not the family, not neighbors, not law enforcement bloodhounds or drones.

"When did the family call 911?" I asked Nate.

"About eight thirty."

"And how long had he been missing?"

"Since about four."

Four and a half hours! "Why'd they wait so long?"

"Don't know. Local police and volunteers searched until ten," Nate said, "then asked for help. We're to report at 0700, so if you want to go, I'll pick you up at six."

"I'll go. Let me check with Scott. I'll text you to confirm when he gets home."

SCOTT WAS fine with me doing the search, so I packed my SAR bag on Friday night and set an alarm for 5:00 a.m. I didn't need it. I woke up on my own. I guess I was excited to go on a search.

I got dressed and went downstairs. I let Luke out and gave him a light breakfast, then I snuck back upstairs and kissed Scott goodbye.

The sun had just come up when Luke and I stepped out on the front porch to wait for Nate. Dew glistened on the fields, and the dawn chorus was in full throat—Carolina wrens, cardinals, and blue jays, and some birds I could not yet identify. I took a deep breath of fresh air just as Nate pulled up.

We took his Tahoe, because the FBI still had my Jeep. Ember was in the back and Nate had loaded a spare crate for Luke. Which dog we used remained to be seen.

Scott had calmed down a little since the tracker was first found on my Jeep, but I knew he felt better when I was with Nate on a search. Between Nate, my Garmin inReach, my cell phone, and my gun, even Scott figured I'd probably come back alive.

Once we left our farm we'd have about a forty-five-minute drive to get to the far reaches of Warren County. I was happy about that, because it would give Nate and I time to talk.

I'd told him about the tracker and so had Scott. "Who do you figure done that?" he asked.

"I don't know. Honestly, I think it was intended for somebody else with the same vehicle. And with the Jeep sitting at the FBI now for two weeks, I'm hoping they'll get the message that one's not worth tracking."

"Was it the same brand you used?"

"I never saw it. I'd have to ask Scott. I ... haven't wanted to bring it up."

Nate grinned. "He told me he'd blown it. Gone nuclear on you."

"And I reacted with calm, loving reserve."

Nate laughed. "I'm sure you did."

I looked over at my friend. "I never got to ask you about Henry. You stayed in Chincoteague an extra day."

"That I did. That boy needed to talk. He didn't want to lay it all on Amanda."

"You know they're getting married."

"He texted me. I figured that's what October 11 was all about."

I paused, waiting for him to continue. He didn't. It really wasn't any of my business what he and Henry talked about. I knew that. I didn't care. But I wanted to know. Everything Nate had to say was interesting to me.

When I couldn't stand it anymore, I said, "Is he doing okay? Henry?"

Nate didn't respond.

"I mean, when you think about it," I said, continuing, "he got hit multiple times in just a month or so—getting hurt, then his brother showing up, his brother overdosing, and his father going off on him."

Silence. We were winding our way through the mountains. He needed to watch the road, I told myself. That's why he's not talking. "I like Henry. Amanda and I have talked. She calls him 'weird' because he won't let her move in. But I think—"

He interrupted me. "We only talked about you."

I whipped my head around.

Nate stared straight ahead. "About how you keep trying to fix everybody. Make them love Jesus like you do."

"You did not!"

He laughed. "You're right. We didn't mention you at all." He worked his way around a series of tight turns. "You can pray for him. He's carryin' a lot. Grief. Anger. But he's also askin' questions, a lot like you did back in the day. He's a smart man. He was blowin' my mind with some of 'em."

I wanted to know more. I wanted the whole conversation. Not to be nosy, but just to hear what insights Nate had given Henry, what theological points he'd made. I rubbed the knuckle of my index finger against my thumb, something I do when I'm thinking hard about something. Several miles later, I had a flash of insight. "What books did you send him?"

Nate looked at me and grinned. "What makes you think—"

"Because I know you! Look, Nate. That's not gossip. I'm asking you about something *you* did, not about anything Henry did or said. Or felt."

We slowed down as we went through Washington, Virginia, seventy miles outside of DC, a tiny town whose famous inn had a dining room with three Michelin stars. Three! That's a lot. Even I knew that. Who sets an amazing inn and restaurant in a town so tiny, so far from the big metro areas?

As we went by, Nate nodded toward it. "You ought to have Scott bring you up here for your anniversary."

"Scott? The one I'm married to? The one who hates spending money on restaurants?"

Nate shrugged. "Y'all clean up good."

He accelerated as the town slipped by.

"What books did you send him, Nate?" I wasn't letting him off the hook.

He folded, shaking his head. "Just three. A study Bible. *Surprised by Joy*."

"C. S. Lewis? Interesting!"

"Some parallels with Henry's life. Mother died of cancer. Father absent or abusive. Trauma from World War I. A long period of intellectual achievement before the Lord opened his eyes." He glanced at me.

"I know," I said. "You gave me that book too. Lewis fought God like a lion. Called himself the most reluctant convert." I paused. "What was the third book?"

"It was about Pascal."

"Who?"

"French mathematician, lived in the sixteen hundreds." He glanced at me. "Had an interestin' experience late one night. You maybe should read that one."

I reached over and touched Nate's shoulder, smiling. "You're such a good guy."

"No. I'm not. But I do know who is good. And I'm jus' followin' him, best I can."

34

JESS

We arrived at the search site, the home of William Sears, the missing eighty-one-year-old. His son stood talking to cops in the driveway of the small rambler nestled in the shadow of a mountain.

"Lived here all his adult life," I heard the son say as we got out of the Tahoe. "Knows these woods like the back of his hand."

Four teams from Battlefield responded. Bill acted as incident commander. He briefed us on the search subject. "His son says he's pretty fit for an eighty-one-year-old and pretty independent. Used to taking walks in the woods. But he does have a heart condition. The son talked to him about four o'clock yesterday, and his dad said he was about to go for a walk. His son tried to reach him about eight, and when there was no answer on his phone, he came over. No sign of his dad, but the car was in the driveway."

Bill gestured. "As you can see, there are no close neighbors. The cops went up and down the road, on the chance someone had seen him driving by. No one had. William doesn't carry a cell phone."

"Did he have a dog with him?" I asked. A lot of older people have a dog to walk with. I mean, I certainly would.

"No." He handed out maps, marked with designated search areas.

I looked around. Jason and Kristen would work as a team. They were young and strong but fairly new to SAR, as was their dog, a Malinois. Emily was there with her border collie, Flash. She would work with a deputy as a walker. The other team was late.

Nate and I were definitely the most experienced. Bill assigned us a complicated area with a stream, some fencing, and a big open area. I wondered how Nate's leg would hold out.

After a few more questions, we were set to go. "Which dog should we run?" I asked my partner.

"Let's give Ember a try."

That meant Nate would be the dog handler and I'd be the walker, in charge of the GPS, the map, the radio, making notes, and generally paying attention while Nate focused on the dog. "Give me a minute to let Luke out, and I'll be ready to go," I said.

I let Luke out to water the bushes and stretch. He was disappointed when I put him back in the crate, but he laid down with a huff. "You may get a chance," I told him, "if we don't find him."

Nate had obviously been working with Ember on his own. The black shepherd kept her eyes focused on him as we walked to the start area. He primed her with treats and she shook with excitement as he put her in the heel position. "Alright," he said to me, "let's pray."

"Right," I said, as if that had been first on my mind as well.

He prayed, then checked the wind, calculated the direction,

coordinated that with me, and then he sent his dog. "Seek!" he said, his arm shooting forward. "Seek!"

He moved forward, doing his best to keep up with Ember as she quartered back and forth through the woods, trying to catch a whiff of any human. Nate's fancy, electronic artificial leg helped him move across the uneven ground and hiking poles helped him keep his balance. Both had helped him hike the Appalachian trail just over a year ago. He wasn't fast, but he made good forward progress, even in this hilly area.

I was so used to working Luke I found myself enjoying observing Nate work with Ember on this search. I'd been on many outings with him and Sprite, his now-retired springer spaniel, but not nearly as many with him and Ember. She was fast, alert, and smaller than Luke, so she could shinny under fallen trees and through the underbrush well. He was so in tune with her he wasn't paying attention to me at all. Soon I was out of breath. Nate was still going strong.

We searched for three hours, with a short break in the middle. Sweat stained the back of Nate's khaki field shirt. My hair and the back of my neck were dripping. The day had turned hot; the forecast was for a high of ninety. The bugs in the woods swarmed us as soon as we stopped moving.

The last area we needed to search was the big meadow. Actually, it wasn't a meadow; it was part of the cut for a big powerline that ran up and over the mountain. Nate had us make the climb up in the morning, which was smart. Now the last part of our search would be downhill.

After hydrating and grabbing a protein snack, we set off again, moving into the powerline easement and, thankfully, downhill, although Nate said that was just as tricky for him as going uphill.

We were almost at the bottom, when Ember came racing back to Nate, sat in front of him, and barked. My heart jumped. That was her indication, her signal she'd found a human! And since she was only trained for live finds, that was a good sign.

We found Mr. Sears about a hundred yards away, sitting in the shade, his back propped up against a tree, right on the edge of the easement. He seemed disoriented. He didn't know what day it was or what time or where he was. He did know his name.

Nate was so gentle with him. The first thing he did was crack open a water bottle and give it to him. I radioed in the find and gave Bill our GPS coordinates. Then I did a brief medical assessment of Mr. Sears while Nate gave Ember her play reward.

It took rescuers about thirty minutes to reach us. By then, Mr. Sears was a little more coherent. He and Nate were swapping stories. The EMTs arrived with a rescue board. Nate had to talk Mr. Sears into allowing them to carry him out.

"He's a feisty old guy," Nate told me later.

"You are kindred spirits," I replied, grinning at him. We packed our gear back up and followed the crew out. Ember seemed a little sad the game was over.

WE ARRIVED BACK at my house at about four. I retrieved my pack and my dog out of the back of the Tahoe and gave Nate a hug. "You did a great job, Nate."

"Good working with you, kid," he said.

"You sure you don't want to stay?"

"I got just enough energy to get home," Nate said. "Thanks, though," and he climbed back in his truck and drove down the lane.

Inside, Scott looked past me. "Nate's not staying?"

"He's tired."

"Okay. Guess what? Henry called. He said you were looking for a pony!" The expression on his face was about the same as an eight-year-old boy's who'd just been told he could have ice cream for breakfast.

"Oh, really?" I responded, smiling at my guy. "*I* was looking for a pony?"

A moment of doubt crossed his face. "That's what Amanda told Henry."

"I'm kidding," I said. "I did ask Amanda about working with Maddie with one of our horses. She said our horses were too 'hot' and suggested looking around for a pony instead."

Scott recovered his smile. "Yeah? Well, guess what? One of Henry's clients has a pony her kids have outgrown. He's a Chincoteague, a gelding, about eight years old, gentle and smart. Here's a picture." He turned his phone toward me, showing me a brown-and-white pony. "Henry knows him well. He says he's healthy, about thirteen-and-a-half hands and safe under saddle."

"How much?"

"Henry said she'll give him to us! She just wants him to have a good home."

"She'll give him away?"

"To us. Apparently, Henry saved her favorite mare and her foal last spring. She says she owes him."

"What do you think?"

"Well, I'd have to see him," Scott said, "but if it would help Maddie—"

"And coincidentally, let you start teaching Mike to ride."

He grinned. "Okay, there is that."

I shrugged. "Whatever you think, Scott. We already have two horses. I don't see that adding a pony will be all that much more work."

"Thank you." He kissed me.

I like what horses do to my husband.

"By the way, did you find your guy?" he asked, suddenly remembering where I'd been all day.

"Our search subject? Yes! Let me go clean up and I'll tell you all about it."

THAT NIGHT, we spent a quiet evening at home. Scott had worn Little Mike out with all they'd done that day and he went to bed at seven thirty. Scott and I talked for a while, then we snuggled on the couch and watched a movie. I may or may not have dozed off through part of it.

I knew once I said 'okay' to the pony it wouldn't take long for Scott to act on it. Sure enough, he made arrangements to meet up with Henry the next Friday. It would be a two-day trip, which meant I wouldn't be able to respond to a callout during that time. As it turned out, my human SAR partner, Nate, was going with him. I was a little surprised about that.

"A boys' trip, huh?" I said to my husband.

"I think he wants to check up on Henry," Scott responded.

I felt a little left out, honestly. I decided to plan a fun hike for Mike and Luke and me, an adventure that, while it didn't involve horses, would still get us out of the house and wear both dog and boy out.

SCOTT WORKED REALLY HARD all week to make sure I didn't have extra work to do while he was gone. He mowed and brought hay down for the horses. He cleaned the stall for the new pony and bedded it with straw. He washed a water bucket and the grain feeder. He even did laundry and vacuumed the whole upstairs of the house. I wanted to tease him and tell him he was a "good, good boy," but instead, I hugged him and gave him a sincere thank you.

Little Mike and I stood on the front porch and waved goodbye as Scott and Nate pulled out in Scott's truck, pulling our horse trailer. Mike cried. "I get it, buddy," I said, picking him up. "Wherever they're going must be more interesting than hanging out at home." I gave him a kiss on his cheek. "Hey, you want to go climb some rocks?"

I'd chosen a trail not far from our home in an area we used for SAR training sometimes. I knew the trail would be well-marked. There'd be a creek, a generally easy climb, and one really fun rock scramble. I filled a backpack with a change of clothes for Mike, water for the three of us, sandwiches, an apple, protein bars, and a snack for Luke and put the Garmin inReach into the cargo pocket of my pants.

I drove to the parking area for the trailhead, singing songs all the way because Mike was restless and a little out of sorts having seen Daddy and Uncle Nate drive off without him. If he knew they were going to see 'Ree, I would have really been in trouble.

The upside, I decided, was my son would have a lot of strong men around him growing up. And that was a good thing.

The weather that morning was beautiful—sunny and in the high seventies. The forecast had us topping off in the eighties. I planned for us to be back at the van by then. We started off up the trail with Luke leading us and Mike running as fast as his little legs could carry him. He was pretty adept at running. In less than a month he'd be two years old. Hard to believe.

When the trail moved near the creek, we stood on the edge and threw rocks in it while Luke waded through it, splashing and chomping the water. I didn't want Mike to get wet just then, so I moved us on.

I pointed out things to my son—a bird's nest, some mushrooms growing on a fallen tree, a hawk soaring overhead. I wanted him to observe nature, not just crash through it. Ever since he was old enough to talk, we'd played a game in the car, categorizing everything as either Things God Made or Things People Made. He was good at it now, and we played that game as we moved along. In the woods, God scored a lot of points.

When we got to the rock scramble, I had to be on high alert for snakes. We have three kinds of venomous snakes in Virginia. One is the timber rattlesnake, officially *Crotalus horridus,* which, in my opinion, is a really great name for a poisonous snake. I'd seen them before in this area, and I sure didn't want my son grabbing for a handhold and coming up with a snake.

We made it through without seeing a single rattler. At the top of the rock scramble was a field of big boulders and a beautiful view of a valley. "Let's stop and have lunch," I said to Mike. I pulled our food out of my backpack along with my dog's collapsible water bowl. "Here, can you pour a drink for Luke?" I handed Mike an open bottle of water and watched as he carefully poured it into the bowl. "Good job!"

"Sit down," I said, "and we'll have lunch."

I had just handed Mike some sliced turkey when my phone rang. Thinking it was Scott, I pulled it out of my pocket and answered it.

It wasn't Scott. It was Brett Hudgins. "Hey, Brett," I said, wishing I'd looked before I'd pressed the green button.

"Hey, where are you?"

I frowned. "On a short trip. Where are you?"

"I got her! She came back to us."

"What?"

"Brittany! I'm so excited. We met so she could see the girls and, well, we talked her into coming home."

My frown deepened. "Okay. So where are you, now?" All kinds of thoughts were racing through my mind.

"At our house! The townhouse."

"*Her* townhouse?"

"Yes!"

My blood pressure was rising with every answer.

He continued, "This is where she wanted to come. She's asleep now. She's exhausted."

"And the girls are with you?"

"Yes! We're all back together. She's even considering that rehab place I told you about."

I swallowed. "Brett, you shouldn't stay there." I handed Little Mike another slice of turkey. My hand shook a little.

"What? Why? We're together!"

I might as well have been talking to my two-year-old. "The people she's been hanging with, they're not good people," I explained. "They may come for her."

He sputtered, sounding confused. "But why?"

"Because she knows about them. Whatever they're doing, she knows about it, and so she's a threat." *And they may be making money off of her, you idiot.* I somehow kept from saying that.

"But how would they know where we are?"

"She might have told them. They might be tracking her car. If they want to badly enough, they can find you." I could see Mike was starting to lose interest in food. He was looking around, and I knew soon he'd be climbing the boulders around us. "Brett, it's not safe there. Why don't you leave? Take a different car. Go to your house in Crozet." I did not get an instant objection so I riffed on that. "Show her what peace looks like. Get her out in that natural beauty."

"Yeah, maybe," he said, softening. "Maybe that's a good idea."

"Do it, Brett. I've got to run. Let's talk later, okay?"

"Okay."

I clicked off my phone and grabbed my son, just as he reached the top of a three-foot boulder. *Man is born to trouble as the sparks fly upward.*

35

JESS

I was dying to know whether Brett Hudgins had taken my advice, but he hadn't called me, and with Scott out of town, I had my hands full with Mike and the farm. Scott had texted me around four and said they'd seen the pony, and he liked him a lot. I was not surprised. I mean, did the thing have four legs?

Their plan was to load him up in the morning and drive home. So they'd be home about two or three. He asked me to go to the feed store and get a special grain the pony was used to eating.

Mike and I fed the horses and I let him feed Luke. I made an easy dinner and then played with Mike until it was time for his bedtime routine.

It's funny. I don't remember ever having a bedtime routine when I was growing up. It seems to me I'd just put myself to bed, especially after my father died. But with Mike, it was a nightly ritual, instituted by Scott, and continued by me. Bath. Book. Bedtime prayers.

After he was down, I sat in the recliner rereading *Surprised by Joy*. I wanted to refresh my memory of it in case it ever came up in conversation, either with Henry or Nate. I loved the honesty of that book. I identified with the stubborn resistance Lewis clung to even as his atheism was being chipped away. He finally decided there had to be intelligence at the core of reality but he still was not ready to embrace Christ. That came later, when suddenly, he could *see*.

The part of Lewis's writing that struck my heart like a hammer striking a bell came in another of his books, *Mere Christianity*. That is the "Great Trilemma" argument for Christ's deity. People everywhere, all over the world, recognize Jesus as a great moral teacher, yet he went much further—he equated himself with God. "Before Abraham was, I AM," Jesus said, invoking the sacred name of God. He claimed the authority to forgive sins, something only God can do. And he said he would return one day in the future to judge the world.

Would a "great moral teacher" lie about those things? Would he make these insane claims if they were not true?

Logically, Jesus was either a liar, or a lunatic, or exactly who he claimed to be—the Son of God.

Liar, lunatic, or Lord. The Great Trilemma.

I do not have the skills in dialectic or philosophy or even moral reasoning that Lewis had, but when I read that for the first time, I could not let go of it. It stuck to me like fly paper. It ran around in my mind for days like a loose dog I could not catch or contain.

Finally, it caught me.

God opened my eyes. Changed my heart. And now, here I am, a very imperfect Jesus follower, stumbling toward eternity, committed to him in all my fallen humanity.

I put my book down and thanked God for coming for me, his lost sheep, wandering in the wilderness of my own will. I prayed for Henry and also for Amanda. I prayed they would see the light, that their eyes would be opened, and that they would know the truth, and receive his love. I prayed God would give

Nate and Scott words to use that would unlock the mystery for them. And while I was at it, I prayed again for Little Mike to come to know Jesus. "Thank you, thank you," I whispered.

Then it was time for bed.

I have trouble sleeping when Scott is gone. If I don't get upstairs during my first sleepy cycle in the evening, or worse, if I doze off downstairs, I'm a mess. I'll go upstairs, get ready for bed, and lie awake for hours. So I've disciplined myself to catch that first cycle and go up as soon as I feel sleepy. Call it my grown-up bedtime routine.

I let Luke out for his nightly perimeter patrol, finished cleaning up the kitchen, turned off lights downstairs, let Luke back in, and then we both climbed the stairs and went to bed.

I fell asleep right away. Two hours later, at 11:52 p.m., my phone rang, jolting me—and Luke—awake. *Scott? Nate? A call-out? What?*

I didn't recognize the number. I answered it anyway. "Hello?"

"Jessica Cooper?"

I can recognize a cop voice any time of the day or night. "Yes." I sat up and swung my feet over the side of the bed. *Was Scott alright?*

"This is Detective Jay Pittman, Charlottesville Police."

Charlottesville. My heart started beating hard. Luke put his head on my knee.

"We are investigating a homicide that occurred tonight at ..." He gave me the address. I recognized it as Brittany's townhouse. "We found your name and number in the victim's pocket. Do you know a man at that address?"

"Can you send me a picture?"

He hesitated. "It's graphic."

I squeezed my eyes shut. "Send it." He did. When I heard the text come in, I opened my eyes and saw a man lying on his back in a giant pool of blood. "That's Brett Hudgins," I said, my stomach roiling. "The address is Brett Hudgins's ex-wife's townhouse. Brittany. Brittany Hudgins."

A sudden thought jolted me to my feet. Luke jumped away, alarmed. "Is she there?"

"No."

"Where are the girls?" I demanded.

"Who?"

"Brett's girls. Nora and Ava. They're nine and seven. They were with him and her earlier today." I heard paper shuffling.

"I don't see anything about—"

"Look," I said, beginning to pace, "I am a private investigator and a former homicide detective." I rattled off the most important facts about Brett and Brittany. "These people she's been involved with are under investigation by the Alexandria police and the FBI for drug and human trafficking. They're bad actors. If they have those girls ..." I couldn't finish, couldn't bear the thoughts that jumped out in my mind like spooks in the night.

He asked me the names of the detectives and FBI people investigating the case. I didn't know. I only knew John Welsh, with Alexandria PD. Scott was the one who'd interacted with the agents on the case, and I'd never asked him for their names. How stupid of me!

"Can you come in and give us a statement and a positive ID on the victim?"

"My husband's out of town. I can't leave my two-year-old alone. You can send somebody out."

He hesitated, then asked for the address.

"Make sure they identify themselves clearly," I said, "and tell them I will be armed."

I CLICKED out of that call and stared at my phone. *What do I do now? Call Scott? He's sleeping, I'm sure!*

I decided to think about it while I got dressed. I slid into my khaki cargo pants and a short-sleeved shirt, brushed my hair and teeth, then went downstairs where I put on a pair of short boots. I pulled my gun out of the safe in the front hall closet and clipped it onto my belt. I turned on a lot of lights and brewed a pot of coffee.

Downstairs, I was less inclined to call Scott. The only thing he could do is give me the name of the agents who he'd talked to. I suspected John Welsh could also do that. Calling him would wake Scott up, disturb his sleep, and hurt his chances of driving back safely tomorrow.

At 12:40 a.m. I heard wheels crunching down our lane. Luke jumped to his feet. I unholstered my weapon and looked out of the window. A black sedan was moving toward the house. I couldn't see the driver, but I saw a uniformed officer in the passenger seat. "It's okay," I said to my dog's low growl. *Please don't bark and wake up Mike.*

Two men got out of the car. One was dressed in a detective's business suit and tie, and the other was in uniform. They walked up, knocked, and the detective pressed his creds against the window beside the door.

"One second," I said. I unclipped my gun and put it on the side table. "Come in. My gun is on the side table."

Cops are nervous around guns except for their own. The two men stepped inside the door, glanced at the gun, then saw Luke. Their eyes widened.

"He's okay."

They took my word for it.

"I'm Jessica Cooper. Come in. Would you like some coffee?"

I led them to our farm table. The uniform cop's utility belt squeaked as he moved, a sound I both remembered and liked.

I poured us all coffee, put cream and sugar on the table, and sat down with them. I gave each of them a business card, and asked for theirs. The cop gave me his name and badge number, which I wrote down on a notepad. Then they started asking questions. How did I know Brett? What was I investigating? When's the last time I had contact with him? And on and on it went.

I've rarely had a more surreal night. Awakened from a dead sleep, now here I was, sitting across the table from two cops talking about Brett Hudgins's murder.

"I warned him," I said to the cops. "I told him it wasn't safe there. I told him to leave. He said that the townhouse is where Brittany wanted to come." I shook my head. "He was a smart man, but she was like a drug to him."

"And where were you tonight between the hours of six and ten?"

I raised my eyebrows. Were they seriously thinking of me as a suspect? "Right here on the farm. In the barn feeding the horses, in the house feeding my son, then sitting in the living room reading C. S. Lewis after Mike went to bed."

"Is there anyone who could vouch for you?"

"Above the age of two, no." I shook my head, a little frustrated. "Look, I had no reason to kill Brett. I liked the guy. I felt sorry he was so ... so trapped by his wife's problems." I tapped the table.

"When you say you 'liked the guy...'"

"It was strictly a professional relationship."

"Are you married?"

"Yes."

"Is your husband at home?"

"He's out of town, over on the Eastern Shore, and he left early this morning." I looked from one to the other. "Anything else?" They didn't respond. "I didn't have anything to do with Brett's death, and neither did my husband. Brittany was mixed up with some awful people. Violent people.

"Here's what I'm concerned about." I tapped the table for emphasis. "Those girls. Brittany lost custody of them after making some really poor parenting decisions. Brett thought she was bipolar and needed help. I thought she was under the influence of drugs. That she was addicted, and her supplier was using her. Now, is her dealer also planning to use those girls? *That's* what I'm concerned about!" I leaned toward them. "And you should be too."

The detective pushed his chair back. "Our job is to find out who killed Hudgins."

I stared at them.

And that's it. They left.

36

JESS

I spent the rest of the night obsessing about Nora and Ava. I went over my notes. I emailed Brett's lawyer, the guy who'd hired me originally, and expressed my concerns. Then I emailed John Welsh and filled him in.

I read online about drugs and trafficking in Northern Virginia. I already knew this much: There was a time when if a teenaged girl ran away a parent might worry she would get hooked up with a less-than-desirable boyfriend. In comparison, those were innocent days. These days, if a girl fell into the wrong hands, she could be videoed, threatened with being exposed online, and forced into prostitution. Trafficked.

Oh, Brett. You were supposed to protect your girls, not sacrifice them to your own foolishness!

I sketched out ideas about searching for the girls. I made lists of things I could do once Scott got home to take care of Mike. I drank the rest of the coffee. I tried to read but the words just swam around on the page. I prayed, yes, I prayed as hard as Nate would for those girls.

Around 4:00 a.m. I suddenly had a thought. Had I asked

Brett for the phone number for Nora's watch? Even if I didn't, I knew I had Brett's phone number, so would his service provider give me the watch number?

I started searching through my notes on his case. A lot were on my laptop, more were in notebooks and file folders. Some were in my phone. I'm not the neatest detective. While I was searching for the number, I started making a list of facts about the girls. Names, ages, where they went to school, grades, friends, hair color, distinguishing features, and so on—anything I could remember and anything in my notes.

Then I made a fact sheet on the case. The lawyer who hired me. Where I met Brett. How I went about working it. The yoga studio where I attached the tracker to Brittany's car. The type of car she drove. The car Brett drove. The address of the Section 8 apartments where the girls had been taken and where Brett rescued them. The address of the "office" in Alexandria where Brittany visited. Detail after detail in two quick reference sheets.

Then, the names of the investigators I'd worked with. The name of the judge. Brett's father's name. And a description of Glowering Man.

I'd left out one critical point—the discovery of the tracker on my Jeep. That twisted my stomach, thinking of it now. Why hadn't we pursued that more vigorously? I tightened my jaw and added it to the list anyway.

I sent my lists to two people—John Welsh and Frank Sinclair, the lawyer who'd first hired me to help Brett Hudgins. As an afterthought, I also sent a copy to Scott. Maybe he'd be able to use it to put a fire under the agents looking into that group.

By 5:00 a.m. I had a plan. First thing, I wanted to get that pony feed for Scott, so whatever I got involved in later, the pony wouldn't starve. The feed store opened at eight. Before that, I'd feed the horses, Luke, and Little Mike. We'd be at the feed store when it opened. Come home. And then I'd make my phone calls, first to Scott, then to John Welsh, the lawyer, and maybe even to the Charlottesville police chief.

Somebody needed to find those girls.

MY PLAN SET and my lists sent, I sat down in the recliner to rest a little. Luke had been following me around all night, lying near me, dozing, sometimes whimpering and huffing his way through a dream. I always wondered what he was chasing or searching for in those dreams. Dogs are so funny.

I had the baby monitor near me but I didn't need it. As soon as Little Mike's feet hit the floor, Luke leaped up and started for the stairs. Mike was in a big-boy bed now, and once he was awake, he was on the loose, and there was no more rest for the weary.

We went through our usual routine. I changed Mike's pants, dressed him in daytime clothes, and together we fed Luke. I gave Mike breakfast and made three eggs for myself, because who knows what I was going to get into later. I needed the protein. We fed the horses, then I told Mike we were going to the feed store.

That was fine with him! He loved that place. There were so many interesting things to look at, from bits and bridles to hoof picks, dog beds, grooming supplies, buckets, and sometimes baby chickens.

We could even take Luke with us into that store, but this time, when Mike asked, I told him no. Luke would stay at home. I'm not even sure why I made that decision. Maybe it was because I wanted to keep a straight-arrow focus on my plan. That would be hard enough with a two-year-old in tow. Add in a dog and it might derail me. Or maybe I was just tired.

We arrived at the store just as it opened. I found the pony feed, no problem. Scott had asked me not to tell Mike about the pony, so I just said it was a special kind of horse food. We explored the store a little. Mike fingered the bridles, pointed to a hoof pick, and laid his face down on a saddle blanket. Then we went to the dog section, where he suggested we buy Luke a new bowl (I said no), and then some dog treats. I said yes and added those to our cart.

I guided us toward the checkout. At 8:20 a.m., we left the store and walked back out to the van. I remember so clearly what a beautiful day it was. The sky was impossibly blue, cloudless and clear, without the usual midsummer haze. A wonderful day to be outside, playing in the yard, while waiting for Scott.

I opened the sliding door, set Mike inside, and told him to climb into his car seat while I loaded the bag of feed into the cargo area and closed the liftgate. Mike put on his safety straps. He asked to hold Luke's treats, so I handed them to him.

"Daddy's coming home today," I told Mike as I buckled him up. "He's bringing a surprise." I snapped the last buckle shut. "I'll put the cart back, and then we'll go home and see Luke."

I hit the van's "door close" button, opened the driver's door, and tossed my purse into the front seat. Then I closed the door and turned toward the cart. I heard a sound behind me. My heart jumped. Then I felt a gun on my neck.

Men speaking Spanish surrounded me, grabbed me. My adrenaline surged. Instinctively, I yelled, dropped low, threw my elbow back, twisted, and turned. I hit "lock" on the key fob and threw it as hard as I could, into the retention pond next to where I was parked.

Whoever this was might take me. They were not taking Mike.

One second later I was down on the ground, face in the asphalt, someone's heavy weight on my back.

37

SCOTT

Scott checked his watch. Nine-fifteen. A little later than he wanted, but they'd had a great breakfast, with strong coffee and good conversation. The time spent was worth it. They'd still get home in midafternoon in plenty of time for Mike to see the surprise he was bringing him.

He tried calling Jess to tell her they were just about to load the pony. Across from him, Nate and Henry leaned on a fence, looking out over a field full of horses, still talking. Was there anybody Nate couldn't talk to? He said the most interesting things, but somehow, he never made himself the center of attention.

No answer on Jess's phone. She was probably in the middle of something. She'd call him back. She always did.

He was sliding his phone in his pocket when it signaled another call. *Jess.* No. A different number. He didn't recognize it. "Hello?"

"Mr. Cooper?"

His heart rate accelerated. "Yes."

"This is Deputy Thomas Graves, Madison County Sheriff's Department."

What happened? Jess? Are they ... "Yes?"

"Sir, a citizen reported a child locked in a van and in distress. We got him out and he's fine, but sir, we believe he may be your son."

"Mike? Where is this? Where's my wife?" Scott looked up. Nate stared at him.

"It's in the parking lot of Madison Feed and Supply. We tracked the license plate to you, sir. As I said, the boy is fine. The clerk inside said Mrs. Cooper purchased horse feed at 8:16 a.m. this morning, sir."

"What happened to her?"

"We don't know. We're checking security camera footage now, sir."

"She wouldn't have left him. She would never have left him in that van alone. Not for a second." Scott ran his hand through his hair. Nate walked toward him. Henry followed. "Look, I'm like five, six hours away, over on the Eastern Shore. Can I reach you on the number you're calling from?"

"Yes, sir."

"I'll get back as quickly as I can. The sheriff knows us. Tell him about this. Call me as soon as you guys know anything. I'm with the FBI. If she doesn't turn up quickly, the bureau will get involved."

"Yes, sir."

"Where is my son now?"

"We're still at the feed store. I've called CPS."

Scott's heart did a double beat. *CPS? For Mike?* "Can I have a friend pick him up?"

"Yes, sir."

"Okay. It'll be Ellen Davidson. I'll call her now. She lives in that area. Thank you, deputy. If Ellen's not available, I'll call our pastor." He clicked off his phone, fear and anger stiffening every muscle in his body.

"What?" Nate asked.

He told them.

"That don't sound right," Nate said.

"I need to call Ellie to get Mike. Then I need to get a hot ride back."

"Is this 'bout that lawyer?" Nate asked.

"I don't know. Let me call Ellie." A few minutes later, Scott clicked off his phone and said, "She's going to get Mike. Now, I just need to get home."

"Don't the FBI have choppers?" Nate asked.

They did. Scott called his boss. Five minutes later, Scott hung up and told Nate and Henry, "He's trying to arrange for a ride. Meanwhile, he's also calling the agents who were working to identify that tracker on her Jeep."

"No way would she have left Mike," Nate said, repeating what they all knew.

"What can I do?" Henry said.

"I don't know."

"Want me to drive the pony to your farm?"

Scott shook his head. "I may not have time to acclimate him right now."

Henry nodded. "I can drive him up there later, when things settle down. Let me go tell Julia what's going on."

"Tell her I'm sorry, but we do want him. Just not ..." he hesitated, his voice catching.

"Scott!" Nate said. His tone made Henry stop and turn around. Nate put his hand on Scott's arm. "This ain't no surprise to God. He's still in charge."

A nod was all the agreement Scott could muster right then.

Henry came back. "Julia's cool with it," he said. "You can get the pony whenever."

"Hold on, hold on, hold on," Scott said. He stared at his

phone. "Look at this!" He turned the phone around, but neither Henry nor Nate could really read what was on the screen. "At 4:27 a.m. this morning, Jess sent me an email with an attachment. Brett Hudgins was found murdered."

"The lawyer?"

"Right! Man! She's documented everything!" He looked up at Henry. "Does Julia have a printer?"

"She must. Come on!"

She did. Scott forwarded the email to her and in short order, the three men were standing around, each staring at his own copy. "I've got to send this to my boss," Scott said. "This is gold." He pulled his phone out, sent the email, then called his boss to alert him.

"So this dude Brett gets back with his ex and goes to her house. Jess tells him to get out of there, then he ends up dead." Henry looked up from the paper, his eyes wide. "Man!"

"And now his girls are missin', plus Jess," Nate said. "That ain't good."

Scott came back to the group. "He's taking the ball and running with it—straight to the assistant director. He's still trying to get a chopper."

Henry spoke up. "You know you can charter a private jet in Salisbury. My dad's done it."

"How much does that cost?"

"Not as much as you'd think. A couple thousand?"

"Worth it," Scott and Nate said together.

"Let's go!" Henry said.

"Nate, will you drive my truck and the trailer back?"

"Let's get them later. I want to go with you. We can split the cost."

"Why don't you leave the truck and trailer here?" Julia said. She'd been standing in the room and heard everything. "I've got plenty of room."

Scott nodded. "Okay! Thank you."

"I want to come," Henry said suddenly.

The other men looked at him.

He checked his calendar app. "Wait, I can't. I gotta work."

Nate grinned. "Don't worry, boy. You'll have another chance at a Cooper Family Adventure. Trust me. They come around pretty reg'lar."

"Let me drive you to the airport," Henry said. "I can get you there fast. All the cops know me." He grinned. "Let's go! You can call on the way up and book a flight."

38

JESS

I spent a long time—one hour, two?—in the trunk of that vehicle obsessing about who had me and why, and, most of all, about Mike locked in that van.

Someone would see him, right? Surely someone would notice him and rescue him! Before the van got hot?

I could only hope. And pray.

Finally, hands tied behind my back, I was hauled from the vehicle I was in, marched into a building, taken up in an elevator, and thrown into a room. My captor shoved me, and I slammed against a hard piece of furniture and fell to the floor. When I was able to sit up, I rubbed my face against the bedcovers next to me and worked the mask off one eye.

I was in a small bedroom. Shocked, I saw I had roommates. Nora and Ava.

The two girls, dressed in pajamas, sat huddled together on a bed, their backs against the wall, their eyes closed. They didn't say anything. They didn't move. I wondered if they were drugged.

As I looked at them, I felt a wave of sorrow. Their dad, who I actually liked, was dead. Their mother was, well, out of control. Who knows what these men were planning to do with those girls!

I tightened my jaw. I was going to save them. I prayed, right there and then, that God would let me do it.

I had a boatload of problems to overcome. First, there were the men I could hear shouting in Spanish in the other room. Second, we were trapped in a bedroom with just one small window. It had two beds, a small dresser, and dirty wall-to-wall carpeting. Third, my watch and my phone were both missing. Fourth, my hands were tied behind my back.

Would the girls cooperate with me or were they too traumatized? Why was I here? Why had they tracked me down and grabbed me? If they wanted to silence me, why hadn't they just killed me right there in front of my son?

Sadness washed through me as I thought of Little Mike's scared face. I squeezed my eyes shut against it. I'd done what I could to keep him safe, I told myself. He's in God's hands. Still, my mama's heart ached.

Scott. He'd be so angry, furious, not at me, but at these men who dared touch me. His search for me would be intense. I knew that. "I'm alive," I whispered. "Scottie, I'm alive. Come find me."

My head hurt. I tasted blood on my lip. Those guys had roughed me up. I had to figure a way out for all three of us. Before anything worse happened.

There was a small window in the room, but we were up on the third or fourth floor of an apartment building. No way to climb down outside. Or was there?

I forced myself to my feet and made my way to the window. I scraped the mask away from both eyes and peered out. A sheer drop. Four floors. No balconies, no fire escape, not even a drainpipe to climb down.

The second bed in the room had a sheet on it. A white

sheet. Could I hang that out of the window? Like what you do when your car breaks down?

No. The bad guys might see it and retaliate. Plus, no way could I open the window with my hands behind my back.

I sat down on the second bed to think. I looked at the drugged or sleeping girls. Nora's watch. Where was Nora's watch? If I had that, I might be able to make a call or, at the very least, fake a fall and let it call 911. I peeked around the girls. It was not on Nora's arm.

What stuff did they have with them? Backpacks? Suitcases? What?

I looked around them. Nothing. The small dresser stood below the window. Standing with my back to it, I eased open the drawers one by one, turning around to look at each drawer. They were all empty. I carefully closed the last one.

I heard a noise in the hallway. Someone was coming!

I dove back to the place they'd thrown me and pretended to be out cold. I heard the door open. Heard breathing. Then the door shut again.

I stayed still for what felt like forever.

I was just about to move when I heard quick footsteps. The door flew open and Brittany strode into the room, her hair disheveled, her face twisted in rage. She attacked me, kicking me over and over. Pulled me up by my hair. Threw me on the bed. Jerked me around.

A cold chill ran through me. Her eyes looked demonic.

Greater is he who is in me—

"How dare you!" she screamed.

I blinked. "What? How dare I what?"

She slapped me hard across the face and cursed me.

My heart beat hard. "Brittany!" I said sharply. "What's wrong with you?"

"You wanted him, didn't you? And when you couldn't have him, you killed him!"

"Wanted who? Brett? No way! No way, Brittany!"

She wasn't listening. She put her hands on either side of my head and raked her sharp fingernails down my face. I twisted away from her, blood seeping from those wounds.

"Mama?"

She whipped around and pointed her finger at Ava. "You... you... Julio!" A small, mousy man responded to her summons. He had a syringe in his hand. She pointed to Ava.

The little girl began to cry. He gave her a shot.

"And her."

He turned to me. A different needle. Bigger.

Just then, someone else stepped up behind Julio.

I saw Brittany's face fill with fear. Her eyes widened. She looked away quickly and slithered out of the room.

The man stepped out of the shadows. My heart jumped. The Glowering Man!

"Yes, *jefe*?" Julio said.

Jefe. Boss. I stood. His dark eyes ranged over me. I felt a chill run down my spine. *Greater is he who is in me ... greater is he ...* I straightened my back and set my jaw. "What do you want with me?" I asked.

The surprise on his face spoke volumes to me. He wasn't used to women speaking up.

I tossed my head. "Why did you bring me here?"

He moved closer. I could smell alcohol on him. Whiskey maybe. "You block me," he said, his voice low and threatening. He was a good bit taller than me, but not as tall as Scott. He was lean and fit, with high cheekbones and a low brow. He might have been considered handsome but for the evil he projected.

I had a running prayer going on in my mind: *Oh God!* Fear swept over me. My head started spinning. This man. I was at the mercy of this man! My very soul trembled. All my bones shook.

I felt like I was going to pass out. Then Glowering Man

turned his attention to the girls. He walked toward them, lying helpless on the bed. Nora's pajama top had risen up, exposing her belly. He looked them over ... like ... well, I didn't like the way he was looking at them.

Something happened inside me. A shift in my thinking. Because of this man, Brittany was hooked on drugs. Brett was dead. Now Nora and Ava—who knew what could lie ahead for them?

I hated the thought of that. I had to do something.

"I blocked you?" I said, drawing his attention away from the girls. "From what?" Glowering Man turned around. "What did I block you from? Abusing women and children? Getting access to these girls?"

His eyes glittered, fueled by the anger just beneath his skin. He took a step toward me and slapped me, hard. My head twisted. My lip split against my teeth and once more I tasted blood.

I turned back to him. "Is this how you prove your manhood? Hitting a woman whose hands are tied? It does kind of go along with abusing women and children. Is that because you can't go one-on-one with a man?"

Julio's eyes widened. He took a step back.

I kept going. "What's your name anyway? Or do you just go by 'boss'?"

He grabbed me by the throat and shook me like a cat shakes a mouse. My vision grew dark. I couldn't breathe!

Then suddenly he let go. My throat expanded. I gasped for air, choking and coughing, spit and blood stringing toward the floor.

I gathered myself together. I used my shoulder to wipe spit off my mouth. I faced him again. "Look, jefe. You can keep Brittany. You've ruined her anyway. I don't know where we are. I don't know who you are. I can't turn you in. Let us go. Me and the girls. We are nothing to you. Let us go."

A dark smile spread across his face. "Oh, you are not nothing." He jerked his head toward the girls. "And they, they are much more." He looked at Julio and jerked his head toward me.

Julio moved swiftly, and before I knew it, I was on the bed. "No," I whispered, "no." I tried to pull away.

The needle plunged into my arm.

39

SCOTT

Scott's chartered jet flew them to Stafford Airport, just south of Quantico. After they landed, Nate rented a car and headed for the Coopers's farm. He told Scott he'd be back with Luke, and when Scott asked him why, he said, "'Cause I'm the dog man. It's what I do."

A young FBI agent, dispatched by Scott's boss, picked Scott up. He was supposed to take him to Quantico, but Scott had found out the search headquarters would be in Alexandria. So he talked the kid into taking him there.

On the drive up, Scott called Ellie to check on Little Mike. "He's a little weepy," she told him, "but don't worry. We'll take good care of him."

He also called Henry to thank him for the suggestion to charter the jet. "Less than fifty minutes," Scott told him. "It was great."

"So what happens next?" Henry asked.

"The bureau is assembling a CARD team," he told him, "a Child Abduction Rapid Deployment team. It has a boatload of agents, some profilers, technicians who can track cell phones, computer techs, evidence techs, and a lot of state and local law enforcement officers."

"Child abduction? What about Jess?"

"Once they realized the two cases were related, it made sense to combine them. They'll work them both together."

"Do you have any idea who's involved?"

"We have security cam video of the guy in the courtroom at Brett Hudgins's hearing. Jess didn't like the looks of him. The assistant director has lit a fire under the facial recognition people in West Virginia. Hopefully, we'll have a name soon."

"What about the tracker someone put on her Jeep?"

Scott's eyebrows raised. "No prints on it. They're trying to establish who bought units like that from the manufacturer. That can take a while. It's a Chinese company."

"Okay, well, update me when you have time. And if there's something I can do, let me know."

"Will do, Henry."

"Hey, I'm praying for y'all."

His eyebrows raised, Scott responded, "Thank you. That's exactly what we need."

After that call, Scott checked his watch. An hour to go. Traffic seemed to crawl on I-95. "This is why I didn't want to be stuck in Quantico," he said to the young agent.

"Yes, sir."

Nate should be at the farm by now. He'd already given permission for agents to go in and look for evidence on Jess's computer and pick up her hairbrush or toothbrush, so they could gather her DNA. And he'd told Nate to let them in if he was there.

The command center would be at the Alexandria Police Department headquarters. The new building, brick with an airy, glass atrium, stood near the Washington Beltway. As the young agent pulled into the parking lot, Scott said, "Just drop me off."

The guy glanced at him, but complied. "Yes, sir."

"Thanks for the lift." He grabbed his gear bags, went inside, showed his creds, and a sergeant directed him to the conference room, which would serve as the command center. Already the logistics team was there, running wires, setting up tables and computers, arranging whiteboards and projectors. He was staring at it all when a voice behind him pulled him out of his thoughts.

"Scott?"

He turned around to see a newer member of BAU approaching him. A tall, striking brunette, Special Agent Elizabeth Rodriguez always turned heads when she entered a room. "Elizabeth," he said, acknowledging her.

"It's just Beth. Might as well keep it short. We're working together on this."

He turned toward her, questioning.

"I'm your babysitter." She smiled. "Get used to it."

Scott rolled his eyes. By all rights, because he was personally involved, Scott shouldn't have been anywhere near the investigation. But he knew the most about the case Jess had been working, and he was, after all, an experienced, senior agent. Beyond that, he knew his boss figured a team of horses couldn't keep Scott away. Not with Jess missing.

"You're hard to catch." Beth said. "I was waiting for you at Quantico."

His jaw shifted.

"I'm here to protect the case," she said. "When we get these guys we don't want anybody getting off because we messed something up."

By "we" Scott knew she meant "he."

"I've arranged for motel rooms," she said, "in case this goes long."

"Let's hope it doesn't."

"From what the boss tells me, your wife is no shrinking violet. She's tough. She'll stay strong."

He nodded, his throat tight.

SCOTT TRIED TO KEEP BUSY, reading Jess's email over and over, trying to make connections. Formulate questions. Gradually, the room filled with agents and officers. Some Scott knew. Many he didn't.

At 1300 hours sharp, James Berkley, one of two case agents assigned to oversee the CARD team, convened the meeting. He began by giving a brief summary to bring everyone up to speed.

"At 2257 last night, residents of an upscale townhouse community in Charlottesville called 911 and reported hearing gunshots. Responding officers found the door to the residence standing open and Brett Hudgins dead from multiple gunshot wounds.

"The house belonged to the victim's ex-wife. Investigators found a paper in Hudgins's pocket with the name Jessica Cooper and a phone number written on it.

"Jessica, it turns out, is a private investigator, who had been working for Hudgins on a custody case. When police contacted her, she asked about the children, Nora age nine, and Ava age seven. When told they weren't in the townhouse, Jessica told police they might have been abducted by their noncustodial parent, their mother Brittany. She gave them the number of Brett's lawyer, who verified her concern at 0830 the next morning. Investigators then contacted state police, who issued an Amber Alert.

"Twenty minutes later, at 0850, a sheriff's deputy in Madison, thirty miles away from Charlottesville, responded to a 911 call from a citizen who'd found a young child alone and in distress in a locked van in the parking lot of a feed store. After extricating the child, the deputy talked to the checker in the store, who said the child had been in the store with his mother between eight and eight thirty. Security camera footage revealed her being abducted. The deputy called the sheriff and by 0920, state police were notified. No one at that point knew the two cases were connected.

"At 0940 that morning, FBI Special Agent Scott Cooper, who is Jessica's husband, received word that his son had been found alone in the van. He was in Accomack County, Virginia, on personal business. Knowing his wife would not willingly abandon their son, he called his boss. A few minutes later, he transmitted an email his wife had sent to him, Hudgins's lawyer, and to Alexandria Detective John Welsh.

"That email outlined the Hudgins's case, which Jessica had worked on, including recent developments and her concerns about the children. The email established the connection between her abduction and the kids' and gave us a path forward, which we are now pursuing.

"Let me introduce you to Special Agent Sherry Dickinson from the Washington office, who is my co-case agent. Sherry has already been working a case we believe is at the root of these abductions."

Agent Dickinson was a petite, bob-haired blonde whose no-nonsense personality came across right away. "Before I begin, Special Agent Cooper, would you like to say something?"

That surprised him, but Scott welcomed the opportunity. He strode up, took the mic, and said, "First off, I'm thankful for every one of you here. I know you will put your heart and soul into this case, just as if it were your own wife or your own children at the hands of these criminals. Anything you need to ask me, about my wife or anything else, feel free. I've been around a few years.

"I'll tell you this much, Jessica is strong. Smart. Fearless. And physically able to handle herself in a fight. She was a Fairfax homicide detective before I met her. She risked her life for me just last year. And you know what? She'd risk her life for you too. Let's find these guys. I want my wife back."

Scott's voice caught a little at the end, but he walked back to Beth with his head up, praying silently.

Agent Dickinson then briefed the crowd on the investigation into drug and human trafficking in the Alexandria location on King Street near the Potomac River. Dickenson then presented the evidence the team of FBI, DEA, and local police had developed. She outlined the methodologies of the group, the suspicion that the gang had moved into making adult videos using underage "actors" as well as some salacious websites. And she said, "We were just about to move on them when this latest development occurred."

The two co-case agents had already decided on the CARD team's first move. "We know," Agent Dickinson said, "that Brittany was with this group many times recently, and that she left her kids in this housing complex in Hybla Valley, south of the city." She had a map projected on the screen. "I've given you maps, and pictures of the girls and Mrs. Cooper, as well as pictures of the main players in this gang.

"We have surveillance teams on both locations. We also want a door-to-door search in both neighborhoods. I have given you a list of license plates on the vehicles they've been using as well as the prior addresses we have so far. Our drone team is already monitoring these places and the streets around them.

"As soon as we have warrants, we are going in. Let me remind you to consider these players desperate and therefore dangerous."

She looked up. "Tom, will you explain the software we'll be using to track leads?"

The computer expert, dressed in a gray suit and white shirt, stepped up and explained what they needed to know to access and use the lead tracker.

The district attorney assigned to the case spoke, then finally, assignments were passed out. Agent Berkely announced follow-up meetings at 2000 hours and 0800 every day. And then the meeting was over.

Scott approached Agent Dickinson. "Could I have a copy of your handouts?"

"Two copies, please." Beth had followed him.

Scott glanced at her. This was going to be annoying. He started looking at the documents while he walked away. Pictures, maps, drawings of the two locations, and profiles on the identified gang members. Which one was the guy Jess was concerned about?

"Agent Cooper?"

He looked up. An older man in a brown suit stood before him. He looked vaguely familiar.

"I'm Detective John Welsh, Alexandria police. My brother Brad worked with your wife last year."

"Oh, right! Brad! Yes, I've met him."

"When he found out what was going on, he said if I didn't volunteer he'd never speak to me again." The man grinned. "He's my older brother, so I've got to do what he says." He grew serious. "I was on it anyway. I met your wife. I like her. She handed me a ton of leads in that email. We will find her, Scott. I promise you that."

Scott nodded. "I'm glad you're here. Thank you."

"Here's my cell." Welsh handed Scott a business card. "If you need local knowledge, or anything else, call me anytime."

"Thank you."

As Welsh walked away, Scott simultaneously turned to Beth. "I need a bucar."

"I have a bucar."

"But..."

"I'll take you anywhere you want to go."

He grimaced, then tried to regroup. "Okay. I need a third room in the hotel, near me."

She raised her eyebrows.

"I have a consultant coming to help. Nathan Tanner. He's coming with Jess's search dog."

She raised her eyebrows more.

"You're going to have to trust me on this."

She shook her head, took a deep breath, and said, "Alright. I will."

When she walked away to arrange the room, Scott approached the tech guy. "Tom, I need a laptop and the password to the lead tracker."

Tom's gray eyes searched Scott's face. Then he nodded. "I'll hook you up. Give me a minute."

Having the computer kept Scott occupied. He could watch leads being posted, watch drone footage, and in general, keep up with the investigation. When Beth came back and saw it, she questioned whether him having a computer was a good idea, for his sake.

"Look. I want to be out there busting down doors and shaking down scumbags," Scott explained. "If I can't do that, at least I can track the progress."

She yielded. Plus she'd brought back food. A big, warm, steak-and-cheese sub. "Keep your strength up," she said. "You might need to bust heads tonight."

"Ours or theirs?" Scott said.

She smiled. "That remains to be seen."

40

SCOTT

The first action was set—twin raids on the gang's two known locations at 1800 hours, 6:00 p.m. Scott could hardly wait.

He'd asked Beth to take him to King Street, but she talked him out of it. "Let's stay here," she reasoned. "With the drone footage, we can watch them both go down."

That made sense, even to Scott.

THE RAIDS WENT DOWN SIMULTANEOUSLY, conducted by FBI SWAT teams and the Alexandria Police Department's Special Operations Team. Using drones and flashbangs and battering rams, they busted down doors and entered the buildings, ready to take into custody whoever was there.

Scott paced in the conference room and watched the reports come in. Empty. Both places were empty, of people anyway, which is all Scott really cared about.

He'd been hoping the "woman" the surveillance team had

been seeing at the apartment was Jess. It wasn't. In fact, nobody was there.

Which meant Jess wasn't there. She wasn't safe. She wasn't back with him.

He was beyond frustrated.

"Just wait," Beth said. "Let's see what the evidence teams come up with."

"I want her, not her DNA!" Scott thundered.

Beth didn't respond.

What's next? He started to walk toward the case agent, James Berkley, his pace reflecting his frustration.

Beth stopped him with a hand on his arm. "You'll be a lot less happy if you get kicked out of here."

He looked at her, hard, a thousand retorts running through his mind. Then he took a deep breath and ran his hand through his hair. "You're right." He saw the relief in her face. *What could he do?* Then her eyes shifted behind him. He turned to see James Berkley approaching.

"Scott?"

"Yes."

"Want to collaborate with us?"

"Yes, yes I do."

So the four of them sat down—Berkley, Dickinson, Scott, and Beth. Then a detective from Alexandria joined them. They got a break almost immediately. CJIS in Clarksburg confirmed the name of the Glowering Man Jess had seen in court. He was Emilio Lopez, the leader of the gang Agent Dickinson's group had been looking at.

That connected him with Brett Hudgins and with Jess. Lopez was in the courtroom when Jess testified in favor of Brett. That established Lopez's motive.

Dickinson briefed Scott on the basics of the joint Alexandria Police/FBI's investigation. Lopez, age thirty-nine, had a wife and four children in Mexico, but he was not shy about connecting with other women in the DC area. Four women admitted to having been in a relationship with him during the last five years. Three of them had complained about domestic assault when he lived with them. One admitted to participating in drug distribution and adult film production while dating him.

"Let's go after these women," Scott said. "They're probably scared of him, but a lot of times women will cooperate with us when they realize children are at risk."

"Right," Berkley said.

"I'm guessing there are more women out there who've had dealings with him," Scott said. "Where is he finding them? Bars? Social clubs? Dating apps? And these other guys, where do they live?"

"Most are living together in one apartment over in this area," Dickinson pointed to public housing in Alexandria.

"Do we have eyes on that place?" Scott asked.

"Yes, we do."

"Talk to the women who live around them. They're living like a bachelor herd, and I'm betting they've been on the hunt." He ran his hand through his hair. "What about license plate readers?"

"Yes. We have them and we're watching for the plates we know about. But we just got a report of plates stolen off a car in long-term parking at Reagan National. So, we've got those plates in the system on the hot list."

"We seized computers at the King Street location," Berkley said, "as well as cameras and recording equipment. We have techs going through them now."

Scott tapped his thumb on his leg. "Lopez will run."

"Why's that?" Dickinson asked.

"We've interrupted a major part of his money-making operation. Two arms, right? Drugs and women. Plus the films, so three. He's got the drugs somewhere else. Plus a stash of money.

Where is that? Because he'll make a move to collect them and run."

"Without his guys?"

Scott waved a hand. "They're expendable. Do you know where the drugs and money are?"

"No."

"Maybe a storage facility?" Beth suggested.

"Are all the women past tense?" Scott asked.

"Yes."

Scott's jaw shifted. "He's got another one. He's got a new woman somewhere, and she's holding them for him."

"He's got Brittany."

Scott shook his head. "He just used her. He doesn't want her. Maybe he just wanted the girls."

That thought made everyone flinch.

"We need to get eyes on him. And his gang members."

Silence.

"Go out on the street and round up some junkies," Scott said, continuing. "See if any of them will play with us. Offer them cash. Tell them he's about to go down. See if they'll give us anything on him. Second, go to some bars and talk to the bartenders. They know everything. Third, are there any storage facilities owned by members of the community? Find out, because he'd probably rent from someone who at least speaks Spanish."

Unable to remain seated any longer, Scott stood. "We need to turn this town upside down and look under every mattress," Scott said, "or wait for this guy to make a mistake. I'm big on mattress-turning."

41

JESS

When I awoke later, the room was darker. How long had I been out? I didn't know. Groggy and nauseated, I forced myself to my feet. Drugs. How I hate drugs.

I could not let that happen again, I told myself. No way. No more drugs.

My stomach churned. I turned away and threw up.

Someone was playing music in the other room. I heard laughing and loud joking. I heard bottles and glasses clinking.

Scottie, where are you?

I closed my eyes and prayed, my face stiff with dried blood.

I lost consciousness again. When I came to, the other room was quiet. Were they sleeping? Could I sneak out?

I crept over to the door and turned around to put my hand on the knob. The door opened a crack. I heard voices. Apparently, not everyone was asleep.

I quietly closed the door. Discouraged, I sat down again and forced myself to think. How could I escape?

I didn't see any options. I couldn't go out of the window. I couldn't go through the door. What else was there? Helplessness and panic grabbed me. I trembled in fear.

Desperate, I prayed. My mouth was dry, my tongue thick. I was thirsty, hungry, and oh, I wanted to get back home! I slumped down onto the floor, my back against the wall, my head drooping.

I begged God to help me. I bargained with him, promising a deeper walk, a greater obedience, if he'd just get me out of here. I started to cry.

Then I stopped myself. *Don't be stupid. He already loves you with an eternal, everlasting, steadfast love. You can't earn more.*

Then I remembered something Nate told me. *The walk of faith is a walk into death. Dying to self, living for Christ. Jesus wants all of you, all your life, everything.*

I'd had a lot of deep conversations with Nate, especially after his beloved Laura was killed. Even Nate had to learn more about dying to self and about God's sovereignty—and his love.

My favorite quote from The Heidelberg Catechism popped into my head. *What is your only comfort in life and in death?* I could use some comfort right now, I thought. *What is your only comfort in life and in death? That I am not my own, but belong, body and soul, in life and in death, to my faithful Savior, Jesus Christ.* Body and soul. In life and death.

I took a deep breath and settled myself. I reminded myself what I believed. I gave up control, not to Glowering Man, but to God. He knew where I was. He could save me—or not.

I prayed, whispering my words. "God, if you want me to die here, so be it. I want to live, but I release it all—my life, my son, my husband," I caught a sob in my throat. "Nate, Luke, everyone I love, to you." A shiver went through me.

"Use this day to shape me into the image of Christ. Help me to love you the way Jesus loves you and help me to trust you with all that I am. But please, please, please don't let those men harm these girls!" Tears streamed down my face.

I got hold of myself again, blotting my face on my sleeve. "God, if you will allow me to live, open my eyes and help me see the door out, the door back to life. I love you. I trust you. I put my life in your hands. Help me glorify you in the way that I live or in the way that I die. Help me walk out my faith. Help me run the race and finish the course with joy. And help me save those girls!"

My own bold prayer actually encouraged me. I felt a deep calm come over me.

Trying to sustain that calm, I imagined myself back at home, sitting in the recliner. I saw in my mind the couch, the fireplace, Mike's toys at the end of the room. I was sitting in the recliner reading ... what was I reading? Oh, yes, C. S. Lewis's *Surprised by Joy.* I forced myself to remember it, trying to ground myself in what was real. Lewis would say Heaven is more real than anything on earth, but I couldn't imagine that as easily so I stuck to the reality I did know.

In the book, Lewis describes his childhood in Northern Ireland, with his brother Warnie. He talked about the little garden Warnie made in the lid of a biscuit tin and how that was his first taste of beauty. Nate told me that beauty was a key to finding God.

Lewis described exploring the house his father had bought. The house was big, with long corridors ... lots of books ... and sunlit rooms.

My heart quickened. *Oh, what I wouldn't give for a sunlit room!*

I allowed myself to dream. I wondered if we could build a sunroom on the east side of our house, a place where I could greet the sunrise each day, a cup of coffee and my Bible in my hands.

I stayed with that idea for a while, imagining the beauty of it, the peace.

What else did Lewis describe in his father's house?

Gurgling pipes. And attics. There were attics to explore, which gave him hours of pleasure.

My heart thumped. *Attics!*

I knew I was on the top floor. Did apartment buildings have attics? Certainly they must have at least space to run pipes. Was there an attic above this apartment and was there access to it?

I had to unbind my hands to explore that. Absolutely had to.

I got up. I felt around the room in the dark, mostly using my feet, searching for anything, any edge I could use to cut myself loose. I tried the edge of the metal bedframe. That didn't work. I found some debris under the second bed but nothing that would help. Then I started searching under the bed the girls were on. Ava woke up. "What ... are you doing?" she whispered, staring down at me. She yawned.

"Looking for something to cut my hands free," I whispered back.

Bless her, she slid off the bed and crawled under it. She emerged several minutes later empty-handed. Inspired, though, by her efforts, I tried quietly scooting the small dresser away from the wall. She crawled back there. She found a small sock, some paper, used tissues, and then, holding up a small pair of fingernail scissors, she said, "Would this work?"

"Good girl!" I said. "Can you cut these ties?"

She nodded. I turned and felt her touching the plastic zip ties that bound me.

It took a long time, but that girl kept at it. Then suddenly, my hands were free!

Oh, that felt good! I rubbed my wrists and gave her a hug. "Thank you!"

Nora began to stir. "What's—"

"Shh," I cautioned. "Be real quiet."

"I need to pee," she whispered.

"Use the bucket," Ava said.

The bucket?

"In the closet."

What closet?

When Nora was finished, I found the closet, which I hadn't noticed before, that held the bucket. It was so dark! But when I looked up, I saw something. A square, framed. And I knew, that was my attic access. *Thank you, Jesus!*

"Girls, girls, come here!" I said motioning them close. "Look up. See that square? It's a way out. It'll be dark and it may be scary, but it is a way out of this room. Do you know what's going to happen if that man, Julio, comes in again?"

"Shots."

"That's right."

"They make me feel sick," Nora said.

"And sleepy," Ava chimed in.

"Right. I don't want that anymore. I'm getting out of here. Now here's the deal. I can go alone and bring someone back to save you, but that man may come in again before I can get back. Or you can come with me. You'll have to be very brave and very quiet."

"It's like going through the wardrobe," Ava said.

I blinked. "What?"

"In that book, *The Lion, the Witch, and the Wardrobe,*" Nora explained.

"Daddy read it to us," Ava said.

Bless him!

"Mommy's turned into the White Witch," Ava said, continuing.

"Ava!" Nora said. "Stop."

"She's mean!"

I hushed them again. "We can talk about that later. Right now, you need to decide. Do you want to wait here or come with me into the attic? Yes, it'll be just like going through the wardrobe into Narnia. There may be scary things, but it'll be an adventure."

The younger one, Ava, spoke first. "I want to go home. So I want to go with you. Even if it is scary."

I nodded. "Nora?"

She pressed her lips into a straight line. "I'll go. I'm afraid, but I'm scared here too. So I'll go."

"You are good, brave girls."

"Like Susan and Lucy." Ava looked up at me. "Can we pretend we are going through the wardrobe and Aslan will come and find us?"

Tears sprang to my eyes. I smiled. "Yes, honey. We most certainly can. And I believe he will. Let's go!"

42

JESS

The only attic I'd ever crawled through before was the one in my mother's house in Burke, where I spent my teen years. We kept Christmas decorations up there, and it was always my job to get them down in November and put them back up when the holidays were over.

I knew there should be boards to walk on and that deviating from that path could send you right through the drywall that formed the ceiling of the top floor.

I warned the girls to stay on the boards and hoisted them up into the attic of the apartment building. They were troupers and did exactly what I'd asked.

There were shelves built into the closet. I used those to climb up to the attic hatch. Thankful for the upper body workouts I got rock climbing, I managed to get myself into that dark space as well, although I did partially dislodge one of those shelves in the process.

I don't know what I was expecting to find. A window? A door out to the roof?

Logically, there should have been firewalls between the

units. There weren't. Anyone could do what we did and have access to any other apartment through the hatches. Should I try to drop in to someone else's apartment and get help?

No. First things first. Get far away from those men.

There was equipment up in the attic, HVAC maybe, and other equipment, with tiny little operating lights that gave me just enough light to see. There was also a path, three one-by-six boards side-by-side to walk on. But if you lost your balance or tripped or got dizzy, you could easily fall through someone's ceiling.

I just didn't want it to be Glowering Man's.

I replaced the hatch we'd just come through and whispered to the girls. "Walk as far from here as we can. Don't hurry. We don't want to fall." Ava, the first one through the hatch, would lead. There was no way to get around each other to change positions.

They crept silently down that path, holding on to rafters on the slanted part of the roof when they needed to balance. In the middle, I could see some heavy equipment. When we got closer, I realized it was the elevator.

Just past the elevator, Ava stopped quickly and gave a little scream. It made my heart race. "What?" I whispered. But then I saw what—mice. There were mice in the attic. Nora started to cry, then turned toward me like she wanted to go back.

"Shh. Nora, stop. We're going on." They didn't move. I tried again. "Girls, listen. Those are very friendly mice. I think I saw Reepicheep." Ava giggled. "Keep going. They'll scamper away from you."

"I c...c...can't," Nora said.

"Yes, you can. You are Susan, Queen of Narnia. And you can do this!"

Slowly, we began to move forward again. I counted eight hatches, eight apartments, and then we reached the end. I thanked God for whoever had not installed firewalls in this place!

At the end was a door. Ava turned around and looked at me. "Open it," I whispered.

She did, and we found it was a utility room of sorts, some kind of maintenance or mechanical closet with a metal ladder fixed to one wall. We stepped inside the small space. "We're going to go down. Can you do it?" Both of them nodded yes. "Let me lead," I whispered. I guess I thought I might be able to catch them if they started to fall. "Should be just four floors."

Just as I was closing the door to that closet, I heard a loud noise. The elevator was moving. Had they found out we were gone?

I couldn't do anything about that. I got in front and went down one flight to an identical closet with an identical door. The girls followed. Two more flights, and we were on the ground floor. There was another door. Unlocked. I quietly opened it a crack. And I saw grass! Trees! Sky! All robed in darkness studded by streetlights.

I closed it again and said to the girls, "This door goes outside. I can see a bunch of trees, like woods, across the lawn. We're going to make a run for it.

"If anyone starts to chase us, I'll try to hold them off. If we get separated, I want you to run as far from here as you can. Find somebody in uniform—a police officer, a fireman, a soldier, a nurse. Find a helper."

"Like Mr. and Mrs. Beaver," Ava said.

"Yes, just like Mr. and Mrs. Beaver. Find a helper like Mr. and Mrs. Beaver and ask them to help you."

"Got it," Nora said. Maybe her confidence in my crazy plan was growing.

. . .

It was one thing to crawl through an empty attic and quite another to go out into the dark, the two girls dressed in pajamas and barefoot, with a passel of scary men ready to grab us again. My gut was tight as a drum.

I opened the door just far enough to stick my face out and look around. I didn't see anyone. "Okay," I said to the girls, "we're going to walk very quickly. Don't run unless someone yells at us or comes out after us. Are you ready?"

They said they were. I breathed a silent prayer.

We walked out into the darkness. The air was cool and clean and I took deep breaths and felt grateful. Nora held one of my hands and Ava held the other. We walked steadily toward the trees, oaks they looked like in the dark. I could see houses well beyond them on another street. I guessed we were somewhere in south Alexandria, the Mount Vernon area or Hybla Valley, but I saw nothing distinctive that would verify our location.

We were about ten yards from the trees when I heard a shout. From a man. In Spanish. I glanced back and saw him coming around the building.

"Run!" I said to the girls, and I let go of their hands. "Run like the wind!"

Heart racing, I ran in the opposite direction, back toward the building. I pretended to stumble, acted like I was confused, and moved as if I was going to go around the other side of the building. I was so much closer to the man, he chose to chase me, not the girls. And that was my plan.

I put on speed and glanced back. The girls had disappeared into the dark woods. I dashed around the building. As I reached the front, two men came out.

Seconds later, I was on the ground, face in the asphalt. Again. *Run, girls, run!*

. . .

THEY SHOVED me into the trunk of a car. *Where were we going?* I thought about disabling the taillights, but with my hands, once again, secured behind my back, I couldn't manage it.

I tried, though, and I was still trying when the car stopped. The truck lid flew open, and I was marched into another apartment building, up an elevator, and into a different apartment, which looked, oddly, a lot like the other one, that is, disheveled. Cheap, hand-me-down furniture, and bottles and cups on the floor. Trash.

Brittany came in after me, along with two men.

I expected them to beat me. They did. I expected them to curse at me. They did that too. I was scared they'd rape me. They didn't.

Thank God.

They tied me to a chair at a small kitchen table. I was aching all over, thirsty and tired, and I wanted to go home. I let my head droop. It was about the only part of me I could control. Well, there was one more thing. My feet were tired of being in shoes. Under the table, I worked my shoes off. No one noticed.

And I prayed. These men couldn't take that away from me. My heart and my soul were free even though my body was tied up. I prayed for myself, for Scott, for Mike, and for those girls, with all my strength.

El Jefe was nowhere in sight. Brittany sprawled on a chair in the living room, and soon she was head back, snoring. The men, three of them, argued with each other.

I pretended to be less conscious than I was. Actually, every one of my senses was on high alert. I could feel their tension and smell their fear. I could see it in their eyes.

I sensed their problem. They'd lost the girls. They were afraid to leave me guarded by just one of them, but they'd need two to corral the girls.

Mostly, they were afraid of El Jefe.

Which is probably why they weren't touching me.

Scottie, where are you? Come find me.

43

SCOTT

"We've got the girls!"

Scott jumped to his feet. "What?"

"Nora and Ava, we've got them," Agent Dickinson said.

"How? Where?"

"An older woman in a house off Route 1. She was letting her dog out before going to bed when the girls came running up, asking for help. She took them in and called 911."

"Where'd they come from?" Scott asked.

"An apartment building nearby. They were a little confused about which building. It's a large complex, four stories, and they all look alike."

"What about Jess?" Scott's fists were clenched. If it had been good news he would have gotten it right away.

"We're going through the buildings now. The girls know they were on the top floor." Dickinson told Scott about the attic escape, and then about the race away from the building. "From what they're telling us, when the man started chasing them, Jessica acted as a decoy."

Of course she would. Scott shivered.

"She ran toward him, away from the girls, forcing him to decide who to chase. He chose Jessica." Dickinson touched his arm. "Your wife is very brave."

"I know," he said, his voice catching. "I know. But where is she?"

Dickinson started talking, something about checking for security cameras, but Scott's head was buzzing, and he thought he was going to throw up. He clenched and unclenched his fists. Finally, she stopped talking. "I want to talk to the girls," he said.

"That won't be possible. They're at the hospital."

"Look, it's my wife! I need to talk to them. Find out if she's hurt, if she's ... suffering. What they've done to her. I need to know what the girls know about Jess."

Dickinson looked at him. She hesitated, then said, "I'll have to ask the boss."

"C'mon, Scott. Let's get a drink," Beth said. "Tea, maybe."

He let her lead him to what passed as a break area, where coffee and tea, muffins and cookies had been set up. Food to keep people going.

He sat down in a chair while she made tea, his anger and fear throbbing in his head. And suddenly, he saw himself, sitting on the beach with Amanda after Henry got hurt. They'd been having a deep conversation and those were few and far between.

Henry's accident had scared her. They were talking about how love could be risky, but he was saying it was worth it. She wanted to know how people survived the loss of a partner. He could still hear her words.

But what if we all died? All at once? she had asked.

Even if everybody died, he'd responded, *I'd still have God. I would depend on him.*

Now this was his "even if" moment. Because Jess was everything to him. Yes, he had Mike. And friends like Nate. And

Amanda and Henry. But no one could replace Jess. If he lost her, could he truly depend on Jesus? Was Jesus enough for him to survive?

Beth came back with tea and a blueberry muffin. "Want to talk?" she said, scanning his face.

He shook his head.

She sat down with him and her own tea and muffin. "In English mystery novels, whenever something upsetting happens, they make the person a strong cup of tea with a lot of sugar. They probably have scones or 'biscuits' instead of muffins, but that's the best I could do."

Scott wrapped his hands around the paper cup, ignoring the chatter. The steam rose from the tea. It was somehow comforting. He looked up at Beth but couldn't hold her gaze.

"My friend Nate lost his wife and it nearly killed him. I just .. I just don't know if I'd survive if … if Jess is …"

Beth stopped him. "She isn't. She's going to make it. She's smart, resourceful, and we will find her."

Scott trembled.

Dickinson found them. "It's a hard 'no' Scott. They're protecting the girls. But John Welsh has permission to talk to them. I told him what you wanted to know."

Scott nodded. And he downed the hot cup of tea all at once. He had no stomach for the muffin.

44

JESS

Evening faded into night. It must be at least ten o'clock, I thought. The men were sitting around drinking beer. They'd ordered food from somewhere, burritos or something similar. The delivery guy had stood in the open door, with a clear view of me tied to that chair, and said nothing.

People! My dog has better instincts.

I amused myself by cataloging descriptions of the three men. I noted height, approximate weight, skin and eye color, all of which were about the same by the way. But the tattoos! Ah, now that was a gold mine for individual identification. Women's names. Slogans. Gang signs. Facial teardrops noting kills. Initiation markers. I memorized every one of them, attaching a name if I could.

Around ten twenty—I read Juan's watch upside down—the main guy's phone rang. He had a serious conversation with someone—short, terse sentences, quick responses. Then he said, "Yes, jefe. We will be there."

We were moving. Again.

They walked me into the elevator, into the darkened

parking lot, and into the back seat of the car, a gun in my ribs. They didn't notice I was in my sock feet. I counted that as a victory. Then Brittany was crammed in on the other side of me, her eyes rolling, unfocused, blocking me in.

Where's a cop when you need one?

Scorpion—he had one tattooed on the back of his neck and another one on his hand—drove us. I read the street signs. We were on King Street going south, past fancy shops and restaurants, headed toward the beltway.

They hadn't bothered to mask my eyes. They were going to kill me.

He turned off of King Street toward the Potomac. Soon I didn't know where I was. There was so much redevelopment. Tall townhomes, nice bars, and restaurants.

And then we turned. Into a park. Under the Wilson Bridge.

No one was around. I mean, no one. Not a jogger, not a dog walker, not a homeless person. And certainly not a cop.

White concrete arches supported the Wilson Bridge, which crossed the Potomac, connecting Virginia and Maryland, or maybe DC, I couldn't remember exactly where the line was. Oddly, I noticed how beautiful those arches were, how graceful. I'd never really noticed them before.

Brittany and Scorpion got out of the car. I saw her stumble as she walked.

With her gone, I could possibly have tried to escape on that side, but the gun in my ribs and the fact that my hands were tied kept me still. I leaned my head back.

We were waiting for someone. Who? El Jefe, I presumed.

Jets landed nonstop at Reagan National Airport, just upriver from us, probably by a mile or two. I began to count them, to focus on the sounds of their engines, to try to discern the differences in pitch and tone, as if learning about jets landing at Reagan was important at this stage of my life.

Doesn't anyone look out of the windows of a plane anymore? Long enough to see a single car in a darkened parking lot?

Meanwhile, Chain Man, who had a chain tattoo all the way up his right arm, emerging out of his collar and onto his neck, and Julio, talked quietly. Their voices sounded worried, although since they were speaking Spanish, I had no idea what they were saying.

One of them got a text. I heard it bing. And Julio said, "Let's go."

They dragged me out of the car. We walked toward the river, under the bridge. It's massive, by the way. The traffic overhead seemed as loud as the jets landing. *Where are all these people going so late at night?*

We passed Brittany, who was collapsed on the ground, weeping. *What's wrong with her?* I heard the response in my head. *No hope.*

She had no hope, no hope beyond this life, which she'd just about used up.

They took me down a gravel path, which, in my sock feet, hurt like crazy, but you know what? It was my hurt, one I'd selected, and so I embraced it. We walked under the bridge to a place full of weeds and some concrete slabs next to the water. Probably, I thought, an area prone to flooding.

They forced me out onto the slabs. I realized what they were going to do—shoot me and shove me into the river. Probably film it and send it to the FBI. I refused to imagine the impact on Scott.

I expected El Jefe to show up any moment.

To the left, upriver in the distance, I could see the Washington Monument. I think Washington, DC, is a gorgeous city, especially at night. Clean, white-marble monuments. Classic buildings. Beautiful.

To my right, on the Maryland side of the Potomac, was Washington Harbor, a relatively new development whose main feature was a fancy hotel and a big casino. Oh, and also one of those big "eye" Ferris wheels. And lots and lots of lights.

The sky was black, and although I could not see stars, the blinking lights of the planes and helicopters created their own display. The moon was up, a half-moon. My father had told me that in the Southern Hemisphere, the half-moon is lit on the other side. I don't know. I've never seen it.

He also told me about the Southern Cross, the beautiful constellation we can't see in the north.

There's a lot of things we can't see.

There was no boat traffic at this time of night. The Potomac stretched before me, black, empty, and probably cold, beautiful in its own way. A little breeze came from the south, ruffling my hair. It was refreshing.

As I stood there staring at it, quietly awaiting my own execution, I heard Nate's voice in my head from when we saved Jamie and Maddie from the flood. *When you pass through the waters, I'll be with you.* I took it then as both a prayer and a statement of faith.

When you pass through the waters, I'll be with you.

Like Noah in the ark. Like Moses in the basket. Like the children of Israel in the Red Sea. In my mind I went through God's faithfulness to his people.

When you pass through the waters, I'll be with you,

Then I remembered the next part: *and through the rivers they shall not overwhelm you.*

Like the Jordan River when they entered the Promised Land.

I started thinking, what if I just stepped off? Into the river? Why give Glowering Man the pleasure of killing me? Why not take my chances with God?

When you pass through the waters, I'll be with you, and through the rivers they shall not overwhelm you.

I'd been so quiet, Julio was getting sloppy about holding that gun on me. El Jefe was nowhere in sight. I could just jump.

I began to argue with myself. *But my hands are tied behind my back. I can't swim.*

So what? Flip on your back.

I could do that. But my shoes will weigh me down.

You took off your shoes!

Oh, right.

When you pass through the waters, I'll be with you, and through the rivers they shall not overwhelm you.

But what if I jumped and the river turned out to be, like, a foot deep? Too shallow? Is there current that will pull me away?

When you pass through the waters, I'll be with you, and through the rivers they shall not overwhelm you.

Where would I end up, even if I did survive? In the Chesapeake Bay? The Atlantic Ocean? How would Scott find me?

When you pass through the waters...

Over and over that phrase ran through my mind. Then I heard one of the men say, "He's here." And even though it was in Spanish, *El esta aqui*, I knew what he said.

I heard footsteps crunching on the gravel behind us.

I jumped.

45

SCOTT

"Gunfire! A lot of it," an officer sitting at a monitor said.

Scott jumped to his feet.

"Where?" James Berkely asked.

"South. Near the bridge. Hold on. Jones Point Park! Jones Point Park."

"Get a drone down there now. And let's roll! SWAT 2. This is yours."

Scott turned to Beth. "Let's go. I want to go."

"I don't think—"

"I'm going. Whether you take me or not." He slid into his vest and grabbed a water bottle. He stopped and looked at her. "You coming?"

She blinked and slid on her vest.

The radio in Beth's bucar narrated the story. Drone footage showed four men and a woman at Jones Point Park, under the Wilson Bridge. Then, *Officers under fire!*

"We're going nowhere near that," Beth said.

"Right."

The small road leading to the park was totally jammed with

law enforcement vehicles. Beth parked at the end of a long line and radioed their location.

Ten minutes later, the radio reported, "Drone indicates all five neutralized. Approach with caution."

"Will you ask Berkley to send me pictures of the woman?"

Beth nodded. "Good idea." She picked up her radio and made that request.

A few minutes later, Scott's phone indicated a message. He looked at the footage using the map light in the car. "Hard to see, it's so dark. Wait. No. That's not Jess! Definitely not Jess." And he was glad, because the woman definitely looked dead.

Beth relayed that information. "We'd like access to make a positive ID," she told the dispatcher.

"Roger that."

It took more than twenty minutes for the scene to be secured and permission granted for Scott to go in. He and Beth left her bucar and walked forward.

Two of the male suspects plus the woman were dead, their bodies fallen like weeds cut down by a scythe. Blood everywhere. Two were still alive, barely, and being attended by EMTs prior to transport.

"That's not Jess. So what happened to her? Did they have her? Where is my wife? I want to know before they take them away." Scott's hopes and fears swirled together in a toxic mix in his gut. His blood pressure soared.

"I'll ask."

Scott watched as she walked forward to the head of the SWAT team. He saw the guy shake his head, saw her body language as she pressed him for information, then she turned and motioned for Scott to hold fast. And she climbed into the ambulance.

Scott prayed.

He saw her emerge, go over to the SWAT team leader, then turn toward him.

He couldn't read her face. It was too dark. "You speak Spanish?"

"Yes. Walk with me," Beth said. He followed her down a dark gravel path, under the bridge, to a place full of weeds that looked like a dump for leftover concrete. Crime scene tape surrounded them.

Then she turned to face him. "One guy, Julio, said El Jefe told them to bring her here. They did. He thinks El Jefe was going to shoot her. Instead, she jumped into the river."

A little hope sprung up in him.

She continued. "Then they shot her."

His eyes flared. "She jumped and then they shot her?"

"Right. Plus, when she jumped, her hands were behind her back."

Scott's whole body sagged. He groaned and staggered back.

Beth grabbed his arm.

He squeezed his eyes shut and shook his head. "I want the dog here."

"There's no point, really," she said, her voice gentle. "There's no—"

He stopped her before she could say *body*. "I want the dog here."

She took a deep breath and blew it out. "I'll ask for authorization."

Scott didn't wait. He called Nate.

THEY ALLOWED NATE IN, but with an agent escort to make sure he didn't mess up the crime scene. They had at least two people to prosecute now, and that was their focus. The boss, El Jefe, AKA Emilio Lopez, was dead. So was Brittany Hudgins and a man they had not yet identified.

As for Jessica Cooper? Everyone shrugged. They didn't want

to say what they believed to be true. Her body would surface eventually.

Nate's escort was Bill Chandler, an agent from the Washington field office. He loved dogs and took a liking to Nate right away, so he was a good pick. Chandler had been instructed not to tell Nate what they knew about the crime scene. "Do whatever Scott wants," he told Nate. "All I ask is that you keep the dog on leash."

"Right."

Scott met them well away from where he'd been told Jess jumped into the water. When he saw Nate his heart jumped. He hugged him, and then dropped down and embraced Luke, who was ecstatic, whining and licking him and wagging his tail. Scott was surprised at how much he needed that right then. He soaked it in and then stood up. "What I want you to do, Nate, is just let Luke tell us if someone was here, you know?"

"Absolutely."

"Don't mention the name."

"Right. Y'all move back a little and we'll give it a try."

Nate had a thirty-foot leash on the dog. He made him sit-stay, then he crouched down and talked to him. "Okay, buddy, this here is a special job." He stroked him. "We need you to use that nose of yours real good." He stood up so Luke was at heel position. "Okay, buddy. Now, seek, seek!" His hand shot forward and Luke took off.

At first, the dog worked normally. He quartered back and forth, nose up, trying to air scent a live human. He walked down the path toward the rough area, sniffing, stopping, and sniffing again. When he got to the concrete slabs he went crazy, sniffing, and whining, and barking, staring at Nate like, *can you smell her? Can you?* Then, to everyone's shock, he leaped off the slabs and into the water.

Scott rushed forward to grab Nate as the thirty-foot leash played out in his hands and Luke started dragging him.

"Thanks, brother. He was about to pull me in!" Nate said. "Luke, come!" It took a lot of encouragement to get that dog to turn around and swim back.

The dog came back to shore, stepped out, and immediately shook off. Then he tried to go back in the river, and he barked at Nate when he wouldn't let him.

"So what could you tell from that?" Bill Chandler asked.

"Luke's trained to scent any live human in the area I point him to. I didn't mention any names. So he started out, jus' reg'lar, sniffing the air, sniffing one or two things on the ground.

"He got real focused at the end of the parkin' lot and then comin' down the gravel path. When he got to them slabs, though, he went nuts. Did you see him? He lit up. And then he leaped into the water. He's trained on water searches too.

"So the way I see it, there were several people here abouts, but Jess was one of 'em. That got him excited when he hit her smell. She left quite a lot of scent in that one place, and then, she went into the water."

Scott groaned and turned away. His stomach lurched.

"So what do we do now?" someone said.

"I guess there's nothing we can do," Beth said.

"Just wait until ... until the body surfaces," Chandler said.

"Y'all are sayin' give up? Give up? Are you crazy?" Nate shocked everyone. "Y'all can give up, but I'm not!" His eyes flashed. "Jesus Christ is alive. Sittin' on the throne. Anything can happen. Anything! I'm goin' downstream with a strong light and this here dog. I ain't givin' up. Not yet."

Scott looked up. "Thank you! I don't want to give up! I'm going with you, Nate."

The other two remained silent, then Beth said, "Well, I guess I'm going too."

"I'm in," Bill Chandler said, "for whatever it's worth. Let me tell the boss what we're doing."

"Hold on." Scott had his phone to his ear, making a call to

John Welsh as they moved back to the parking lot. "Wait a second."

"What's going on?" Detective John Welsh jogged up to the group.

"John, this is my friend Nate. Nate, this is Detective John Welsh, Alexandria PD. He knows Jess."

Nate shook his hand.

"And this is Luke, Jess's dog. We think he's indicated that Jess was here, and that she went into the water."

"Which matches what that suspect said," Welsh responded.

"Right. We're looking at following up downstream."

"That's a good idea. In fact, I think we should get on that. Launch a boat." He gestured to the water.

Nate spoke up. "What's that down there?" He pointed to a string of lights in the distance.

"What you're looking at is a marina," Welsh said. "There's a pretty big creek, Cameron Run, coming into the Potomac this way. Lots of mud right there. And then the lights you see, that's Foster's Marina."

"How do we get there?" Nate said.

"South on Route 1 to 629. That'll take you there."

"Can you see about a boat? I can take the dog out, but I'd sooner check the land first."

"Yes, sir. I'll do that now."

"Let me get your cell. How 'bout this: We head for the marina. You arrange for a boat. If we've got nothing at the marina, have the boat pick me and the dog up there and we'll work our way back. He's trained in water searches." Nate looked at Scott. "You okay with that?"

Scott nodded, unable to get even one word out.

"I'll get some officers to help you search down there if you need them. Just let me know."

"Send 'em down. C'mon, Scott," Nate said. He slapped him on the shoulder. "Jesus is alive. Anything can happen!"

. . .

Jesus is alive. Anything can happen. But what if it doesn't? What if? Scott shook his head. He couldn't go there.

Traffic on Route 1 was heavy. Beth talked nonstop. Scott wondered if she was nervous, if that was why the words were pouring out. Talking about "back home" and "at Quantico," and a thousand other things.

He tuned her out. He could think of only one thing—Jess.

He got a text. *Still praying.* An odd text, he thought, for Nate to send. Especially since he was driving.

Then he looked again. Henry. Henry had sent that text. *Still praying*, he'd said. Well, that's a miracle right there, Scott thought.

Scott texted back. *Making progress.* That wasn't the complete story, but it was true.

Text me even if it's in the middle of the night, Henry typed.

Beth turned onto 629 as instructed. A smaller, darker road. Nate was right in front. They found the marina, parked, and Scott got out of the car.

The night was cool and clear, a beautiful night, really, with a half-moon. There were docks filled with sailboats off to the right. He could hear the halyards clanking in the breeze. The dark expanse of the Potomac River lay straight ahead. He shivered a little, from nerves not the chill. More agents and officers pulled up. One was carrying a big red bag with a white cross on the side.

Nate took charge. Later, Scott would wonder at how a bunch of agents and cops would automatically fall in line behind the dog man. He told them where to walk, where not to walk, and when they'd be free to fan out.

Then he brought Luke out.

Scott realized he was trembling. *C'mon, Luke!*

Nate was going to start at the dock, then move northwest. If the dog didn't find anything, he'd start again at the dock and move south.

Please God, help us.

Luke was already nose up, sniffing the air. Nate talked to him quietly. The dog whined and half-jumped onto him, putting one paw on Nate's thigh. He seemed anxious to go.

He set the dog up in the heel position. Nate wore his SAR backpack. Scott thought that was odd and almost volunteered to carry it for him. But he stayed quiet and just watched. *Please God!* He saw Nate check the wind, which was coming from the south. Then he unclipped the dog's leash.

"Seek, Luke. Seek!" Nate's hand shot out and Luke started quartering. Scott knew he was trying to catch a scent. Luke moved left, toward the north, quickly, into the woods that bordered the river and marked the edge of the marina property.

As Luke and Nate searched under the trees, it became harder to see them. Everything in Scott wanted to move, to follow them, but Nate had been clear. They were to stay back. And the last thing Scott wanted to do was distract the dog.

Beth tapped his arm. He turned. She handed him binoculars. Not night vision, but better than what he could see with his naked eyes. "Thanks," he said. He lifted the glasses up to his eyes and tracked Luke through the woods and along the shoreline. But then, the oddest thing happened. He saw Luke stop. Sniff the air. Look back at Nate. And then Luke dove into the river.

Scott heard Nate call Luke. Saw the dog swimming straight out into the channel. What was he doing? Scott's heart beat hard. He saw Luke turn. The current began carrying him southeast.

Nate had been trying to keep pace with the dog on the shore, but Scott could tell that the combination of shoreline debris and his artificial leg slowed him down. Then Nate stopped, turned toward Scott, pointed, and called him to come, gesturing with his arm.

Scott handed the binoculars back to Beth and took off running, triangulating between Nate and where the dog was headed. Luke barked. Was he in distress? Drowning? The dog changed direction, headed for shore, fighting the current in the channel. As Scott got closer, he saw Luke was headed straight for the water's edge. He pulled his flashlight off his belt and began scanning the water.

And then he saw her. "Jess!"

Scott ran into the river. The dog arrived and started going crazy. Jess lay in the water, at the edge of the river, her face resting on a flat rock, her hands still behind her.

"Call an ambulance!" someone yelled.

"I got it, Scott," Nate said, and he pulled out a Leatherman tool and cut Jess's hands free while Luke danced around them. Scott felt Jess's neck. "I got a pulse!"

And Scott turned her over and picked her up and carried her out of that river. He lifted her close and kissed her muddy, bruised face.

Alive. His girl was alive! Tears blurred his vision. *Thank you, God!*

46

JESS

"Scottie. I knew you'd find me." Those were my first words when I realized I was in his arms. As soon as I warmed up a little in the ambulance, I asked about our son. "Mike?"

"Ellie has him. He's fine."

I closed my eyes. Then they flew open again. "The girls!"

"Nora and Ava are safe, Jess. You saved them."

I smiled, tears welling in my eyes.

I REFUSED to stay in the hospital more than twenty-four hours. All I needed, I insisted, based on my extensive medical training, was hydration, food, rest, and a shower.

Especially once I found out about Luke.

"He's fine," Scott insisted. "Nate has him."

But he wasn't fine, and I knew it. Apparently, while he was dancing around me in the river, he got cut on something. Scott downplayed it, but any injury was serious to me.

"I want to go home, Scott. I need to go home." I'd just

survived a fifteen-hour ordeal. I felt I had a right to demand release.

So he pushed the doctors and we agreed that, if nothing weird showed up, I could leave the hospital the next afternoon. Thankfully, my prescribed detention went fast, largely due to the nonstop visits from investigators. I told my story over and over. Every one of those cops was impressed by my catalogue of the guys's tattoos.

Around noon the next day, I had a surprise—a visit from Brett Hudgins's father—and the two girls! Oh my goodness, what a lift I got from seeing them. They gave me hugs and told me how they'd gotten help. I assured them that, except for a few bruises, I was fine. And we retold our adventure, adding in the Narnia twist.

Scott, observing our affectionate reunion, exchanged his contact information with their grandfather.

After they left, I said to him, "Are you thinking they may need some pony therapy?"

"I'm sure they'll want to see you again."

TWO WEEKS LATER, Scott and I sat on our front porch on what promised to be a sunny, hot August day, pretty typical for Virginia. Little Mike, one week away from his second birthday, played with his toy riding tractor in the front yard. It came complete with a rechargeable battery, so he could "cut the grass," a job he performed with precision.

Luke lay on the porch next to me, his back leg bandaged, watching Mike intently.

I found out what happened to him that night. Scott had just pulled me from the river. Everyone was focused on me, and no one noticed Luke was hurt and bleeding badly until the ambulance crew took charge of me and someone pointed out that

Luke was in distress. Nate found a bad cut on his leg. He had lost a lot of blood.

One of the local cops contacted a K-9 officer who called in the vet they used, and he agreed to meet them at the clinic. By the time Nate and Luke arrived, my dog was starting to go into shock. The vet saved his life, but it turns out, he had severed his Achilles tendon. He had surgery to repair it, but Nate told me gently his SAR career was probably over.

I cried about that, until I realized God had prepared me for it. Weeks before, when I found that lump on his side, it had prompted the thought that maybe it was time to start another dog and ease Luke out of SAR. He was, after all, nine years old.

There would never be another Luke. We all knew that. I reached down and scratched behind his ear, happy my guy was at least still with me.

Scott and I had been talking about building a sunroom off the side of the house. He was open to that idea. In fact, he had already called a contractor to see what it would take. He was so happy to have me back in one piece I think he would have built me a castle if I'd asked.

I heard the gravel in our driveway crunch. Scott had told me he had a surprise for me that day, and I wondered if this was it. Nate's Tahoe pulled in and my friend got out, along with Ember, his black shepherd.

That prompted Mike to jump off his mower and hug Naa'. Luke started to rise, but I told him "down." He needed to heal; he just didn't realize it.

Nate pulled up a chair, and we started talking. By then, he'd already heard all the stories of my capture and escape. He still got misty-eyed when it came up.

"Hey, I learnt somethin' you might want to know," he said to me.

"What's that?"

"You know how TSA has those dogs that check the baggage and walk through the airport and all?"

"Yes."

"Well, sometimes they get one that don't work out for one reason or another. And they're looking to place them."

"What breeds?"

"Labs, GSPs, sometimes shepherds and Malinois. The website says they're active dogs that aren't necessarily house-broken. They're usually about two years old."

I looked at Scott. "That's how I got Luke, remember? He was a police tactical dog that wouldn't bite."

"Maybe you should look into that," Scott said.

I heard more gravel crunching. Luke pricked up his ears. So, I swear, did Scott.

"Mike, come up on the porch," he said to our son.

Scott's truck came slowly down the driveway with Henry driving. Pulling our horse trailer. That's when I knew what the surprise was.

"Truck, truck," Mike said, pointing.

Henry parked and got out of the truck, followed by Cash, and Scott let Little Mike go running to him. "'Ree, 'Ree!" he cried, and Henry picked him up, while Cash and Ember started chasing each other around the front yard. Henry walked to the porch and we all got up to greet him. He gave me a really long, gentle hug, then held me at arm's length and looked at me long and hard. "You're really okay?"

"All better. Where's Amanda?"

"She said she had to work," Henry said, averting his eyes.

A red flag popped up in my head. Maybe our trauma had stressed her. Maybe she was angry about something. Maybe ... well, I didn't know what else, but the flag stayed.

Henry put Mike down and stepped up on the porch to see Luke. "What's up, big man?" He petted him gently around his ruff, scratching him under his chin. "A lacerated Achilles, huh?"

"Yes," I said. "He must've clipped something underwater that sliced him."

"A jagged piece of metal, I'll bet," Henry said. "I'm so sorry." He stood up and looked at me. "He'll heal. He won't be as strong or capable as he was, but he'll still be here."

"He's been such a great SAR dog." I turned so Henry wouldn't see the tears in my eyes.

"He'll still be a great family dog. I'll change that bandage for you later if you'd like. I'd like to take a look at it." Henry looked at Scott. "How do you want to do this thing?"

"Let's put the dogs inside," Scott said, "just to minimize any distractions."

"Good idea."

"Luke will stay on a down," I said. I didn't want to put him inside. I'd have to put him in the crate so the other dogs didn't do something that would hurt him. And I didn't want to do that.

Scott nodded. "Okay. I'll hold Mike, and Henry, you do the honors." He picked up our son. I got ready to take pictures.

Henry walked over to the trailer, unlatched it, and dropped the tailgate. Then he stepped inside and came out holding a beautiful chestnut pinto pony. "This is Bree, although you can change that if you want."

"Oh no!" I said, my heart pounding. "It has to stay Bree." Everyone stared at me. My face grew hot. But Scott, though mystified, nodded and "Bree" the pony's name remained. In Mike-speak, the name was "Bwee" for quite a while.

What followed was a magical day for Mike, for Scott, for all of us really. Seeing the joy, not just on Little Mike's face, but in his whole body, did a lot to dispel some of the lingering trauma we were all still holding. And Scott, well, it was like he was the one getting the gift. Honestly, I have never seen him so happy, at least when nobody had just been rescued.

I took pictures that documented those precious memories.

Mike trying to wiggle out of Scott's arms. Scott gripping him, while he gently stroked the pony. Having Mike let the pony smell his hand. Then finally, putting him on the pony's back and Mike leaning over to hug Bree's neck. *A horse and his boy.*

Tears popped into my eyes, tears of joy mostly, but mixed with sorrow, because of what I'd seen and experienced and how my dog was now injured.

Isn't that the way life is? Sorrow and joy?

SCOTT HAD to wrestle Mike away from the barn at the end of the day. We managed to get some dinner down him. He played with Nate for a while, and then we told him it was time for bed. He went around the room and said nite-nite to everyone, but protested loudly because he hadn't said nite-nite to "Bwee."

Scott and I had both about reached our limit, but Henry bailed us out. "How about if I take him down to say good night?"

We gladly handed our son off, and after a walk down to the barn in the evening darkness, and ten minutes of saying good night and a kiss on the pony's nose, Mike was satisfied and went to bed.

I suppose getting your first pony is just too exciting for a boy to go to sleep easily.

I was puttering in the kitchen later when Henry walked in. "Can I help?"

"Sure!"

I let him wash while I dried, since I knew where things went. Cash came into the kitchen and laid down under the table. I liked the way he followed Henry whenever he could. I felt tears jump into my eyes again, thinking about Luke.

I bit my lip hard, suppressing my grief, and I asked Henry about his job, his ribs, the Chincoteague ponies, surfing—

anything I could think of that would take my mind off my own problems. Why was I so emotional?

We were finished in short order. "You want a cup of tea?" he asked me.

"Sure. There's decaf in there. Lemon and ginger sounds good to me."

So he made two mugs and set them on the kitchen table and that's when I realized he wanted to talk.

"Can I ask you a question?"

"Yes, sure." I expected him to ask about Amanda. Or marriage. That's not what I got.

"Were you terrified when those men had you?"

My throat thickened. I wrapped my hands around the mug, grateful for its warmth. "Yes." I swallowed.

"How'd you get through it?"

"I mean, how much do you want to know?"

"As much as you'll tell me."

Maybe it was Henry's broad, friendly face, or his brown eyes that looked so much like Luke's. Or maybe I just felt like sharing. Whatever it was, I started talking, and the story poured out of me like the river current that had eventually taken me to safety. The shock. The fear. The horror at the thought of what they might do to those girls.

Tears came.

"I didn't mean to upset you," he said, concerned.

"You're not. It helps me to tell it." I took a deep breath, grabbed a tissue, and dabbed my eyes. "I don't know, Henry, just how to say this. Don't think I'm a spiritual giant or a hero or anything. I'm not. I was desperate, trapped, at the mercy of those men. I started to panic. I was so scared my bones were shaking.

"Then I thought of something Nate always says—that the walk of faith is a walk into death. Dying to self, living for Christ.

Jesus is Lord. Period. And he wants all of you, all your life, everything."

Henry's eyes never wavered from mine.

"As I thought about that, what came to mind was my favorite line from The Heidelberg Catechism."

"The what?"

"It's a statement of faith from like the fifteen hundreds. Anyway, this came into my mind: 'What is your only comfort in life and in death? That I am not my own, but belong, body and soul, in life and in death, to my faithful Savior, Jesus Christ.' Body and soul, in life and death," I said, repeating those words.

"Here I was, trapped by these men, but I belonged body and soul, in life and death, to Jesus. Did I believe that? Right in those circumstances?" I paused. "I decided I did believe it. I did and I would believe it, and I released everything into his hands —my life, my husband, my son, my dog, my friends, everything."

I went on to tell Henry how I decided to trust Jesus whether I lived or died. "I knew he was with me," I said. "Still, I begged him to save those girls."

"Wow," Henry said.

I told Henry about finding the attic access, about climbing up there, and walking through that dark attic, about pretending we were on an adventure, like the children in *The Lion, the Witch, and the Wardrobe*. "And that's why the pony has to be called Bree, because there's a talking horse in that series by that same name."

"What a coincidence!"

I raised my eyebrows. There are no coincidences, not with God.

I continued. "We got out of that building. A man came after us, but the girls escaped. Once they caught me again and didn't bother putting a mask over my eyes, I knew they were going to kill me. I spent those hours silently praying, thinking about eternity, and Jesus, and all he went through for me. And ... I can't explain it, but I had a peace come over me, Henry. A peace. I felt the presence of Jesus and I drank him in. It was the strangest thing."

"You weren't worried about Mike? Or Scott?"

"I couldn't. There was nothing I could do to save myself for them. I was trapped, helpless, but I knew Jesus was present, and that he was still in control.

"Standing out there by the river," I closed my eyes and shook my head, imagining it again, "Henry, it was so peaceful, so beautiful. I loved it—the darkness, the black night sky, the beautiful bridge, the feel of the breeze, even the blinking lights of the planes. Just beautiful." I looked at him. "I should have been full of fear. Angry and afraid. I wasn't. I ... I can hardly explain it, but I knew I was alive 'in Jesus' at that moment, and I knew that if I died I'd be alive 'in him' in eternity. And somehow, it would all be okay."

"You found a 'thin place,'" Henry said, his eyes bright.

I cocked my head, frowning, studying him.

"That's what Nate calls them, places where the veil between Heaven and earth is thinned, and ... and you can almost see into eternity. Like what happened to him on the AT."

Oh, they had been talking! When Nate was walking out his grief on the Appalachian Trail, he had a breakthrough. Afterward, he saw a magnificent, healing sunset that felt like God was enveloping him in love.

"Maybe it was a thin place," I said. "Standing there, drinking in that beauty, I heard these words in my head, *When you pass through the waters, I'll be with you.* That's a Scripture verse, and I heard it in my head over and over. *When you pass through the waters, I'll be with you.* After a while, I decided maybe it wasn't just a memory, maybe it was a promise."

"So you jumped in; you took that leap of faith."

I studied him for a moment. Was he drawing inferences? I

could tell something was stirring in this young man. "I trusted God and I took that leap."

"What an incredible story!" Henry shook his head. "You are amazing! I think the fact you survived is an absolute miracle."

I studied him. "Henry, I think there are miracles around us every day. The sun coming up. The precision of the tides. Our hearts beating. A child being born." I paused. "You surviving that cow falling on you. These are everyday miracles. We just need eyes to see them."

Henry looked like he was trying to process that thought, but before he could respond, his eyes flicked to a spot behind me. I turned. Nate had come into the room. I could tell he'd been standing there, listening, because his eyes were full of tears. I stood and embraced him.

Nate kissed me on my cheek. "God bless you, girl." He squeezed me then looked at Henry. "You ready?"

Henry was staying with Nate that night. He would drive him across the Bay Bridge the next day, where a friend would pick up Henry and take him down to Chincoteague.

"Yes, sir." Henry looked at me. "Thank you."

I hugged him goodbye.

Scott joined us and shook Henry's hand. "Thanks again for driving the pony up here."

"I'm just sorry I can't stay to see the fun you have with him these next few days."

Scott grinned. "Come back whenever you want to. And tell Amanda we missed her."

Henry nodded. "I will."

Scott walked them out to Nate's Tahoe. I stayed inside, thinking. Nate's job, the way he made money, was a lot like my work at home. Repetitive. He cut the grass. A week later he cut it again. He painted a room; sometime later, he'd paint it again. Over and over, just like me changing Mike's pants, doing dishes and laundry, and cooking, and sometime later, doing it all over again.

Nate's repetitive job was important. It paid his bills and put him in contact with a lot of people. But his truest identity was not in his job, nor was it in his work with dogs. It was in his faith, grown strong through years and years of Bible study and prayer and reading and trusting God even in terrible times. His search and rescue work literally saved lives. His faith helped change people for eternity. It had impacted me and Scott and now I could see it impacting Henry.

What was the truest part of my identity? SAR? Being a smart PI? A mom? A wife? All those things are good and important, but you know what? Standing out there on that river facing death only one thing mattered: that I knew the One standing with me.

ACKNOWLEDGMENTS

As always, I am indebted to a vast array of people who help me with my writing. The SAR people, and in particular, Jessica Burnside, my FBI person (and friend), Dru Wells, my Beta readers, and of course, those of you who read these tales of mine and encourage me on. My daughter Becky gives me great feedback on the storyline and helps me publish the book. Amanda Geaney, my invaluable assistant, keeps up my presence on social media and gives me wise counsel. Janet Grant, my long time agent, is a steady hand for me as is Barbara Scott, my editor. And Hannah Linder has ably added her artistic talents and picked up the cover design task for this book.

While the main storyline of my SAR books revolves around Jessica and Luke, Scott, and Nate, I've recently added a subplot involving Scott's grown daughter, Amanda and horses. I've lived with dogs my whole adult life and while I've ridden horses, I've never owned one. I have to pick up the nuances of interacting with them from others.

As if that wasn't hard enough, suddenly young Henry Bunting III, a horse vet, walked into my storyline. A horse vet! For the Chincoteague ponies! What in the world? Cleary my writing had the bit in its teeth and was running away with me.

Enter Allison Dotzel and Tipson Myers. Allison is a vet and Tipson raises Quarter horses and helps Allison. They both live in Pennsylvania, and Allison is the official vet of the Chincoteague pony herd. Thanks to a Q&A they did at Pony Penning last year and Allison's response to my requests for specific help, I've learned a little about what Henry's job would look like, and how to depict him. Whew! Allison and Tipson love horses and the Chincoteague ponies in particular and I'm very grateful for their help.

Way back in Book 2 I introduced you to Hope Ranch. That fictional equine therapy place on the Eastern Shore of Virginia is loosely based on Hope Reins in Raleigh, N.C. Hope Reins rescues and rehabilitates horses, then pairs them with children with needs. The magic that can happen when a kid finds a gentle, twelve-hundred pound friend is amazing. Emotions become regulated, confidence improves, and hope blossoms. As the child learns to trust, communicate, set boundaries, and lead, his or her resiliency grows and healing follows.

Some friends and I visited Hope Reins in September 2025. I'd been there several years ago. All of us were wowed by the peaceful feel the place and the emphasis on compassionate care for horses and people. The ultimate goal of Hope Reins is to help kids learn to trust animals, then people, then God. The program introduces them to Jesus and the love He so faithfully shares. Over a hundred volunteers help run the program, which has been so successful it's been studied and lauded by the University of Kentucky. I encourage you to visit their website, HopeReins.org, and check out their program.

I am so grateful for the privilege of "writing for Him" and thankful for you, dear readers, for joining me on this journey!

Blessings,

Linda

SDG

ABOUT THE AUTHOR

Linda J. White has loved dogs and a good dog story since early childhood. Family allergies kept her from having a dog as a child but seven dogs have enhanced her adult life. She lost her most recent buddy, a twelve-year-old Sheltie, Keira, in 2024.

Linda has been a government worker, a mom at home, a Bible study teacher, a freelance writer, and the assistant editorial-page editor of a daily newspaper as well as being the author of award-winning, bestselling novels. Her late husband, Larry, a graduate of the American Film Institute, made training films for the FBI Academy for nearly thirty years. Linda has three grown children and five grandchildren and lives in Yorktown, Virginia, where she enjoys hiking and watching birds migrate and grandchildren grow.

For more about Linda see her website, www.lindajwhite.net.

ALSO BY LINDA J WHITE

The K-9 Search and Rescue Series:

All That I Dread

The Fear That Chases Me

When Evil Finds Us

My Darkest Night

Winter Flight

A Great and Terrible Darkness

I Call Her Brave

FBI Thrillers:

Bloody Point

Battered Justice

Seeds of Evidence

Sniper!

Words of Conviction

The Tiger's Cage

www.ingramcontent.com/pod-product-compliance
Lightning Source LLC
LaVergne TN
LVHW091107080826
845145LV00008B/1833

* 9 7 8 1 7 3 7 2 3 5 6 9 9 *